GHOST CATS II

Jaycee Clark
Michelle M. Pillow
Mandy M. Roth

Erotic Paranormal Romance

New Concepts   Georgia

Be sure to check out our website for the very best in fiction at fantastic prices!

When you visit our webpage, you can:
* Read excerpts of currently available books
* View cover art of upcoming books and current releases
* Find out more about the talented artists who capture the magic of the writer's imagination on the covers
* Order books from our backlist
* Find out the latest NCP and author news--including any upcoming book signings by your favorite NCP author
* Read author bios and reviews of our books
* Get NCP submission guidelines
* And so much more!

We offer a 20% discount on all new Trade Paperback releases ordered from our website!

Be sure to visit our webpage to find the best deals in e-books and paperbacks! To find out about our new releases as soon as they are available, please be sure to sign up for our newsletter (http://www.newconceptspublishing.com/newsletter.htm) or join our reader group (http://groups.yahoo.com/group/new_concepts_pub/join)!

The newsletter is available by double opt in only and our customer information is *never* shared!

Visit our webpage at:
www.newconceptspublishing.com

Ghost Cats II is an original publication of NCP. This work has never before appeared in book form. This work is a novel. Any similarity to actual persons or events is purely coincidental.

New Concepts Publishing, Inc.
5202 Humphreys Rd.
Lake Park, GA 31636

ISBN 1-58608-784-3
2005 © Jaycee Clark, Michelle M. Pillow, Mandy M. Roth
Cover art (c) copyright 2006 Kat Richards

NCP books are available at special quantity discounts for bulk purchases for sales promotions, premiums, fund raising, or educational use. For details, write, email, or phone New Concepts Publishing, Inc., 5202 Humphreys Rd., Lake Park, GA 31636; Ph. 229-257-0367, Fax 229-219-1097; orders@newconceptspublishing.com.

First NCP Trade Paperback Printing: June 2006

Clark/Pillow/Roth

TABLE OF CONTENTS

Revenge II   Page 5

Carnal Instinct   Page 99

Dance of Souls   Page 170

REVENGE II

Jaycee Clark

Thanks Mandy and Michelle for always being there, for dragging me back to the chair when life was too hectic to even think of writing. And to Syd--here's to thinking out of the damn box.

Prologue

Istanbul; 1806

He looked at her crouched in the corner. Almost broken, but yet there was fire in those dark eyes. Eyes normally as dark as sin, were wide with fear ... no terror. He'd done this. The edges of her eyes were speckled with green and gold. Lovely eyes.

"Precious," he chided. "You know I prefer you ready for me."

He motioned to the bed hung with thick ropes of silk, the canopy bannered in deep sensual colors.

She hissed at him. He kept her here, right here on this edge between her human form and that of shifting into her werecat. A lynx. He found it fascinating. She was so much fun, so enticing. So *his.*

He waited, held his hand out as if he had all the patience in the world. "Don't make me ask again."

He watched her eyes widen more, watched as she began to mutter something, something he had never heard before, in that tongue she often used when he'd humiliated her down to the very essence that lived within her. A place neither good or bad, light or dark, simply being.

A brutal, raw and completely arousing place….

He waited, irritation growing in him. He took a deep breath, smelled the jasmine and spices of his incense heavy on the air.

Her chanting continued.

"Precious," he warned. Then he tried to move, but couldn't. What? He frowned.

And in that instant he knew.

She shifted, seamlessly into her cat and leapt. Straight at him. Her claws extended, he tried to deflect her, but could do nothing. Claws, sharp as razors raked across his arm, he tried to throw her off.

The damn cat sank her teeth into the muscles just between his neck and shoulder.

He yelled and fell to the floor. Anger rose in him.

Her jaws tightened, her claws continued to shred. Growls and roars filled the air, yet he still heard her chanting, in that soft husky voice of hers, in his head.

Blood hot and thick ran from him, he could feel the silk of his shirt sticking to his skin, saw the walls waver.

Still the voice chanted in his mind.

He tried to call on his own power.

The teeth sank again and again, claws still shredding.

Then he felt the damned feline move away.

"I'll … kill…." He coughed. Blood rained down on his face. The mythical beasts and beings painted on the ceiling seemed to sneer at him. "…kill … you…," he whispered.

He heard something crash to the floor, smelled the oil from the lamp seconds before he saw flames shoot up the banners and bed hangings.

Bitch. "You're … mine…."

She carefully walked to him, now in human form. She kicked him, then jerked the key from the chain on his neck.

"Never."

He smiled up at her even as the world grayed and the flames licked closer….

"Precious…." He coughed again. "My precious."

He felt her feet on the floor, heard the door slam shut, the lock click into place.

"Precious…."

Chapter One

He looked into the pool of water, deep in the forgotten caves, waiting. Waiting to see what the spirits would show him. To see if he were destined as he'd believed.

What he craved was so close.

He'd seen the one he wanted. Whispering to another. Laughing in the fading light of day. And for a moment, just a moment, she'd paused, scanned the crowd.

He liked to think she knew, some part of her knew that he was watching. Waiting. Perhaps some part of her recognized … remembered.

And she damn well should remember.

He'd sent one before to bring Precious to him, but that had been his mistake. He'd entrusted too much to another.

Once a lesson was learned, he didn't make the same mistake again.

This time, this time he would simply *use* the other--no more, no less. Then rid himself of the idiot. For now though, he needed the other to obtain what he desired.

He glanced to the side, to the female wolf who was only partially transformed.

Her wrath had been great enough that the magick she'd used in destruction had come back on her. She'd wanted too much. Too much power and revenge.

Not that he didn't understand revenge. In fact--he touched the mottled and scarred skin on the left side of his chest and neck. The skin smooth and puckered under his fingers--he understood it all too well. His was more focused, sharpened, and honed. He didn't burn with hatred, but with *affection* … with desire…. He would not make the same mistake Selinna did last year.

Yes, last fall had been a mistake. Now the spirits nudged him to move back to what he wanted.

And what he wanted was the love of the woman he'd once possessed not so long ago. He'd worked too long, set up too many things, to let this go, to let it slide.

The wolf in the corner whimpered. He ignored her and

breathed deep the scent of incense and smoke, the fainter smells of dry sand and the dankness of the cave.

The pool of water was deep, the edges clear, the center an intense turquoise. He was more interested in the fact that the pool was sacred, the waters a mirror to fates.

So he waited. And in his waiting, lusted for that which would be his again.

* * * *

A month later

Reya Lynx wished the customers were out of the gallery. Energy hummed under her skin and she wondered if anyone else felt it, wondered what exactly it meant. The late summer air pressed hot and dry against the large windows of *Horizons Gallery*. As the sole owner of the artistic jewelry shop in the trendy New Mexico town of Taos, she normally wanted customers in, wanted them to browse, wanted them to buy. Today she was ready to leave.

She scanned the street beyond the windows.

Could it be Lorenzo?

At the thought of her husband, she rubbed the ring on her finger, a symbol, more modern than a tradition for either of them, but it served its purpose--a reminder, a hope.

Reya glanced down at the wide silver band, the carvings to ward off evil, the edges lined with tiny marbled turquoise, to let her know when danger approached--or so legend went. She smiled. Lorenzo had given it to her not even a year ago.

It had nothing to do with the normal marriage proposal. For they were neither lovers nor haters, estranged, engaged nor married. They were mates--for the most part. Of course their relationship was rather confusing. It didn't matter that they had loved, and lost, hated and blamed, worried and hoped for the other through the centuries. What was, simply was. No matter the time, sooner or later they found their way back to each other. Then again, sooner or later something usually ripped them apart.

Lorenzo Craigen, as he was currently known, was her mate. He always had been and he always would be.

She knew that, even loved him for it. He was, at present, pissed at her for the fact that she still wasn't living with him. He currently didn't demand her acceptance. He understood she needed to sort through things. Theirs was not a normal union either by human or were nature. Both were strong, willful, and independent.

They'd met so long ago in the village in the canyon, its terra cotta walls protecting that lost civilization. A canyon that would become known as Chaco Canyon. They had lived with the Anasazi. Young, they'd fallen in love. A forbidden love it seemed. The shaman of their people had wanted her.

At the memory of Sael, she shivered. The dark shaman had ripped them apart, cursing the young lovers, sending them away. Lorenzo had been turned into a werecat under the instructions from Sael, to be a descendant of the great mountain lions while she'd been consigned to the shifting forces of the lynx felines. For years she'd been at the mercy of Sael until Lorenzo had rescued her.

Then had come the most peaceful time. A time for many of her people to fear when the Spanish came. But for her, for Lorenzo, living in the pueblos, it had been perfect. She could close her eyes and remember the sacred lake nestled higher in the mountains, the peace of unadulterated nature, remember the sound of the ceremonial drums deep in the kiva rumbling through the ground. But that time too, ended in pain. Pain of losing Little Moon--their child. A child of blessings, or promise--dead by Sael. Again dark years followed and yet again, Lorenzo found her, finally hunting down Sael and killing him. That should have been the end, but lies, illusions and heartache tore them apart again.

Most mates were together, always, forever, without any breaks or questions. After Sael's death she, however, denounced her bond with Lorenzo. Not that it broke it.

Now though, over two hundred years later, they were together again. She just wasn't certain she wanted to become his … possession. In her opinion, Pride Law of mates was a bit antiquated. Not that she really wanted to lose him.

Not that he'd let her.

So *why* the hesitancy, she wondered. He didn't demand answers. She figured it was only a matter of time before he did.

He told her she was being stubborn. Probably right. She was stubborn, but then she'd learned to be. If one were stubborn, they didn't let others rule them, didn't become a damn doormat or worse. And she'd been both at the hands of men who only wanted to control.

Shaking off the thoughts, she knew her time of reprieve was up.

She rested her hand on her still flat stomach and shivered.

What if she was wrong? She thought she *might* be pregnant, the thought brought excitement even as it brought horrible fear.

What if she lost this child as she had the last?

Pain at the thought of losing Little Moon washed over her. It hardly mattered it happened hundreds of years ago. Some pains should never be.

Swallowing, she looked out at the bright street again.

"Excuse me, miss?" The patron in a sundress, glasses shoved up over her blond hair motioned to the glass case before her.

Charles, Reya's assistant walked around from behind the counter. His sharp hazel eyes studied her. "Did you want to try on the strand of coral and turquoise?" He hurried over and Reya walked into the back, her thoughts too muddled and confused to mess with her customers. Charles was capable. Hell, she'd bought the place from him, expanded their selections, and renamed the gallery.

Now it was hers and he was still here, guiding and protecting.

She shut her computer down after checking her email. The rumble of Charles' voice and the tinkle of the bell above the door told her the customers were done. Or did someone else step in?

She glanced out her small office and saw the shop was blessedly empty. Sighing, she picked up her jacket and reached for the lights.

The phone rang.

Hurrying to her desk, she answered.

"Is this Reya Lynx?" a man's voice asked.

"Yes. Who's calling please?"

"This is S. Whitehall out at Cuba. Well, near Cuba. I have a conflict with our original meeting." A moment of silence.

Whitehall, the newest artist she'd found and was still trying to sign.

"Yes, Mr. Whitehall, what can I do for you? Do we need

to reschedule at a later date?"

A moment of silence greeted her, before wind hushed on his end of the line. "I was wondering if we could meet this weekend. I'll be leaving in a few days and not sure when I'll be back."

She thought for a minute. If she rearranged some things.... Lorenzo had mentioned doing something this weekend, but maybe he could go with her. Nodding, she asked the caller. "Just a minute please." She hit the hold button and hollered, "Charlie?"

"Reya." He stood behind her in the doorway.

"Oh, sorry. Didn't know you were there. Can you watch the shop this weekend? Or at least tomorrow? I need to go see that new artist I was telling you about. Out near Cuba."

Charles frowned. "What's his name again? Whitehall?"

She nodded.

Charles shrugged. "Well, you know me. Where else would I be?"

She set up a time to meet the potential artist and hung up smiling. Maybe she'd finally sign him. His work was phenomenal. Slightly pagan in a Celtic influence, but predominantly Southwestern. He worked with silver and copper mostly. No bead work, no flashing colors, just … earthy. Charmed and energized pieces, or at least that was what she saw when she looked at his work.

"Lorenzo going with you?" Charles asked as they walked up front.

Ever since last fall, it seemed someone was always watching out for her. Something she herself was pissed about. But Lo would not back down. He'd almost lost her too many times he'd said, including last fall when she'd been the object of revenge. Sael's sister, Selinna, had created a nightmare. The only good thing was that it brought her and Lo back together.

It hardly mattered if she wanted their interference or not, she got it.

"I don't know, haven't talked to him about it yet. We'd thought of going camping or something this weekend, just to get away. We'll see."

Charles was fifty-two with dark, graying hair, a goatee and a penchant to sprouting out tidbits of wisdom she usually found annoying. He was handsome with his sharp features and habitual khakis and pullovers. His hazel eyes narrowed. "Be careful."

She nodded, gave him a quick hug and said, "I'll call you and let you know how it goes."

"Do that."

The doorbell tingled as she walked through it. The cool mountain air was crisp this evening, promising colder temps before too long. The trees were bursting in bright yellows and orange. She loved this time of year. Next was the long cold winter, summer was often hot and spring was generally muddy thanks to snow melts. But fall…. Fall was her favorite.

She tugged her leather jacket tighter around her and strode down the sidewalk towards her house several blocks from the gallery. She enjoyed living in town, the hustle and bustle of the shop keepers, gallery owners, tourists.

Yet part of her knew she didn't belong here. She belonged with Lorenzo. That was simply Pride Law. Where the alpha was, so was his mate. Period.

So she didn't *exactly* accept all of being his mate. Not yet. Maybe that was what kept her. Their history was too confusing for anyone to set by simple laws.

Okay, that and fear.

She really hated fear. But there had been so much pain in their past, and fear of pain had turned her into a sissy.

Reya touched her stomach and tried not to hope. Tried not to see what could be, forced herself not to remember what had been.

Again, she felt it.

A faint humming itch under her skin.

Something black slithered up her spine halting her.

Reya looked one way then the other. Motorists were parked at the red light, tourists walked hand in hand and in groups to restaurants or shops. Laughter floated on the air.

An image long buried, long shielded rose in her mind.

"Please," she begged.

"Please what, Precious?"

She hated that name. Hated the way he said it.

She knew he loved it when she begged, when she pleaded. The cage she was in barred her view of him….

Reya shook off the dark memory.

Where the hell had *that* come from? She'd blocked that

time of her life. Blocked it from herself and from Lorenzo for *years*. There were some things she knew, he wouldn't be able to deal with.

All the thoughts of the past had messed with her mind. That was all it was.

Deciding she needed a bit of help, she hurried the rest of the way home, daring herself not give into the fear that suddenly seemed to surround her.

She needed to see White Lilly.

Opening the door to her house, she felt someone inside and froze. Her heart beat kicked against her ribs.

"No need to fear, for love's sake. Come in. In my old age, it's cold already and winter's not even here," a robust voice said from the kitchen area.

Reya huffed out a sigh of relief. Seems the *bruja* always knew when she was needed. Something Reya couldn't quite understand.

"Lilly, what are you doing here and how did you get in?" Reya tossed her jacket over the chair back and stared at the woman calmly drinking a cup of tea at the kitchen table.

White Lilly was almost seventy, her hair still long, but gray, worn in two braids on either side of her head and lay like forgotten ribbons on her chest. She wore a pouch around her neck, the leather almost as gray as her hair, the bead work broken and frayed. Inside were protection bundles of special herbs to ward off evil spirits.

Some of Lilly was eccentric and for bluster, some was for the fact she appreciated the old ways, but most was simply because she believed. She was known as one of the strongest *bruja*s in the region.

They'd become more than mentor and student in the last months. They were friends and Reya loved the lady like her grandmother.

The eyes staring out of the wrinkled face always took Reya by surprise. Blue as the Caribbean.

Lilly raised an arthritic finger, the knuckles worn from Lilly's hobby of weaving--of which she really wasn't all that proficient. It hadn't stopped the woman from continuing the practice throughout her entire life.

"You, child, need to be careful."

For a moment, Reya held that blue stare, then she looked down and ran her hand over the smooth tan leather of her jacket.

"Why?"

Lilly snorted. "You don't know? I just sense things, for crying out loud. I'm not omnipresent. I just pass on the knowledge I know, not guesses." Lilly's oversized sweater engulfed her small frame.

Reya turned and sure enough, there was Lilly's walking stick, complete with her dangles of feathers, leather, beads and strips of neon pink and tie-died green.

Eccentric might be a bit of an understatement.

The gnarled hand pushed a leather pouch towards Reya across the table. "Wear this. I made it for you after my dream."

Tentatively, she reached for the pouch. "What's inside?"

Lilly smiled. "I can't give away all my secrets." But the smile didn't reach her eyes. "Perhaps, Reya, you should think of the importance of the future and claim before The Council to be Lorenzo's mate. You would be protected then."

Importance of the future? Her hand went again to her stomach. The Council? The Council, like any government had many and varied levels. The Council ruled the immortals, shifters, the living dead. She often thought of them as the legislative branch of the immortal world, more an oligarchy than a normal democracy. The Council had local levels, regional and international levels. And admitting to accepting Pride Law and being Lorenzo's mate before The Council…. Lilly was right, she would then be completely under protection simply because she was Lorenzo's. And he was the ruler of the werecats of this region.

Those blue eyes offered no quarter, but seemed to see right through Reya. "Yes, you would be well protected, and so will those you carry."

"Those?" Reya asked startled.

Lilly smiled and stood. "Wear the protection. Watch your back and go to Lorenzo. He'll be at my door otherwise and the man gives me hot dreams I shouldn't be having at my age--at least not about him."

With that, Lilly grabbed her walking stick, thumped to the door and let herself out. But Reya had heard her, heard the chants the old witch had muttered as she left.

Protection.

What or who did Reya need to be protected from?

The house was empty, the energy inside calm. The fear that had followed her from the shop stopped at the door.

Lorenzo.

Perhaps it was time. Wasn't it? She wanted to be his mate, and was in his eyes and half The Council.

Chapter Two

Detective Lorenzo Craigen of the New Mexico State
Police pulled his pickup truck into the driveway of his
ranch. His ranch house sprawled across the land, the adobe
a deep orange in the setting sun. Reya's car was already
parked out front under the golden leafed cottonwoods. He
relaxed at the knowledge she was here, with him--at least
for now. Damned stubborn woman. She was his mate. Her
place was with him, yet half the time she chose to stay in
town, needing her space--whatever the hell that meant.

They had some things to discuss.

Stepping from the truck, he breathed deep and shut the
door. Simple day, all around, thank goodness. No local
murders. Two days ago there was the old man that died in
his sleep. Lo and two others had to go out to the nursing
home and investigate another passing. The surviving
daughter of one of the guests had thought her mother had
been killed by negligence. If only the rest of the day had
been that easy. Instead, he'd had to meet with The Council.

As the werecat leader of this region he had much to
answer for. The Council was still pissed at him for the
battle last fall between the allied wolves and coyotes
against his cats. Against him. Against Reya. They seemed
to think he could have negotiated a more peaceful outcome.

Not when it was Reya. If anyone harmed her, it was
death. Plain and simple. No negotiating about it.

He sighed and realized part of him looked forward to the
fight he knew they'd have. Then again, maybe he'd wait
until this weekend.

It was Thursday. He planned to take Reya somewhere. He
had no idea where yet, but he would. His boots were silent
on the rocks as he strode up the walkway. He let himself
into the side door of the laundry room. The dryer whirred,
the air warm and fresh from the white sheets Reya tossed
into the dryer. The air also smelled of burned something or
the other. Reya was cooking? He shook his head. What did
he forget? Not their anniversary--no matter which one they

were celebrating. Not her birthday. Sure as hell wasn't *his* birthday....

Mood music chanted loudly from the stereo in the kitchen. He winced. He didn't mind listening to Reya's music most of the time. Even most of her mood stuff he could enjoy with flutes, strings and the occasional Native American chants. But he had yet to figure out what the hell this was. Every song sounded the same, a constant hum broken only by those little finger symbol things. Sounded like yoga music to him. Far Eastern, maybe Indian.

He leaned against the doorway and just watched her. Twilight darkened and pressed against the windows of the kitchen looking out over the range, the rabbit bushes and sagebrush shadowing the land. He watched as Reya cursed and grabbed a spatula flipping whatever smoked from the skillet on the stove. Her dark hair lay in a sleek long braid down her back. He followed the line with his eyes, noted the way her tight fitting aqua shirt stretched over her breasts and torso, the way her dark jeans molded her ass.

Lo blew out a breath at the fist of lust that hit him straight in the gut.

"What are we having?" he asked.

She whirled, frowning, but he caught a flicker of something in her face ... shock? Surprise? Fear? For a moment, their gazes locked and he felt it, an emotion wrapped in smoke, too elusive to catch, wisp between them.

"Reya?" He took two steps towards her.

She shook her head and looked back to the stove, cursed again and picked the pan up, dropping it into the sink and turning the water on, squeezing soap into the sizzling skillet.

"Forget it," she muttered.

Lo stood behind her at the sink, the acrid smell of burnt grease and whatever she'd been cooking filling the air.

"What was it supposed to be?"

"Squash. I wanted to try a new fried squash recipe."

Reya could cook, spaghetti, anything on the grill. But her new creations were often ... too interesting to put into words.

"Did I forget something?" he asked instead.

"What do you mean?"

"You're cooking something different. I must have forgotten something special."

She shook her head and turned, smiling at him. "No, nothing. I've just been feeling...." She wrinkled her slightly turned up nose. He smoothed the creases between her brows.

"Feeling what?" he asked, softly.

Her dark eyes dropped from his and she shrugged. "I don't know. Like something is just waiting...." Again she trailed off.

"Waiting?"

She shook her head. "Nothing. I haven't been sleeping well. I want to do something different with the shop this fall and want to sign several new artists and get the current list to create new pieces. I'm just stressed, that's all."

He studied her for a moment more, trying to read her thoughts but got nothing. Since they'd grown closer, she was easier for him to read most of the time.

She was blocking him.

Lo leaned back against the counter, watched as she bent over to rummage in the freezer and pull out a frozen pizza. "Pizza it is."

Reining in his anger at her blocking him, he fought to keep his voice as calm as before. "Why don't we just order in?" He grabbed the cordless and ordered a large vegetarian pizza. "There. Done. Put that one back."

"I could have popped this one in the oven."

"Haven't you burned enough this evening?"

Her dark eyes narrowed at him, even as one corner of her mouth kicked up. "Screw you."

"It's my fondest hope."

When her back was to him, he wrapped his arms around her, pulling her closer. Her ass was nestled against his groin, her breasts just above his arm.

"Are you going to tell me what's really bothering you, Reya?" he whispered in her ear before kissing her just there where her neck joined her shoulder.

She shivered. "I told you."

"Guess we'll have to do this the hard way. But that's all right. I like a challenge." He turned her around, shut the freezer door with his boot, and backed her against it.

"Pizza will be here soon."

He smiled, leaned closer and said, "Not for a bit. They're behind and apologize, but it'll probably be at least forty minutes before they get out here."

Her eyes dropped to his mouth. "Oh."

He leaned in and kissed her, gently at first, then more demandingly. Her arms started to come up, but he grabbed her hands and held them to her side.

"My way," he whispered.

He turned her and walked her in front of him to the bedroom, then on into the bathroom.

"I should--" she started.

"Undress," he finished. "Now."

For a moment she stared at him, and then pulled her shirt off. Today she wore an aqua bra, as her jeans slid down the long line of her thigh, he noticed she also wore a matching lace thong.

He closed his eyes and breathed deep, smelled the scent that was only her--reminding him of desert rain off the mountains. Her arousal was heavy on the air, promising the storm to come. When he opened his eyes, she eased back.

"Don't."

She stopped.

"Do you know where I just came from, Reya?" he asked, as he reached into the shower and flicked on the water, jerking two towels out and tossing them onto the vanity.

Her eyes didn't look away from him, she didn't try to cover herself, but he could feel her blocking him and that pissed him off. No matter what the hell else had happened or hadn't between them, he could always find her, always sense her, always--trying hard enough--read her.

Screw waiting until this weekend.

Lo all but ripped his clothes off and gripped her elbow as they got into the shower, the hot spray and warm mist surrounding them.

He pressed her against the stone tiles of his shower, the color of canyon walls. "I was with The Council. I've been given an ultimatum, *wife*." He bit the last word out, leaned closer and let his beast, his werecat tease to the edge, call to hers. "Since our claiming has never run the normal course, they want a declaration from us *both*, or they break our bond. And they want it by the next full moon." He kissed her hard, not wanting to hurt her, but too angry to care.

She'd played her games for too damn long. "I *won't* let you go, Reya," he growled. His hands slid over her wet body, molding her torso, her ribcage, her hipbones. The muscles of her belly contracted at his movements. "You *will* declare before The Council that you are, always have been, and always *will* be mine." His fingers trailed circles on her breasts, now dripping with water, her hair slicked to her head.

He raised his gaze and saw the anger in hers. "Lo," she whispered.

"No more excuses, Reya. No more postponements. Dena told me on the way out, I should give you a choice … woo you." He flicked a nipple with his nail, her breath shuddering out. He leaned closer, pressing harder, his mouth nipping at her chin. "But I'm not in the mood to woo. Not in the mood to seduce."

Her head whipped up, and though there was just a hint of anger, he also saw relief in the depths of her eyes just before she closed them.

"What's wrong?" he demanded against her chest. He held her breast in his hand, teasing with his tongue before pulling the center into his mouth, laving, licking, torturing.

Her sigh moaned in the stall. Still he caressed with his hands and mouth, moving from one breast to the other. He played his hands up and down her sides. Easing down her, he hooked her left leg over his right shoulder opening her to him completely. She brought her hands up to cover herself. He grabbed her wrists.

"Don't hide anything from me, Reya." He grazed his thumb over her from her pubic bone, down her center, to her ass. "Not one. Damn. Thing."

Her eyes locked with his and as if he'd run into a steel wall, he felt her shields.

"Damn you," he muttered. Her wrists strained in his. "Hold yourself open for me," he growled.

He looked from her flesh, up her body into her eyes. "Do it."

Licking her lips, her fingers held open her slit to his eyes, his hands, his mouth.

Reya shuddered looking down into his eyes. Her heart slammed in her chest, her pulse pounding hot through her body.

His eyes, always dark, were leonine, the pupils wide, the irises all but black gold. His beast was so close to the surface, she could feel it batting and playing at hers, teasing, taunting, waiting.

Still watching her eyes, he leaned in and softly blew across her exposed clit. His eyes never wavered as he closed the distance and licked her from bottom to top and down again.

Chills danced over her skin. Tension coiled tightly within her, pooling at the base of her spine, spreading to her gut, wetting her arousal.

As if he had all the time in the world, he licked, teased, stroked and kept her on the brink of insanity.

"You are mine, Reya." He twirled his tongue around the bundle of nerves that begged for his attention. One long finger pierced her. "You are mine to protect, to avenge, to comfort. Now tell me what's wrong."

Then tension coiled tighter inside her. Tighter. His finger stilled.

"Tell me, baby," he whispered.

She opened her mouth, a dark image long buried spiked through her mind.

…You are mine, Precious…

Pain coursed through her and she screamed.

Reya startled, shoving the blackness away.

When she looked down, Lo's eyes were narrowed to slits. Anger tightened the long contours of his face, pulled the skin across his high, wide cheek bones. The stubble of beard he'd had for the last week, made him look lethal.

As if he'd need it.

"What the hell was that?" he asked.

Keeping her gaze on him, her eyes filled with tears. There were some things she could never tell him. Never. Some powers were too strong even for Lorenzo to defeat.

Her fingers speared into his hair. "You're mine to protect as well."

The finger within her moved and she leaned against the tiles, moaning. His mouth and hands were merciless. Finally, finally the brink stood just out of reach.

His hands and mouth left her. Standing, his skin, chest, stomach and thighs brushing hers, he looked into her eyes.

"We'll finish this later." He moved her aside and reached

for the shampoo.

Bastard.

She reached for him, wrapping her fingers around his length. He stilled, sucked in a breath just as he squeezed creamy shampoo into his hand. "We will?"

His eyes, still angry were answer enough. "Yeah, we will."

He quickly washed off, turned her and slathered soap across her skin and shampoo over her hair. She let him, concentrating on keeping her shields in place. Between wondering if she were pregnant, the worry at the back of her mind that something was wrong, and the old nightmare images, there were too many things she wanted to work out herself before talking about them. Everyone deserved some privacy, damn it.

Of course, Lo would never see it that way. She could feel him trying to read her, feel his power pushing against hers. Water sprayed in her face, slicked down her body as he washed her off. Not speaking, his features still hard, he rubbed the towel over her, drying her off. He then wrapped it around himself and motioned her back to the bedroom.

"I need my robe," she said.

Staring into her eyes, he shook his head. "Get on the bed, Reya."

Anger bit through her. Though she knew she'd pushed him enough in the last months, he was normally more patient, calmer over her pushing him away than she'd ever have given him credit for.

Looked like that had changed. He knew something was wrong, sensed it.

Without a word, she walked to the bedroom, and felt him behind her. At the bed, she climbed up and lay down, waiting.

He leaned against the bathroom doorway. His arms were crossed over his chest. He was just under six feet of corded muscle, his biceps bulging slightly, his chest and abdomen tight, yet not overly so. He was lithe and predatorial. His eyes were still narrowed on hers, his wet hair hung over his forehead, past his harsh slash of brows, grazing the tops of his shoulders. The white towel hung low on his hips, a scar slashing across one hip bone, another across his chest.

And still she felt him pushing against her.

"Why won't you claim before The Council to be mine?"

She didn't answer.

"If you, if I, were anyone else, all it would take would be me claiming you. That would be the end of it. But The Council knows you, Reya, they know me, they know our history." He pushed away from the doorway, his steps mirroring his feline therianthrope. Slow. Steady. Stalking.

Reya stayed quiet. What he spoke was the truth.

"They want a confirmation or denial, and I'll be damned before you ever give them a denial," he quietly growled. He stopped at the edge of the bed and his power punched her straight in the gut, pooling and coiling lower.

One corner of his mouth tilted, but his eyes remained angry.

His lids lowered. "Turn over."

Reya licked her lips. Shit. "Uh--Lo, I don't think--"

"Turn over, Reya, don't make me ask again."

For one moment, she stared at him. Yet she complied. The down comforter was soft beneath her cooling skin. What would he do if she *did* make him ask again?

He chuckled. Then whispered warm in her ear. "Do you really want to find out?"

Did she?

Rising up on her elbows, she started to answer but the doorbell interrupted.

Still he only stared at her. The doorbell rang again.

"Do. Not. Move." He turned, grabbed his wallet from the bathroom and strode from the room.

She heard the rumble of his voice as he spoke, heard the door slam, heard the pizza box thud in the kitchen.

Apparently her mate had decided to play his alpha role. Sometimes he could be a royal pain in the ass, but damn if she didn't love him. And damn if she wasn't turned on.

Two could play this game.

She sat up, kneeling on the bed, then curled over, laying her cheek on her stacked hands.

Reya felt him, before she heard him. "I told you not to move. But this…."

Chapter Three

Lorenzo froze in the doorway, at the sight before him. Reya lay on his bed, not lay exactly. Her long, willowy body curled and waiting for him, all of her open and ready.

Damn. He breathed deep and smelled her arousal on the air.

His dick twitched and rose more insistently against the towel. He'd leave it on for now. Taking another deep breath, he strode to the bed and swatted her ass. Once, twice.

"This I could get used to, Reya." He smoothed his hands over her ass, then up her back, before trailing a finger back down again.

The thought she was trying to distract him crossed his mind and maybe she was. But before this night was over, he would remind her who he was, who she was to him.

"God, you're beautiful." He ran his hand down her back again, leaned in and kissed her nape, felt her shudder under him, even before his hands reached around and sought her breasts.

Her nipples, already pebbled, seemed to seek out his fingers. He smiled, tweaked, caressed and breathed deep.

"I'll make you beg tonight, Ree," he told her, pressing against her, still playing his fingers across her nipples. Her back rose against his chest with her inhalation. Lo grazed his hand over her soft stomach, twirled across her belly button, then walked his fingers lower … and lower, stopping at her pubic bone. "But I will *not* give you what you want until you're honest with me, until you tell me what's bothering you." He raked his fingers across her clit, pulling a moan from deep in her throat before he sank one finger deep.

She was so wet and hot.

Damn.

He stroked her with his hands, felt her shudder, loved the way she tried to arch against him, pressed back into him. She moaned again.

"What's wrong, Reya?" He licked a line on her shoulder, up her neck, to behind her ear.

She turned her face, her open mouthed kiss as hot and wet as her slit. Lust whip-lashed him, roared through his blood. But love, the need to *know*, the need to *control*, held him.

He stilled his hands. "Who's your mate?"

She tried to arch into his hand, but his other on her hip kept her still.

"Who is your mate, Reya?" he growled.

He strummed her clit.

"Y-you."

Lo stopped, spread her hair over her other shoulder and trailed his tongue over the nape of her neck. Goosebumps prickled her skin.

"Who?"

"You."

He wrapped her long wet strands, around and around his hand. "And as your mate, I have control over you, don't I?"

He thrust his finger into her wet sheath, then withdrew it, only to sink it deeper. "Don't I?"

She whimpered and nodded.

"Why are you afraid?"

He felt it, the sharp-taloned beast of fear sinking through her shields and straight into him.

He froze.

She tried to pull away from him, but he didn't let her. Instead he moved closer, shifted, so that the towel fell from his hips and his shaft nestled against her naked flesh.

"Lo, please," she whispered.

What the hell had her so scared?

But then he felt her heat, her wetness on him and he strained for control. He played her again, stroked her back to writhing against him, wet and ready and so damn hot. "You'll tell me, Reya."

He unwound his hand from her hair, gripped her hips and played at the edge of her opening. She shuddered, moaned and shifted.

"Lorenzo!"

He inched in, then pulled out, inched in just a bit more, then withdrew. "Do you want me?"

She growled, pissed.

He might have smiled, but he'd felt her fear.

"Tell me," he whispered, gently as he slid back inside her. His hands glided up her ribcage, drew circles on the soft sides of her breasts.

"I--I...."

He withdrew, heard her moan. Once, twice he slapped her ass. "I'm getting tired of this game, but I bet I'd feel better if I had to beat it out of you, than if you withheld it." Again his hand landed, but this time he smoothed it over her bottom, over the pink hand prints he'd left. Lo thrust back into her, balls deep and stilled.

She pulsed around him and he gritted his teeth, pulling out, then thrusting back in. Slow and deep. Just as he felt her tightening, he stopped, changed the tempo.

"Ree?" he whispered, nipping her shoulder, wanting to hear her beg, hear her scream his name, wanting to slam into her until nothing else mattered.

But he waited, swatted her ass again, felt her fist around him and moaned himself.

"I think ... I think...."

He leaned close, brushed the hair from her face as he moved out and in. In her ear, he whispered. "I'm going to mark you."

She started to shake her head. Then nodded.

He froze, frowning. "Is that what you want? Me to make you do it?" Anger batted at him. "Why can't you give me anything?" He thrust back into her, hard and fast, hearing her rising cries. He could go at any minute, but he held on. She screamed and vised around him, pulsing, begging him to empty himself in her.

Instead, he leaned over and bit her on the shoulder, chanted the words in his mind, *What I claim, is mine. My wrath on any who trespass.*

She yelled again and he jerked out, flipping her over to stare down into her wide, dilated eyes.

The room around them shimmered with pale green light, pulsing stronger. He gripped her legs, slid up her body, parted her folds. He ran his fingers up and down, stared back into her shifting eyes and slowly slid into her. She picked up his rhythm, her back arching, her moans heating the breath between them. He kissed her hard and hot, nipping her lips, even as she nipped his. He trailed hot kisses down her neck, shifted so that she arched more, offering her breasts to him. He circled his tongue across her left one, just over her heart. Saw the faint scars where he'd marked her centuries before.

Damn stubborn woman.

He thrust hard, high and deep. Her cry filled the air, as he sank his teeth over the old marks and claimed her again. He sucked hard, tasted the faint copper of her blood and sighed. He licked, laved, sealed the marks then shifted up onto his arms.

"What I claim is mine. My wrath on those who trespass," he growled.

She nodded, cupped his face. "I love you, I always have. I'll announce my acceptance before The Council."

He thrust harder, faster, shifted so that each stroke raked him across her clit. Her moans filled his ears. Lo placed a hand over her heart, just as she arched and screamed again. The storm caught them both and shoved them into the vortex.

And in that instant he saw.

Children. His and Reya's.

Her scream mixed with his yell. They both lay panting until he raised his head enough to look into her eyes, her lashes spiky from tears, the dark brown irises widened and speckled with green light.

He stared at her, the image of his vision so sharp he could still hear the faint giggles in his mind. Children. A boy and a girl. Theirs.

He traced his thumbs along her temples. "Why didn't you tell me of the babies?"

Shuddering out a breath, she tilted her head on the pillow. "I don't know. I'm not certain. I might not be. I might. Maybe it's what will be."

He rolled and pulled her with him. Kissing her brow, he said, "Good thing you agreed to go before The Council. I'd have dragged you there otherwise." Especially now. "And this weekend we're moving you here. Period."

They'd lost a child once. He'd make damn certain they never did again.

He expected her to argue on the last, but instead, she only sighed and nodded.

He wondered what else she might be keeping from him.

* * * *

Drip. Drip. The leaking faucet was distracting him. Everything was almost ready.

"Nybras?" a voice asked him.

He turned, his gaze raking over her. No longer in wolf form, she'd morphed into a man. Selinna was too powerful for her own good. Not only was she a werewolf, but she had the ability to morph into any she'd harmed. Didn't have to kill them to morph into them, just harm them. In her case, he knew she usually killed. She liked it. As a morpher, she could become anyone. Not a simple, or even complicated, glamour--the art of creating an illusion. No, Selinna's power allowed her to *become* whomever she wished.

Her problem was that her anger controlled her and she let it. Stupid woman.

"Will this do?" the medium build man could have been anywhere from forty to sixty with his ash blond hair, tanned line-worn face and straight gray eyes. Faded jeans and a pullover completed the outer shell.

One brow rose. "What? You said a male artist."

Nybras shook his head. "I know what I said. You look more like a movie star than a trustworthy artist. I want her trusting. No feelings of misgivings or worry. That cat she's with will sense it." Nybras brushed his forefinger and thumb across the goatee he had. "I was thinking more along the lines of everyone's favorite uncle. A sort of grandfather figure. You need to be fatter, yet strong. You work with metals and wood, for fate's sake." He glanced at Selinna's male hands. "And make certain you add a few scars." He stepped closer. "You screw this up for me again, and I'll kill you myself."

He'd kill her anyway in the end, but for now she served her purpose.

The man's voice hardened. "I want justice for my brother."

Nybras tsked. "Selinna, Selinna. How many times have we been through this? Your brother got what he deserved. If he'd come along after she'd met me, I'd have killed Sael myself. Her cat just did it instead." He grazed a finger down the male cheek, then tapped it hard once, twice. "Don't be difficult. Get her alone, get her to drink the potion. I'll be waiting."

Selinna morphed, not as silkily as she used to, but even after her near death, still fluid. It was the only thing he found arousing about the woman. She was beautiful, her long jet hair satin down her back, her face smooth and perfect, eyes as green as the most expensive emeralds. She'd glammed over the scars she now carried from her fall into the gorge last autumn. But he knew they were there, just under the surface. Like her true nature.

Beauty was often deceiving.

Beauty was often deadly.

In Selinna's case, both applied.

"What?" she snapped, her long legs pacing away from him, only to return.

He waited. *Drip. Drip.* The water pipes were leaking, he'd have to see about that, figure out if it affected anything or not.

Air and water were paramount down here. The power was working.

He glanced around the bedroom, into the bathroom and smiled. It hadn't been easy tapping into Reya's mind. Her protective shields were strong and he always had to catch her off guard, shift through certain memories so that he'd be able to see.

At least he'd finally seen all he needed to. Down to every last detail. Not an easy feat.

He waved a hand in Selinna's direction. "You get the bath products I wanted?" He walked towards the bathroom.

She sighed. "Yes, Nybras. Both of them. The other scent is under the counter. The ones she uses now are in the shower, the lotion on the counter."

He scanned the bathroom, the tiles differing striated colors of the earth.

All was ready.

Poor Ms. Lynx.

"You know, he'll have the pride looking for you. And if she's claimed to be his, you could be in even more trouble with The Council."

He scoffed. He was Nybras, descendent of a powerful Jinn father and an Aerial mother. He knew his power and for nearly five hundred years he'd walked and flown the Earth, loved and hated, lived and destroyed. He'd fought in battles, helped plan and plot wars. Still he lived. He'd yet to be mortally wounded, and he took extra precautions to prolong his supernatural life. He'd loved, truly, only once centuries ago--a woman he'd known as Reyanna. A powerful woman who had been *his*. His to do with as he would. Anything. Everything. Simply because he could.

He fingered the fist-sized amulet of green Amazonite. Rubbing the silky jaded stone, he closed his eyes, thought through his plans. Amazonite was known for its qualities of clarifying harmful deeds. Whether the user decided to act on those, or change the deeds, aim for destruction or redemption lay in the heart of the wearer.

He had no use for redemption.

He simply wanted … craved … lusted…. Loved.

A picture rose in his mind, the mists clearing away.

Nybras saw her, bound as he liked her, begging as he wanted her. Energy charged through him at the thoughts in his brain.

"On second thought," he said to the woman behind him. "I have different plans for you. I'll be the artist. You will get to play a different diversionary role."

Soon, perhaps tomorrow he would be able to see her, smell her, taste her….

Her body, long and lithe stretched out for him and only for him. Her soft voice floating between them, the way her plush lips made him dream of kisses and more. He loved everything about her. He always had. Ever since the very first moment he'd glimpsed her, seen her, smelled her.

"Ah…."

…The music of symbols and bells floated on the air. He watched the dancers in their diaphanous skirts. The harem moved as one, their bodies fluid and graceful, erotic. Glimpses of skin whispered just under the veils. Yet none of that really moved him. He looked down the food laden table, ignoring the dancers to see if he were the only one bored.

Most here were European dignitaries. With his wealth in trading, many sought him out and invitations to his home were coveted. Tonight the ones around the table were of the European political and business elite. Most were here with spouses, or mistresses.

Women fascinated him. He enjoyed the art of pleasure. The candlelight shimmered on the woman's bracelet. He'd noticed her the moment she'd entered as a guest of a widow. He saw her glance down at her hands, saw her play with a beaded bracelet on her fine-boned wrist. He tilted his head and studied the rest of her. Her arms, clearly seen from the short-sleeved dress she wore, were muscular--not like most women here. Her shoulders sloped to a long neck, her jaw line soft.

The face was one of beauty. Her skin was lighter than some here, yet darker as well. She was no Anglo-Saxon. Dark brown eyes seemed almost lost beneath thick lashes, and appeared bored. Her hair, silky and dark as night was pulled tightly back from her unadorned face. Perhaps she was Spanish or Italian. Yet something told him no.

Beauty called to him, called within him.

She was beautiful. She took a deep breath, the bodice of her dress never shifted, her breasts plumping against the lace covered edge of the dark garnet gown she wore.

Though her head was tilted proudly, something about her, something he couldn't quite put his finger on, seemed vulnerable.

He kept studying her, ignoring the diaphanous dancers and their sensuous moves. The music thrummed through his blood until it felt as if no one but she was in the banner draped room with him. The thick spicy incense clouded the air against the ornate, woven tapestries.

He concentrated, felt a whisper of her pain ... heartache. Bitterness. Anger. Hatred.

And love.

He took a deep breath.

Love.

He knew of love, of desire.

Pushing just a bit harder, he only got a glimpse of a man in bed with a woman before shields slammed against his intrusion.

He blinked, realized her dark eyes were narrowed on his, anger blushing her cheeks.

He raised his cup to her.

She looked away and ignored him.

Not only was she beautiful, but she had power....

He smiled, sipped the heady wine from the golden cup. He would learn all there was to know of her.

Then, he'd possess her.

Chapter Four

...She studied the man beneath her lashes. He was handsome, strong aristocratic features, yet there was nothing soft about him. She could feel the power flowing off of him and caressing her. His eyes were a deep aqua color--like the edge of the Ionian Sea she'd seen before sailing across the Mediterranean. His white shirt wasn't as stiff as those in Europe. The cravat absent, the vest a woven tapestry versus satins or silks she'd become accustomed to seeing on the males in Europe. His hair, unlike his contemporaries was absent. He was bald. She wondered if he shaved his head like many who wore wigs did. But from here, she saw no stubble. Light sand colored whiskers covered his chin in a perfectly trimmed goatee. He sat across the table from her, yet three people down so that he was placed mid table. No one sat at either end. She'd wondered at that, but didn't care.

What was she doing here? At this party? She knew. Rosalyn invited her. They'd hooked up in Rome and had spent the last several weeks touring Italy. She deserved it, she knew, but the melancholy that had cloaked her had grown increasingly heavy. She'd hoped that by coming, she'd alleviate it somewhat. She only accompanied Rosalyn tonight because she was growing increasingly tired of even herself, and her friend had not wanted to attend alone.

She glanced around the table.

Most of the guests' attentions were centered on the veiled dancers. Women enticing men.

Reyanna almost rolled her eyes at the performance. Not that the women weren't talented. They were, sexuality all but hissed through the room, teasing, taunting. With each shift of gossamer, each peek of skin, the males in the room seemed to tighten.

Reyanna strained, closing her eyes and trying to figure out if everyone here was a supernatural, or if it was just her....

And him.

Again she looked at him, saw the corner of his mouth, his lower lip fuller than the top, tilt upwards. Was he laughing at her?

He'd tried to read her. She'd felt him pressing in, knew he'd seen what she'd been remembering. Lorenzo. Her husband. Her mate. Or he had been before she'd found him in bed with another woman and denounced him.

Sadness and anger pricked her heart, again and again.

God she was tired.

Her attention had wavered again. The man across from her narrowed his gaze, again she felt him press against her shields.

This time she shoved back.

His half smirk changed into a full grin. Without a doubt he was handsome. He raised his goblet of wine and sipped. When he lowered the cup, the tip of his tongue darted out and licked the nectar from his full bottom lip.

Reyanna closed her eyes and focused back on the dancers. The tempo had increased, the drums and feet beating a staccato rhythm. The small bells adorning the body jewelry the dancers wore, chiming softly on the heavy air.

They moved separately, yet as a whole, veils were tossed into the air, more skin was shown, jewels twinkled in the light.

She breathed deep and caught a whisper of sandalwood and jasmine. Visual enticements as well as scents.

Or was it just her that smelled it?

The dancers were wrapping scarves around some of the men, others the women, guests had turned to each other and started to kiss. The air weighed with wants and desires.

She wanted none of those. Reyanna let her gaze shift and study the other occupants.

"He's been watching you most of the evening," her companion, Rosalyn stated, sipping her own wine. "Perhaps you should give him a bit of thanks for the dinner."

Reyanna turned sharply and looked at the other woman who'd become her friend over the last few months of hell. "What?"

Rosalyn looked out of the corner of her eyes towards the mysterious man. "His name is Nybras. Everyone wants to

*come here. His parties are legendary. His power is very
great in this region. Yet it's said he never interacts with his
guests other than on a business level." Her full lips tilted
up. "Those looks, my dear, are far from business minded,
I'll wager."*

*A trickle of awareness of him as a male, of herself as a
female spiraled down her back. She took a deep breath and
watched him as he watched her. Their eyes never wavering
from all going on around them. At some point, she felt
Rosalyn shift and move away.*

*The aqua of his eyes was almost hypnotizing. She wanted
to look away, but instead took another drink of the heady
wine.*

*His long fingers tapped on the tabletop. They stilled, rose
and motioned her towards him.*

*The music drummed in her head, beat a hot rhythm in her
blood. All she saw was his eyes. Moans twined in the air,
bodies moved against each other, breathing became
heavier around her. She stared and for a moment, saw
herself tangled with this man, almost felt the slick hot of
heated skin against her own.*

*She stood and walked down the table, started to go to
him.*

*Someone bumped her and she blinked. Her head felt
fuzzy. He stood. Long muscular legs encased in flowing
pants that gathered at the ankles. Like a sultan.*

*Her heart slammed in her chest, a caged bird wanting
flight.*

*Reyanna turned and walked out of the dining hall and
down the darkened corridor. Wall sconces burned shadows
along the way.*

Hurry, she needed to hurry.

*"Why?" a deep voice asked just behind her. "You cannot
leave."*

*She stopped, turned and faced him, willing her hands and
heart to stop trembling. "Why not?"*

*That smile teased the edge of his mouth. He walked slowly
towards her, a wine goblet still in his hand. "I've not given
permission for guests to leave."*

*She frowned as he edged closer, pressing her back into a
small alcove. "We need your permission?"*

He leaned closer, dropped his voice. "In case it escaped

your notice, this is a fortress. This isn't London, Precious. Nor is it Paris. Here in Istanbul, people still guard their homes, still protect...." His gaze lowered from her eyes to scan her face, stopped on her neck to continue. "*Still protect what they consider theirs.*"

Her heart fluttered in warning. She reached out, tilted his chin up to meet her eyes again. "*I'm not from London, or Paris.*"

He smiled. "*I know.*" Leaning closer, he pressed her against the wall. "*You've no reason to fear.*"

Yes. Yes, you should fear *warned her conscience.* He raised his cup to her lips. "*Please don't throw my hospitality in my face. Drink. Just one sip.*"

The music from the hall seemed to thrum inside her, heating, cooling, heating again. What was happening? His chuckle danced between them. "*I'd love to see you dance as they do. Gossamer caressing your skin, yet hiding the prize of bareness from the viewer. Soft and silky, your hair down about your shoulders. The music all but calls to you, doesn't it?*" The cup nudged her lips. "*Here, drink, Precious. You won't regret it.*"

Slowly, Reyanna opened her mouth. An image pierced her mind, of Lorenzo, her mate, and another woman entwined in bed, the sunlight dancing off their shifting bodies.

Closing her eyes, Reyanna sipped the wine, headier than her own, spiced and full. It slid down her throat, warm and arousing.

Opening her eyes she stared into the handsome face of Nybras, into his aqua eyes.

"*More?*"

Without thought, she nodded, closing her eyes as he fed her the drink. She felt his lips on her neck, near her ear. "*So beautiful, my precious exotic one. You'll stay awhile with me.*"

Fear battled in her chest, even as his warm mouth moved from her neck to her jaw to her mouth.

"*No,*" she whispered.

"*Yes,*" he said softly. "*Trust me.*"

* * * *

Reya bolted up in bed, her heart pounding, her breath caught in her lungs. She was hot, aroused.

Oh God. Nybras.

No. No. No. Shivering, she rocked. Please. Not another dream of him. Images, memories long buried, threatened to shatter through her carefully erected shields.

Instead she looked over to the man sleeping beside her and was glad she hadn't awakened him. Easing from the bed, Reya walked silently to the bathroom. She needed a shower. The water was warm, washing away remnants of the dream, of the nightmare that followed, of memories she wanted to erase forever.

And why the hell was she dreaming of the demon now? She knew. No one had ever told her, but Nybras was a demon. Where he came from, she knew not. But he was powerful, controlling the winds, controlling minds, creating heat with just a thought.

Shuddering beneath the warm spray, she concentrated instead on the here and now. On her and Lo. On the future. Not the past and fates knew that they'd had enough of bad pasts neither wished to dredge anything up.

She turned the water off and climbed from the shower. Lorenzo stood against the counter, his arms crossed, his black boxers slightly askew as if he'd pulled them on in a hurry. No longer did anger tighten his features, though it was still there, just under the surface. Worry creased his brow.

"Ree, I can't help you if you don't tell me what else is bothering you," he said softly.

She opened her mouth, but then shut it. Slinging her hair upside down, she quickly wrapped it in a towel and straightened. Think. She looked in the mirror as she wrapped another towel around her body.

"And don't even try a *nothing*," he told her, not moving. He hadn't turned around, she saw his back in the mirror, saw his profile as he stared at her.

"I'm just worried."

"About?"

"The baby, or babies or whatever." She shuddered. "I don't even know for certain that I am pregnant or if I want to be pregnant. I'm scared. I don't want anything to happen and I remember what did the last time. How I had no way to save our daughter. How I couldn't stop Sael from hurting her."

She turned and stared at him. "That worries me. I'd love

children, but at the same time, I'd almost rather not have one, than to have one and lose it. I've lived through that pain and I don't know that I'd survive it again."

A muscle moved in his jaw as he turned to her. "Baby, we can't predict the future. No matter if we're were, human, or some other creature. Not like that. I would that we could, but we can't."

She sighed, and cupped his face. "I know. Thank you for being so patient with me."

Shadows moved in his eyes and he held her wrists. "I have a question and you don't have to answer."

Reya frowned. "Okay."

He took a deep breath, his chest rising. "If not for you being pregnant--"

"Maybe."

He shook his head, his brows beetling. "What?"

She shrugged. "I haven't taken a test or anything. I just told you, I don't know for certain, but I feel different and Lilly said something so I probably am, but I don't know. What if I'm not?"

He kissed her head. "Never mind."

She could hear the smile in his voice. Pulling back, she asked, "What was your question?"

His eyes caressed her face. He licked his lips, and then cleared his throat. "I'd give my life for you."

She startled, blinked. "I--I know, Lorenzo."

He nodded. "And I know you would for me and that scares the shit out of me, Ree." He jerked her close, kissing her hard. "It'd be a hell of a lot easier if you weren't so damned independent."

She licked her lips, leaned up and kissed his mouth. "I know."

Sighing, he scooped her up. "We're going back to bed."

For a moment, Nybras from her dream arose. She shook the image away, yet she felt Lorenzo's shoulders tense beneath her hand. Had he seen?

He laid her on the bed. This time their love making was slow and languorous. Instead of demanding, Lorenzo gave with each touch, each caress, each kiss and whisper.

When she climaxed, it wasn't a powerful shove over a cliff, but a soft rolling wave that went on and on and on.

She drifted back to sleep in his arms, knowing she was

safe.

* * * *

"You're not going by yourself." He glanced through the mail he hadn't looked at yesterday. The sun eased up behind Taos Mountain, casting the ranch in shadow.

Her sigh huffed across the kitchen as she pressed the bread down into the toaster. "Lo, it's only to Cuba. It's not but … I dunno … two and a half, three hours tops. I'll meet the guy, look over his stock, see if I can get him to sign with *Horizons* and then turn around and drive back home."

He reigned in on his temper knowing that the more he made an issue of it, the more she'd go just to spite him. Stubborn. She'd always been so damn stubborn.

"Reya, I want to know you're safe. We need to go before The Council first before you go traipsing all over the country."

She set her coffee mug down and turned to him. "Lorenzo, I love you. I'll announce that I'm your mate, bound and claimed by you. But you don't … you can't…." She stopped, bit down, frowned, then opened her mouth again. But instead, she shook her head and turned back to her toast which popped up.

"I don't what? Ree? I can't what?" He waited.

Her shoulders stiffened and she said softly. "You don't *own* me. You can't just *own* a person. Going in, I want you to know where I draw the line. Your partner, yes. I understand Pride Law as it normally applies. Your mate, yes. Most of the time, I have no issue with your opinions or wants." She turned around and glared at him. "I am a person, a being. *I am me*, and no one will ever take that away."

Again hung in the air.

He studied her for a moment. Scratching the side of his mouth, he said, "Reya, I don't think I've ever taken that away from you."

She sighed, looked at him and anger licked anew at the worry creasing her brow.

"Have I ever dictated to you?"

Her droll look reminded him without words.

He shook his head. "The bedroom doesn't count."

Her brows rose. "Trust me. Men start thinking they're completely in charge of a woman in the bedroom on a constant basis and sooner or later it'll trickle over and smother the rest of their lives."

"Smother?" What the hell was going on with her?

"Yes, smother." She slathered butter and honey on the toasted wheat bread. Today she wore jeans, half ankle boots in dark red leather with a sweater the same color. Her hair was braided and coiled at the nape of her neck.

She wore his ring on her left hand, gave him her love, blessed him with memories, but there was a part of her, some hidden part he'd never been able to read. Ever since Europe when he'd hunted Sael down and killed him. It had been well over two hundred years ago, but to them, that was but a blink. And though he'd finally hunted his quarry to ground, he'd lost Reya then, thanks to another woman-- and his own stupidity.

He sighed, shook his head and focused on the matter at hand. "Ree, Cuba's not far from Chaco."

And Chaco Canyon, the old Anasazi ruins was their beginning. Ages and eons ago, of times and languages most had forgotten. They'd fallen in love amidst the cliffs, their families toiling with the rest of the families, following the gods. But fate had been cruel. Sael--an immortal wolf--in the guise of the wise shaman, had ripped them apart. He'd been in love with Reya and a young boy would not come between Sael and his goal. For years they'd searched, both being changed from mortals to werecats. He was of lions, she of lynx. Their love should have died with their transformations. Instead, their bond had never broken. But through the years, finding each other, hoping, happiness only to be shattered again by Sael, was not something easily forgotten. Through her mind, Lorenzo had seen most of what she'd endured at the hands of Sael, things he'd assigned her to do for his own purposes. It had taken almost a century, but Lorenzo had found them and finally ended Sael's miserable life. All that he knew. All before he knew. After Europe when Reya had again stepped foot on this land, he knew. All of it.

Except one part of her life she kept shielded from him. The time from when she'd walked in on him and another woman after he'd killed Sael until she came back to America years later. He'd searched for her. He'd almost found her weeks later in Italy, but then lost her track. The

years in between, almost three, were a blank. They always
had been. Now he wondered.

"Who's Nybras?" he asked.

Her knife clattered to the floor.

"Damn." She ripped some paper towels off and wiped the
splattered jelly off the tiles, picking up the knife. "What?"
she asked.

Her features were schooled, but her hand had trembled.

"Last night you said Nybras in your sleep." He watched
her. "Is that a person or a thing?"

He pressed, tried to read her. All he got was an image …
a pair of aqua eyes.

She shook her head and shrugged. "Who knows? I had a
bad dream last night."

Lorenzo opened his mouth to say more, but his pager
went off. He glanced at it. Shit.

Hurrying, he shrugged into his brown leather coat. "We're
not through with this discussion."

"One could only hope," she whispered.

He hurried to her, kissed her quick and said, "If we're
done, I'll stop by the shop for lunch." At the door, he
turned back to her. "You better damn well be there too,
Ree."

With that he strode to his truck. The morning wind had a
bite to it, heralding the winter to come. The mountains were
already a patchwork of golds, reds, browns and the green of
pines. One good storm or wind and the leaves would fall.

It was this time last year everything had gone wrong.

As he drove down the drive, he looked into his rearview
mirror. All the trouble last year had started with one
murder.

And now he was going to investigate another. He hoped it
was an easy one.

Who the hell was Nybras?

Chapter Five

Nybras waited for the phone to ring. He hoped she'd done her part. He would have loved to have participated in the murder himself, but alas … he was needed here. He looked at himself in the mirror, he'd glamoured into the illusion he needed to be.

The body did nothing for him, slightly out of shape around the middle, a drastic receding hair line, grey mixed in at the temples. He ran his hand over it. Always bald, the hair felt foreign to him, strange and rather itchy. The mustache was a nice touch if he said so himself. The eyes he'd changed to hazel.

Would she sense something?

He didn't know, but it would be fun finding out.

Turning away from the mirror, he straightened the waffle-weaved red Henley he wore and glanced around the cabin. Jewelry graced the table. Copper and turquoise, red corals, beaten silver. He fingered one long pendant and wondered if she would recognize it. The opal glowed almost red against his palm.

He dropped it, picked up the cup of coffee and sprinkled in three drops of powder. Not too much. He didn't want to kill her, just make her sleep. The last thing he needed was her fighting him. He had to wait until he had her in the house, with its walls shielded and protected so that she couldn't escape or project her emotions out, and if she could, they wouldn't be very clear.

He took a deep breath and closed his eyes. Flutes danced from the speakers of the cabin. The rough wood hewn furniture did nothing for him. He appreciated more classic styles of décor with definite Eastern influences.

He wondered how much she'd changed. If his Precious had changed any at all, or if she was still as perfect and imperfect as she'd been before.

Of course, she thought he was dead. Well, perhaps *hope* was a better word. She'd locked him in the bedroom and set the walls aflame, chanting things she'd learned from someone. Her spell had been to vanquish him. Unfortunately for her, though fortunate for him, she'd mispronounced several syllables. Not that he could blame her.

With a bit more time she probably would have succeeded. But he was willing to let bygones be bygones. After all, she was his precious, precious love.

He closed his eyes and remembered what it felt like to have her body pliant under his, what her lips had tasted like, how in the beginning she'd squeezed tight as a fist around him when he brought her pleasure.

The image of her eyes flashing fire at him as he'd locked her in her cage made him smile. Sometimes she'd demanded he teach her the hard way, poor Precious.

Now, she'd be independent--more so than she'd been before. That was always a heady aphrodisiac. Nothing like weakening, eroding and finally, finally breaking those with too much pride.

He smiled and hummed several measures from a *Rasa* song that was in his mind. Soft light filtered through the windows, the wind chimes from the overhang outside tinkled in the air. He wondered where she was.

He sat at the table, stared at the black bowl of water and concentrated.

Her image cleared and wavered in the liquid. She was driving.

Soon. Soon, Precious.

* * * *

Reya left her Grand Jeep Cherokee running and hurried inside the shop. Charles was already there.

"I thought you were off to Cuba," he said, dusting down one case. "Where's Lo?"

She shrugged, booted up the computer and clicked to the contract files. She printed out two and turned back to Charles. "I have no idea. He went tearing out of the house this morning after getting paged. Someone probably died. When he leaves that quickly, it's either an accident or a death. He had that thin mouthed look that said death." Of course he'd already been pissed at her, so maybe that was the reason for the look.

"He knows you're going by yourself? Maybe I should go with you? Or call up Dena?" He set the rag aside and put his hands in his pockets frowning at her.

She shook her head. "What is with everyone?" She fingered the medicine bag under her sweater that Lilly had given her. Opening it earlier, she'd seen it contained protection herbs, and beads. One bead, the size of her thumb nail was an amethyst. For protection? Clarity? Intuition? When she got back, she had plenty to ask Lilly about. How was one supposed to know what to do with a certain stone if it was meant to be used for several things?

"I'm going alone. This weekend we'll be busy."

"Oh?" he raised a brow.

She smiled. "Yes. Or I assume so. I agreed to claim before The Council that Lo is my mate."

Charles let out a breath, his eyes staring at her. "Did he coerce you?"

An image of them last night flashed in her brain. She on her knees, Lo behind her, demanding, commanding and claiming. She shivered and shook off the thought.

Damn man, he'd always been able to reduce her to a sex crazed female.

Focus, Ree.

She tilted her head and studied Charles, shaking off the thoughts of her and Lorenzo Craigen. Sometimes she felt there was more to Charles than met the eye.

"No, he didn't coerce me." She couldn't hold in the chuckle. "He tried damn hard, but I'd gone over there to tell him anyway."

Both brows rose on that one and Charles smiled. "I must say, it's a relief. Now he'll stop growling at everyone."

She wondered at his choice of words.

The printer spit out the pages and she grabbed them up. Perhaps she should wait for Lorenzo, but if she did that, the artist, flighty as the man seemed to be, might decide not to sign. And he'd said he was leaving.

No, better to go.

She checked her watch. It was just after seven. "Look, I should be there by ten. I hope to be done by noon at the latest. That should put me back here by three or four."

"Got your phone?" Charles asked. "I can go with you, or instead if you want me to."

Reya shook her head. "No, he wanted to meet with me. So I better go. You've seen his stuff. His pieces will bring whatever price we stick on them."

"What's his name again?"

Contracts, brochures of some of their other displays, photos of other pieces they carried….

"Reya."

"Oh, what?"

"What's his name? S. Whitehall. What's that stand for?"

Oh, directions. She opened another email from the man and printed out the directions to his cabin. "I don't know. Sar something. Sarlas? Silas? Sarbin? I can't remember." She hit print.

Charles looked over her shoulder. "That's the way to his house?"

She huffed, grabbed the printed sheets and said, "Yes. Why? You plan to surprise me? Jeesh, what the hell's with all the questions with everyone?"

Palms out, he said, "Sorry, just like to know exactly where you are so that when your *mate* inquires, I can let him know your exact location."

Rolling her eyes, she hurried back out the door and climbed into the car. Time to get going or it'd be even later when she returned.

* * * *

Lorenzo checked his watch. Almost ten. He'd tried the house earlier but no one answered. Reya and he still needed to get a few things straight. Of course, he couldn't worry about that right now.

Right now, he and the other law enforcement officials were trying to figure out how the old man had died out here at Tres Piedras. Well, they knew *how*. The gunshot wounds made that evident. But why? He was just an old rancher. They'd found his wallet several yards away in the brush. Mr. Hamilton owned a small ranch not twenty minutes from here.

So what had Mr. Hamilton been doing out here? They were currently trying to figure out if he had friends in the area, someone who might have seen him. Last anyone knew, he'd had breakfast with his wife at four thirty. He'd then left. She'd assumed to go to the local café in Tres Peidras for his ritual morning coffee with all the other farmers and ranchers.

He'd never shown up.

So what was he doing here with bullet holes in him?

His phone rang. Moving away, he answered. "Craigen."

"It's me," Charles' voice said through the phone.

Lorenzo's hand tightened on his mobile. "What?"

"She left here at seven twenty, or there 'bouts. Was heading to see the artist out at Cuba. Name's S. Whitehall."

Damn it! "I swear, after The Council, I'm chaining her at home."

Charles took a deep breath. "Lilly came by about five minutes ago. All shook up and worried about Reya, mumbling about wind spirits and death. I figured you'd want to know. I sent Darrell to watch her. She didn't need to be driving or alone in her condition. Miss Lilly was not pleased with me in the least."

He took a deep breath and pinched the bridge of his nose. He couldn't just take off. He wanted to know if she was safe. "I'll call her."

"Already did that. She's not answering her phone."

His stomach tightened. He closed his eyes and opened his connection with her. He saw her stepping out of the car and walking to a cabin.

What are you doing?

She startled. *My job.*

Her shields shoved him out and blackened his vision.

He blinked. "Detective?"

Sighing, he held up his hand to the uniform trooper and said to Charles. "We've got contacts over there. Marcos. Get him. Send him with the directions over to S. Whitehall's. I want to know exactly what's going on. If anyone asks, he's her body guard."

"I'll contact him and give him the order. She's going to have something to say about this."

"She said she's going before The Council, it's time she remembers the order of things. Call me back."

He hung up and turned to the scene at hand. The state forensics team was crawling on the ground with tweezers and labeled bags.

A dead body, his wife keeping secrets, and her mentoring *bruja* worried.

Reya was by herself and no matter the age, no matter how independent she was and he knew she could take care of herself--he also knew that evil things still walked the Earth and could still strike when least expected.

* * * *

Reya rolled her neck and wondered when Lorenzo would back off. Knowing him, never. And Pride Law demanded she submit to him as her mate.

Well, she hadn't made the official claim *yet.* So she still had a small window of independence. They had some things to discuss when she got back. Checking her watch, she saw it was after ten. She tightened her hold on the portfolio she carried.

She knocked, heard the music of flutes coming from speakers.

No one answered the door for a moment.

Great. Drive all the way here and the man wasn't home. The sun beat down hot on the barren land, yuccas lancing out from the ground like green swords. Rabbit bushes dusted the land and mixed with brown grass. Tumble weeds walled up against a crumbling fence.

Lorenzo was right.

She took a deep breath through her nose. Chaco Canyon, the old ruins, were not far from here and she could smell the past on the wind. Dark, foreboding, yet nostalgic for all that.

An image of her mother rose in her mind, her hair braided, the leather of her clothes as dirty as the last time Reya remembered seeing her--eons ago.

She frowned.

The door opened.

Reya shook her head and blinked. Her mother? She hadn't thought of her mother since Little Moon had died. She'd seen the image of Singing Flower then.

"You must be, Reya Lynx," the balding man said. He smiled and offered his hand.

A warning tingled through her, but she gazed at him and only saw happiness in his eyes. Slowly, she reached out and touched his hand. The palm was clammy, the fingers stubby, the skin scarred from his work. "I apologize for asking you out here. " He motioned her in. The inside was darker than the porch, but tall windows allowed the morning light in, brightening the place.

Pine furniture, chunky and primitive sat in the living room. The long table displayed some of Mr. Whitehall's work.

"Would you like something to drink? I saw you pull up and fixed you a cup of coffee." He picked a pottery mug up and handed it to her.

She took the mug and sipped, then remembered she shouldn't drink caffeine. She'd read recently that pregnant women shouldn't drink caffeine.

Setting the mug down, she licked her lips, tasting a faint sweet flavor to the brew. "You make a wonderful cup of coffee, thank you."

"Drink up, drink up. I know it's a long drive from Taos. I'd hoped to make it there."

Surely one cup couldn't harm her. Not that she had to drink the whole cup. Just part of it. She didn't want to seem rude. Her gaze scanned the table.

"Wow." Hurrying over to the table, she studied the pieces, the copper glinting dully in the light, turquoise that seemed as pale as a robin's egg and coral as red as blood. Intricate carvings in hammered silver, detailed runes on metal medallions that hung with silver medicine wheels.

Normally, she liked to separate the influences. All her artists were Southwestern by locality and product. She carried some Celtic influence pieces as they were popular but for the most part Celtic and Southwest stayed very separate. However, this man had seamlessly melded the two so that the jewelry had a distinctive pagan feel, yet seemed as one, not two differing cultures.

"Amazing." She leaned down and studied a copper ring that sat on a bed of pine shavings, the stones round and set flush against the band. Coral and jet.

She looked over some of the other pieces then turned back to Mr. Whitehall, startled he was standing so close. "You know, I brought photos of our displays and brochures of our other artists to give you an idea of what we do for our artists and right now I can't even think of the pitch I went over and over in the car." She motioned to the jewelry spread out on the table. "I just want these," she said laughing.

He smiled, two dimples showing in his lined cheeks. "That's what all the women say. But I tend to run them off sooner or later."

She smiled. "I brought two contracts on the off chance I

could get you to sign today and take some pieces back to
get started on your display."

His eye brows rose. "So soon? And here I was so excited
to have a beautiful woman out for the day, I'd planned to
show you around."

"Maybe some other time. I have commitments back in
Taos that I need to return to."

"Oh." His fingers tapped on his thigh, something about
the gesture capturing her attention.

She blinked, her head suddenly feeling warm. Shaking her
head, hoping to clear it, she pulled the portfolio out from
under her arm, jerking out the contracts.

The medicine bag seemed to weigh around her neck,
something in it, heating against her cleavage.

What the hell.

A bag of protection.

She shivered and wanted to leave. Checking her watch,
she said, "Here are the contracts. If you could fill them out,
I'd be happy to take them back with me. Let me know
which pieces you'd like displayed first."

He laughed, a rough deep sound that danced over her. The
corners of his eyes crinkled up. "I hate forms. Why don't
you fill them out for me? Enjoy your cup of coffee and I'll
choose some pieces."

For a moment things seemed to shift around her and she
could have sworn….

"Something wrong?" he asked, reaching for her.

She stepped back and glanced down, shaking her head.
"No, I'm just pregnant. Moments of lightheadedness."

At least she hoped that was all it was.

Dropping her shields and opening her mind, she decided
she'd rather feel Lorenzo.

Yet the connection seemed fogged, clogged, as if they
hadn't connected in a long, long time.

She wanted to be in the car. But she'd come this far, she'd
fill out the damn forms, take the jewelry and go home.
Period. Simple.

"Could I have some water?" she smiled as she sat at the
table and laid the papers before her. "I hate to be a bother
and the coffee is wonderful. What's in it to give it the sweet
flavor, almost floral?"

He waved her away. "My own personal favorite.

Jasmine."

Jasmine? A shiver walked down her spine.

"Pregnant, huh?" A faint line appeared between his brows. "You drove all the way out here by yourself?"

She heard him in the kitchen, couldn't see around the bar area, the sink was out of her line of vision.

"What is it about men? They all think we're wilting flowers as soon as they learn we're pregnant."

She filled out what she already knew onto the contract.

"Well," he said again closer than she'd realized, "probably because it seems innate for men to protect."

She studied him a moment, then took the proffered water with a slice of lemon it and sipped. "Thank you."

Reya motioned to the table. "Get to picking." She smiled at him. "I hate to rush you, but I'm supposed to be meeting another client at three in Taos, which means I have to hurry."

Why she lied, she didn't know. She wanted back out in her car, driving away ... driving back to Lorenzo. Mr. Whitehall didn't look at her, but perused the table of jewels and metals.

She took another drink, glad of the cool liquid.

Again a wave of heat washed over her and she shook her head.

Reya ... not far... sending ... Lo's voice staticked in her brain.

Don't feel well ... she told him in her mind.

He answered but she couldn't make it out.

Mr. Whitehall was humming.

The room wavered. She looked up to the man staring down the length of the table at her.

Picking up the pen, she stared, focused on the paper. Just get it done.

"What does the 'S' stand for?" she asked, surprised at how soft her voice was.

"Oh, Sarbyn with a 'y'." He picked up another necklace and draped it over his arm.

"Could you spell that?" The typed letters seemed to pop from the page.

His voice grounded her. "S-A-R-B-Y-N."

She wrote the letters, watched as they too shifted on the page ... Sarbyn ... Sarbyn....

"I've always liked this piece," he said just to the side of her.

Slowly, she blinked, trying to draw in a breath and looked at the pendant before her. Opal held in a silver fist.... It swung to one side then the other.

"I made it for someone once." His voice soothed, deepened, calmed. "I call it...."

She looked into his eyes.

The bag around her neck heated against her skin. She dropped the pen and clutched the bag hanging between her breasts. As her hand touched it, the man before her wavered.

She blinked.

His face shimmered as if a reflection on water....

Oh God. Something was wrong. Very, very wrong....

Power suddenly flowed off him in a steady stream, washing over her.

She tried to call out.

"I call it," he leaned down, his eyes staring into hers, his nose so close she could feel his breath as he exhaled. His eyes ... aqua behind hazel....

"Precious," he whispered.

Nybras!

The world tilted and she moaned even as everything went black.

Chapter Six

Lorenzo froze mid-sentence.

"Detective?"

He could feel her, not as strong as he should, but her fear still thrummed through him like a faint heartbeat.

What was blocking them?

She was trying to reach him, trying to connect, but something was blocking.

Then, he saw, fogged and blurred, through her eyes. A shadow of a man, a pendant.

Her fear roared to life, terror battling through the block to slam into him.

Nybras!

Lo's phone rang, jerking him out of the vision. "Hello?" he barked, already walking away from the scene. He looked over to Detective Castillo and said, "I've got to go. I'll call later."

Castillo, tanned and green-eyed frowned. "Where the hell you off to? In case you didn't notice--"

Without another word of explanation he climbed in his truck and started it, the engine roaring to life.

"Craigen?" the voice asked.

"Who the hell is this?" he said, shifting the truck into gear and backing away.

"Marcos. There's something not right here."

He'd hoped he'd been wrong, hoped that the feeling, the fear had been off.

Yet, in his gut, he knew it wasn't.

"What do you mean?"

Cuba. He needed to get out there. His truck clouded the dirt road behind him as he sped away.

"The air here is dry, dryer than normal, but storm clouds are building. Winds blowing hot and hard, but the clouds aren't moving. Something, Craigen, is very, very wrong. What do you want me to do?"

Static scratched across the phone connection.

"How far are you from the cabin?"

"Ten minutes ... or take...."

Shit.

"I'll be there as soon as I can. Follow her scent. I want to know where she is."

Because something warned him that if he lost her this time, he might never get her back.

Damn it! He ended the call and tried to dial Charles' number. His truck hit a pothole almost slamming him into a rock the size of his pickup.

He swerved and kept going. If only he'd had his pager off. If he'd just waited. If *she'd* just waited he would have gone with her.

The worry he'd had all morning that something was trying to draw him away from Reya wouldn't go away.

He had to find her.

Finally he hit SEND and waited while the call went through.

"Horizon's Gallery."

"Charles. Something's happened."

He swerved onto the highway, barely missing a semi in the other lane. Heading south on Highway 285. Damn. He checked his watch. It would be hours before he got there!

"What?" Charles asked.

"Reya ... I...."

"I knew she shouldn't have gone alone. Do you want me to call the others? The Council?"

"We haven't gone before The Council yet."

Charles tsked. "They know you claim her. If you say she claimed you and you've got a witness, then it's good enough by Pride Law. You know that."

"There's no witness."

"Oh ye of little faith. The woman was always chatty around me."

With that, the man hung up and Lo tried to think. Tried to reason. Tried to reach her.

Instead all he saw was blackness.

Nybras.

Who the hell was Nybras?

He quickly called Charles back and asked him to look up everything he could find on Nybras.

"Nybras as in an unknown person? Or as in the demon?"

Lorenzo slammed on the brakes at a stop sign out in the

middle of nowhere.

"Demon? What the hell do you mean a demon?"

"Demon, Lo, as in blazing fires of hell, fiends, evil and vile creatures, etcetera, etcetera, etcetera."

A demon? "Find out everything you can on anything with the word Nybras in it. I'm assuming it's a person since every time she's thought of it--him--there were aqua eyes."

"Hmmm.... Male or female?" Charles asked.

"Male," he answered without hesitating. He'd even known that this morning when all he'd seen of Reya's fear was the pair of eyes. They were male.

"Considering what I find, I may call others to meet you at this little locale out in BFE." Charles hung up again.

Lo sat at the cross roads, no one in any direction. He closed his eyes and concentrated, tried to see, to *feel* her.

A chill froze the ice in his veins. He couldn't feel her.

His hands shook as he slammed the gear shift into first, tires squalling as he drove on.

Please, please, please keep her safe.

* * * *

Nybras lifted her against him, smiling as he shed the glamour, the image falling away from his true form.

Leaning close, he smelled her, still the same, sweet, yet faint. Not a floral scent, not a citrus or spice. In all the years since her, he'd never been able to recreate her scent.

He closed his eyes, and strode out into the open. Dust rose in the distance down the long road to the house. Someone was coming, were they?

His laughter danced on the air. He held her tight, chanted the words he'd known for millenniums. Dust and clouds whirled down, hot and fierce throwing up bushes and clods of dirt. Inside, he willed the wind tunnel to stay off the ground. The last thing he needed was anyone tracking them. He could have driven, but this was much quicker.

The air whirled and hissed around him. Shrieks from winged fiends screamed through the whirlwind. Still he kept chanting.

Reyanna--Precious, never moved. Never stirred. In seconds, the wind was gone. Here, miles away, near Pueblo Pintado he was near the ancient ruins. An old ranch house was his destination. The barn to the side where he wanted to go. The wind died down, the heat he'd conjured blasting sand in every direction. Almost noon, but the clouds he'd called forth were still heavy and dark in the sky.

Nearly there. Just a bit farther.

Another wind hit him full in the back, nearly bringing him to his knees. He glanced over his shoulder, wondering where the hell that came from. He hadn't called that gust.

He listened as it again rushed over the barren land, rustling the dirt and sage before it. Then it slammed into him, cold and biting, this time knocking him down. He could have sworn he heard chanting on the howl of the breeze.

Instead, he stood, called forth his own wind hot and scorching from the south as his father's people were known.

Nybras made it to the barn doors. Inside, nothing moved. He'd called forth a protection on it so that it wasn't seen, thus could not be tampered with.

He strode across the way, past the old stalls, tack and tools rusted and corroding on the walls. The smell of decaying hay molded the air. He shifted her so that she stood leaning against him. He reached out and yanked on the rope that hung suspended on a pulley from one of the overhead beams.

A floorboard, complete with attached dirt and hay rose. The dark pit beneath was cool, the slight breeze brushing across his face. Nybras slung Precious over his shoulder and jumped down ten feet. The light came on as he snapped his fingers. He'd tried not to use magic blatantly in the past few years. Things like that were noticed. But here, down in the depths of the earth, no one could see.

Dim lights flooded the dirt, beamed passageway to a metal door at the end.

He unlocked the door and walked into the clean entrance. He smiled and breathed deep, the metal door hissing shut behind him. From this side, it appeared the back of a door she'd know well.

He carried her into the bedroom and laid her on the bed. Her breathing was deep, peaceful.

"It's been so long, Precious," he whispered, leaning over to brush a kiss on her forehead.

He wanted her naked, wanted to see her again, see in reality that which had haunted his dreams for over two hundred years. No other woman had ever had the hold on him that Precious had.

Her eyelids were soft, her lashes long and slightly curled. Her cheeks were still hollowed just below her cheekbones. He caressed her face, ran his hand down her neck. The way she laid, he could see something bulging on her chest.

He frowned.

Nybras walked to the dresser, and picked up the dagger he'd set there earlier. Most of the room was replicated, but some things he'd already put in here were his. He figured it would be fun to watch her wonder … watch the confusion slowly give way to memory … and then? Who knew.

He'd never been excessively cruel to her, but she'd grown to fear him. They'd have to talk about that.

Nybras stood by the edge of the bed, staring down at her. Perhaps he wouldn't need the dagger.

He set it aside and quickly stripped the shirt from her. Her breasts were hidden from him in the modern contraption women wore--a bra. Whoever invented them hopefully died a slow and painful death. Women were meant to be appreciated, their beauty worshiped.

The lace edge tickled along his finger as he grazed the swell of her breast. He grabbed the dagger and sliced the wine material and lace right in the middle. That would just have to go. She would not be wearing that. Her stomach was as perfect as he remembered, slightly dipping, then slightly rising just below her navel. He ran his hand over her, fingers splayed and remembered her remark.

Pregnant.

Rage fired through him, flexing his fingers on her lower abdomen just above the low rising jeans and simple leather belt.

So easy….

All he'd have to do is chant a few words. He rubbed her belly in soft counter circles. Or he could feed her some herbs in a drink or food. He kept his palm flat on her, stretching his fingers straight out so they didn't touch her. His claws slowly grew. Or he could do something a bit more drastic.

He looked up at her sleeping face, no longer smiling, the euphoria gone.

But then….

She needed to be punished. What would be worse, he wondered? To take her children now? Or to let her keep them, let her bear them, then ... then take them away and raise them under his tutelage?

Then again, that was months away. Who knew, he had plenty of time to decide. If they were his, he'd be ecstatic. However, a curse placed on him before he could remember prohibited him from having children. He'd tried every way imaginable to break the curse, but it was no use.

Shaking off the thoughts, he unbuckled her belt, unbuttoned her jeans and rolled them down her long, lithe legs, removing her half boots and socks. He didn't like her underwear either, though they were enticing. He fisted his hand in them and ripped them from her pliant body.

Now she was completely bare to him.

Except for the dirty leather pouch around her neck. Bead work created a wheel with a cross inside. He'd seen the design enough to know it was a medicine wheel. Some of the beadwork was frayed, several beads missing.

Well, that would just have to go. It ruined her image.

As soon as he placed his hand on it, he dropped the bag cursing. Holding his hand, he looked at the scalded palm. There in the center was the broken design of the beadwork branded into his hand.

Anger rose hot and fast in him. Damn woman.

He tried again, chanting words to release whatever protection was on it. Yet when he touched it, he was again branded.

Grabbing the dagger, he tried to cut the leather from around her neck. Smoke rose from the blade, the point where it met the leather thong, getting hotter, black, then red until one point on the blade glowed.

He sat back panting. His gaze flew to her left hand. A ring sat on her third finger.

"You are mine. No other will mark you." Nybras grabbed her hand and tried to pull the ring off. Again the design was burned into his fingers. All but hissing, he rose, his chest panting. It was then he saw the markings on her left breast.

Claimed.

She was claimed.

Damn it! He was supposed to have gotten to her before that happened, captured her before her re-claiming. Made certain she kept putting off going to The Council by filling her head with doubts about binding herself with a man who'd betrayed her once.

Yet here she lay with the other man's markings on her. And a half-breed at that. Not a god, like him, not one descended of a powerful feared race. But of a cat. A damn werecat!

His mobile rang. He jerked it out, and all but snarled, "What?"

Selinna's voice slithered through the phone. "I thought you should know, Lorenzo left a bit ago, driving so fast one of the officers here thought about giving him a ticket."

He closed his eyes, and breathed deep. "You did what I asked you to?"

"Why do you think the man was out here to begin with?"

"Where are you now?"

She chuckled. "Well, there's another body they won't find, yet the woman was needed lest she be missed. I think I played her part here today wonderfully picking up little odds and ends off of the ground."

He had no idea what she was talking about.

"Get back to the house as soon as you can."

She sighed. "What the hell do you want now?"

He thought for a moment. She'd fucked it up last year. "To pay you."

" 'Bout damn time." With that the connection was broken.

Staring down at the woman he loved, he decided to shove his anger away. It didn't offer him anything at the present. He'd use it against her later. For now?

He strode to the bathroom, filled the bowl with warm water, laid a towel over his shoulder, grabbed the cream he'd brought from his homelands of ancient Persia, and a cloth.

Her legs were relaxed as he spread them and climbed on the bed between. He lifted her hips and laid the towel beneath.

The cream was tingling and warm between his palms as he rubbed it in his hands. Already the burns of earlier were gone.

As he slathered her groin with the cream, he wondered what power protected her. Who was strong enough that he'd yet to break their spells of protection?

He waited until he knew it was time, and then slowly wiped the cream and pubic hair away until she was completely bare.

Her skin was as soft as he remembered beneath his fingers.

He'd always liked her bare. She knew that.

Again his gaze landed on the medicine bag and the ring. Could she take them off herself?

Nybras cleaned the rest of the cream off, breathed deep and felt himself harden even more than he already was.

She was so damn perfect. So ... so....

He let his fingers graze her again, glad she wasn't tied down.

He'd have to break her again, he knew that. There was nothing wrong with enjoying her while she lay quiet and accepting to his touches.

No. No. It was all about lessons. She'd run, tried to kill him. He had to remind her who she belonged to.

The air filling his lungs was heavy with her scent so he stood, ripped the towel from beneath her and gathered together his things. Quickly he cleaned up the bathroom. She'd be awake in a little while. He would watch her.

Back in the bedroom, he covered her with the quilt, and then placed the necklace he'd shown her before she'd passed out inside the dresser drawer. She'd find it, and when she did, she would know where she really was, not where she hoped to be.

Smiling, he leaned down and kissed her cheek. "I'm glad you're home, Precious. I've missed you."

Nybras strode from the room. Made certain all the cameras were working--after all, he hardly wanted to miss a single moment--then climbed back up into the barn. Making certain everything was as it should be, he entered the ranch house to wait.

There were, after all, a few loose ends to tie up.

The wall of electronics flickered to life and he watched her sleep.

"Not long now, Precious. Not long now."

Chapter Seven

Lorenzo drove like a man possessed, but it still took him almost three hours to get there. When he drove up, Marcos, tall and lanky was chewing on a toothpick leaning back against his black Jeep. Reya's Grand Jeep Cherokee sat parked at an angle before the house.

He didn't even let the truck come to a full stop before he shoved it into park and jumped from his vehicle.

"Where is she?" he asked. Chills danced again over his skin, prickling his arms.

Marcos' eyes were hidden behind shades, his hair pulled tightly back from his face. "Don't know."

"What?" he roared, fisting his hands into Marcos' shirt.

Marcos, Spanish by his father, Kiowa by his mother, didn't flinch. His long face didn't move. Instead, his calm voice said, "I felt the evil before I got here. The dark clouds were practically touching the ground. Then a funnel came down. It went south, towards the canyon. I tried to follow, no scent, but a trace of energy hung in the air. Or it did until the wind picked up and then...." He shook his head. "Nothing."

"Nothing?" He searched Marcos' expression, his fists loosening.

Marcos reached up and removed his shades, his black eyes crinkled at the edges. "No, Lorenzo, nothing. The trace of energy was heavy, dark, but then," he said, shaking his head. "Nothing. Wind came in, and it was like she just disappeared."

Lorenzo's hands slid from Marcos' shirt. Where the hell was she?

Again he tried to reach out to her.

Where are you? Reya? Reya! Answer me, damn it!

Lorenzo searched and searched, but all he felt was blackness, cold blackness smoked with elusive fear.

Nothing. Not a damn thing.

"Did you follow them?" he asked Marcos

Marcos nodded. "For about ten minutes, then it got so

dark I couldn't see, the wind blew like a sonofabitch for a few minutes and then everything cleared off. Nothing, nada. I'm sorry."

He wanted to rip Marcos apart but resisted the urge. "Your orders were to follow them."

He felt a ripple of power from Marcos. "I know what my damn orders were, but we can only do what we can. I couldn't see, then they were just gone. I traced the traces of evil to Pueblo Pintado. But then I lost it."

Damn it!

"We'll find her."

He stared at the man in front of him. Marcos, as a human, worked in shady places that today's laws would disapprove of. Not that Lorenzo cared either way.

"You better pray we do. Your hide will be my first."

Marcos only raised one brow. "You're welcome to try. I contacted several I know to help us."

The wind was normal, a slight breeze, cool from the north. On the far horizon he could see the bank of dark blue clouds. Northern coming in. Probably snow as well.

Fear licked hot through him, flaming the anger. "I don't recall giving you that order."

Marcos carefully pulled his shades off. "I don't recall asking for it. But the fact remains that whatever the hell took your woman--"

"She's my mate," he interrupted.

Marcos raised his brow again. "Did you both finally go before The Council?'

"I claimed her, marked her."

Marcos stared a moment more. "She agree?"

He frowned and focused on the muscular man he knew many women dreamed about. "Excuse me?"

"Just curious. You know the rules."

"If you're wondering if I forced her, no. God's sake, she's my damn wife. She agreed."

Marcos snorted. "That's where you and I differ, my friend. I'd have simply forced her hand, then claimed her, forget asking her."

Instead of continuing this conversation, he turned and walked to the old house. Marcos was right. There was a feel, not a cold breath as many evils he'd come across. Not like Sael. Sael had been cold. Most were cold. This evil was hot, prickling his skin as if he'd stood beside a blazing fire for too long. There were very few times he ever came across a feel of darkness like this. What the hell?

He shoved the door open and stood just inside, breathing deep.

And he smelled her. That scent of desert rain.

But beneath it, around it, almost smoothing her scent was another--spices. He walked through the room. Trying to read it, trying to see what she'd seen.

He could almost hear her. There was a glass of water sitting on the table, a lemon floating midway in the clear liquid. A crescent imprint of her lips edged the rim from the lip gloss she'd used. He strode to the table, saw all the jewelry displayed.

Bastard. Lured her here, did he?

Lorenzo glanced around and wondered what had happened? He scanned the document on the table, lying atop a folder. Reya's handwriting glared up at him.

He noticed the word at the top of the page. S-A-R-B-Y-N.

Nybras.

He closed his eyes and grabbed the chair. He could see her, feel her here. He could see her writing on the paper, caught the swinging movement of what she'd seen, felt her fear, then terror!

Nybras!

Aqua eyes shimmered at him.

Lorenzo's eyes snapped open and he breathed deep.

Marcos stood just in front of the hearth. "I picked up an old evil. Not cold, but hot. You?"

"Same."

"Any ideas?

Lorenzo nodded. "Some bastard named Nybras. And I'm certain she knew him before. Probably about two hundred years ago."

"That's it?" Marcos shook his head. "She's your mate, don't you know?"

Lorenzo threw him a look and stalked from the house, walking the perimeter. The cabin was quaint.

"Why the hell didn't she sense it?" he muttered, pulling out his phone. He called Charles who answered.

"What? Did you find anything?"

Lorenzo filled him in. "What do you know?"

"Nybras isn't good, I'm still looking. I'll let you know more as I have it. Oh and you should probably know that Darrell is on his way with Lilly."

"What?"

"She refused to stay. Said you were going to need her help. So I sent Dena and Darrell."

"Great, they'll probably kill each other before they even get here."

He took a deep breath.

"Marcos know anything?" Charles asked.

"Not as much as I wished."

"I've alerted The Council. I'm meeting with their liaison now."

He took deep breath. "Thank you, Charles. But you should know--tell them, I don't care if this is sanctioned or not. Whoever took her is dead."

He clicked his phone shut and looked to the southeast, back towards the canyon.

* * * *

Pain spiked through her skull, biting her awake. She waited, tried to breathe.

What the hell?

Slowly, she tried to open her eyes. The room was fuzzy. Reya blinked, hoped that things would clear up but they didn't. Edges were blurred, whatever she was focusing on seemed to be too clear, almost right in front of her. She reached up and touched her forehead. Did she get drunk?

She tried to think.

Breathing deep, she smelled … earth. Damp earth and rock. She frowned and tried to look around. She was in their bedroom. The comforter beneath her was dark blue, the down as soft as always, the quilt covering her as worn as she remembered.

Her heart fluttered in her chest.

Something was wrong. She knew it, could sense it.

Her hand fisted on the medicine bag between her breasts.

Her breasts….

She was naked.

Chills danced and pricked her skin. She moved her head to the side. "Lo?"

Fear taunted deep inside. Something was wrong.

No. No. She was here. Here at home. Lo was just around.

What the hell had happened? Why couldn't she remember?

What did she remember?

Reya took a deep breath and tried to calm herself. Tried to see....

Lorenzo's face, worry creasing his brow, bracketing his mouth. His eyes hard and dark. Just as she started to call out to him, saw his eyes change, widen, heard his voice, edged with fury, "*Reya!*"

Blackness blanketed her mind.

What?

Lo?

Nothing. Her hand trembled. Her fist tightened on the bag around her neck.

Calm down. She just needed to calm down. For whatever reason, she was over reacting.

Remember....

She thought back. All she could remember was being in bed. Making love to Lorenzo. His body moving over hers, demanding her, calling her, marking her, claiming her.

Confusion and peace battled fear. What was going on?

She tried to roll over, but the pain in her head nauseated her. Reya moaned.

Careful not to move, she stretched her hand out. The light from the bathroom was dimmed. The curtains were drawn over the windows.

Fates, her head. If only it would stop hurting. Did she get drunk? Had she and Lorenzo partied? Celebrated something?

Pizza. They'd had pizza, she'd burned dinner.

An image, his voice gruff and growling in her mind, pierced through her. *You're mine.* She remembered the momentary sting of his teeth as he'd claimed her.

Then what?

She frowned, tried to remember, but nothing came to her.

Vaguely, as if through fog, she thought she remembered going to the office. What the hell time was it? What day?

"Lo?"

No one answered her. She listened and wondered what it was that seemed off. Was the air conditioner louder than normal? The ceiling fan? There was a noise, a hum that seemed out of place.

Taking a deep breath, she waited, hoping the pain in her

head would calm, but it didn't. On another deep breath, she tried to sit up. The room spun around her, pain knifing through her skull and she swayed, lying back down.

"Lo!" she called out. She was going to be ill.

No one came. She glanced at the door, saw the faint glow of lights from the living room, but nothing stirred.

If she were hurt, wouldn't he have been here? Yes.

If she was sick, if he had to go somewhere, he'd have made certain someone was there to watch her. Yes.

The ring on her finger seemed to heat a band around her finger. The medicine bag warmed against her chest.

She fisted her hand on it, realized again she was naked.

That just seemed wrong. She wiggled her fingers, her hands, her toes and feet. Nothing seemed to hurt, nothing was broken or sprained. Only her head hurt.

She needed some aspirin.

A noise hissed and she frowned. A light flicked on in the other room. "Reya?" Lorenzo asked.

Relief crashed through her. She closed her eyes.

Again something hissed. She wondered what it was, but hurt too badly and she was too tired to care. She threw her arm over her eyes and waited. If Lorenzo was here, everything was fine.

Yet even as his heels clicked across the tiled floor to the bedroom, her nerves tightened, her stomach tensing….

She held her breath.

"Hey, sorry, I wasn't here earlier. Had some stuff to do. A call came in."

She let her breath out slowly, pain still dancing in six inch heels inside her brain. What the hell was wrong with her?

She heard him move across the room, his boots hushing over the rugs. The tap gushed in the bathroom, but something in the sound seemed … different.

Like the hum, or lack of a noise. Something she couldn't put her finger on.

The bed dipped as he sat on it, and she reached down to pull the quilt up, once again chilled. That was when she realized something else.

Her breath froze and she looked down her body over her stomach to her groin. It was bare.

Slowly, she looked back up. Lorenzo sat on the bed, holding a glass of water and a pill. "Here babe, you need this. You had a hell of a headache, and no wonder."

A hot breeze flowed over her, and she looked again down her body. Her hair was there. Reya blinked, then glanced at him, with his dark slashed brows raised.

"Reya?"

God her head was screwed. "Wh-what happened?" she whispered, reaching for the glass, noticing her hand shook.

His other hand caressed her cheek and she jerked back at the contact. He frowned. "You fell at the shop, fainted and slammed your head into the display case. Don't you remember?"

The deep voice was the same, but it didn't comfort her.

Pain slashed again, white hot behind her eyes. She'd figure it out later. Quickly, she swallowed the pill he handed her.

For a moment, he said nothing, then took the glass from her. "Scared me to death." His hand touched her lower abdomen. "You need to take care of yourself now."

The babe! How had she forgotten?

She blinked as the room spun.

Again she reached for the medicine bag at her neck.

"Why don't you take that off?" He reached for her hands that held it, lifting them. But her hands seemed weighed.

Reya shook her head. "No. No, I want it on."

He frowned, even as her vision blurred more. "You'll sleep better without it."

Her eyes were heavy. What had he given her?

"Aspirin?" she asked.

His chuckle danced as his hand moved lower. He leaned over her. "Don't worry, Precious, just something to make you sleep."

Precious....

She shivered. No. Straining, she opened her eyes, her hand still on the bag around her neck. As if down a tunnel she saw his face. That face she loved, would die for....

Lorenzo....

The face shimmered.

No.

Precious....

Nybras. Her fist tightened on the bag, heating her palm, the bites on her neck and breast on fire.

Lorenzo! Help me!

Chapter Eight

Nybras watched her, saw her eyes widen, the fear shifting in them. He wondered how long it would take her. At first, disappointment had slithered through him, but then he'd sensed her doubts, the edge of fear sharpening her senses. It was like ambrosia.

Granted, he didn't want her to always fear him, but a little fear never hurt anyone. It allowed the soul to search, to seek and find that which bought peace.

"Sweet dreams, Precious." Nybras stood, shook the glamour off and strode from the room. At the door he waited, saw she was still, her breathing slow and deep.

He smiled. She was here, she was his, that was all that mattered. And in time, he'd move her where she would never be found.

The bands around his chest loosened. She was here. Finally, with him. All this time, all the searches, all the long cold nights. All the women he'd tried to bury his want with, all for naught. All because none of them were her. None of them made him smile, made him laugh, had the desire rushing through him. No other had ever survived the pleasure he gave them. Well, there was the vampire in Ireland, but she hadn't really impressed him all that much. He'd used the silver blade on her.

Thinking of that brought him back to the matter at hand.

He slowly pulled the door shut and scanned the living room. This décor bothered him. It was too simple, too plain.

But he only had to deal with it for a while longer. Then she would see it differently. As his, not this other cat's. A damn cat. Nybras shook his head at the vagaries of fate. Why she chose mediocrity when she could have him, he'd never understand, and he'd never give her another chance. This time he made certain. He would not gift her with his trust, or anything else. She had tried to kill him. Which in and of itself still shocked him, yet amused him. She hadn't succeeded, but damn the woman had given it her best.

He strode across the kitchen. His place was more ornate, more sensual…. This whole southwest design with its simplistic bare designs and pastels with the random bright color was beyond him. It lacked feeling and … passion.

Nybras closed his eyes and ended the glamour of the living area and kitchen.

When he opened them, he smiled. This was much, much better. Here he felt at home. Silks draped from the ceiling in golds and reds. Bright blue pillows, their tapestries woven with scenes of men and women in sensual poses decorated the low bed. He pressed a button on the countertop, and a panel of wall slid away to reveal the security cameras. He scanned the area and saw all was as it should be. The old stucco house, its porch sagging, sat still and aging.

Then he saw the dust from the road clouding the air. He clicked on the camera.

Selinna. It was about time. She had no consideration for those around her. For Selinna it was all about Selinna. She hadn't learned a single blessed thing through the ages. He blamed that on her brother, Sael. Not that he'd ever met the man. He'd met Selinna over a year ago by chance. They'd been lovers for a time. It was pure luck--or the hand of fate that had brought them into contact. For Selinna finally confided in him she'd found her enemies. When he dug deeper, he learned more. Nybras realized that Selinna would lead him to Precious and she had. But Sael…. Sael, Nybras had only heard of.

Just the name of that bastard licked his rage. But if not for the sick and twisted man, Nybras knew he would never have met Precious. And she was that. The way she seemed powerful yet vulnerable all at once.

He frowned as Selinna drove up and slammed out of the car. Well, she wouldn't have much to be upset about soon.

She strode to the porch, her black jeans painted on her long slim legs, the sweater leaving as little to the imagination as the pants. Her hair was pulled back into a twist at the nape of her neck. He had to admit, Selinna had a beautiful neck, but he didn't desire her. Not like he had others, not like he did Precious.

He'd thought about putting a bomb there, just there where he'd known she'd step, or anyone else for that matter. But then, he knew an explosion would bring mortals swarming all over the place. If possible, he avoided fighting with mortals. He might be a demon, but he still had people to answer to, and if he caused too many problems, then the greater powers would be down his neck and he'd be consigned back into serving the legions of hell.

He'd rather be here. So he did what he could, kept what he wanted. Searched for pleasure where he found it, where he wanted to find it. And he did find it. He always found it sooner or later.

There wasn't a more sensual creature than Precious.

And she was his.

He knew given enough time, Selinna would end up killing his precious. Selinna's rage went too deep, distorted too much. For him, he didn't care. He just wanted what was his. Period.

Selinna walked around the house. He switched cameras, watched as she cursed, hitting her hand on her thigh.

So impatient.

She could learn a few things, but he didn't have time. Loose ends were best tied, then snipped.

He strode over to the fireplace, the incense inside casting the flames in an eerie green. Above was a box, the carvings ancient and of his mother's people. Aerials had a race of their own, even though he'd always embraced his father's legacy more. He lifted the lid and smiled as the dim lights glinted on the silver blade, its handle carved with incantations and encrusted with amber and bloodstones. He knew the crystals had been carefully chosen. The dagger was often used for negative tasks and the bearer didn't want that coming back on them. The crystals balanced and cleansed the negativity from the act.

Or so he'd been told.

He wasn't quite certain he believed it, but it hardly mattered. The dagger had its uses. It was silver, solid silver. He knew its purpose, the reason for its creation was not a normal weapon of defense, but of that of assassination. It was used to kill immortals. One quick stab straight through the heart and all was over.

He palmed the weapon and glanced into the room. She still slept.

Night was falling. He loved the nights. It had been hours,

and a storm was blowing up from the north. He waved his hand and the room shifted back to the drab living room of her beloved cat. He shook his head and walked out, pulling the heavy door shut behind him.

He flew up the passage into the barn. There was no ladder and he knew the drop down was deep enough that she couldn't jump up and out--if she managed to escape out the two foot thick door. Which she wouldn't.

He smiled, dropped the cover over the hole and walked out of the barn towards the old house.

Selinna was pacing down the dilapidated porch, her squared heels clicking impatiently.

"Where the hell have you been?" she asked.

He didn't say a word as he walked to her. "You should have garnered a bit more patience, my pretty. Impatient people often come to very bad ends."

She crossed her arms over her chest. "I did what you wanted. I still want that Lorenzo bastard. You can have your precious Reya and--"

She'd dared to use her name. Only he called her precious.

"How dare you," he whispered, stepping closer.

She frowned. "What?"

He grabbed the back of her neck, chanted the words in his mind to bind her beast which he could feel her calling.

He smiled at the shock look in her eyes.

"What's wrong, Selinna? Can't find your puppy?" He laughed, flipping the dagger in his hand. Looking into her wide, angry green eyes, he slid the dagger between her ribs, tightened his hold when she would have pulled away and shoved the blade until he felt her heart pop. "No one calls her precious, Selinna. Only I call her that. She's *mine*."

Selinna's eyes clouded, her energy leaving her. He held the blade there, let her blood seep out of her heart, allowed the silver to poison what was left of her.

When she wasn't breathing, he jerked the blade free, wiped it on her sweater, and let her down on the porch. What a waste. She was a beautiful woman, but she let anger and hatred turn her bitter.

Even as he watched, she died like most that passed in the human form when they'd walked the earth too long. At least the more evil ones. He knew all didn't go this way, but just as many did. Her skin shriveled, turned almost green, then grey, fading into paper over a skeleton. Before he blinked, the remains became dust.

Nybras smiled, sucked in his breath and blew hard, until all the dirt was scattered in the air, nothing but particles dancing in the wind.

Humming, he went into the house to get a few things he thought precious might like later, and if she didn't....

Well, she really didn't have a choice anymore did she?

* * * *

Lorenzo scanned the horizon. He and Marcos followed the faint trace of evil on the land. Evil had a way of being traced and they did for a while. Several miles from the canyon. The dead animals and insects littering the ground, scavenging off of each other, were signs enough. The scorched and curled blades of yuccas. Then nothing. Not a damn thing. They followed the trail several miles further than Marcos had originally. Working across the land, they found more death and decay. Then, as if someone flipped a switch. nothing, damn it all. And he was looking, searching.

But then, he felt her, a shimmer, just a shimmer, relief, then fear. He saw their room, from her eyes, yet something was wrong.

Jerking out his cell phone, he dialed home. The phone rang and rang. "Hi, we can't come to the phone right now, but if you'd leave your name and number we'll try to get back with you."

He cursed, hung up and called Charles. "Did anyone check the house out?"

"No, we just raised the alarm because we're all bored. Yes, I closed the shop and checked it all myself. House is fine. Nothing in it to show she's there, why?"

He searched for her again. Saw the walls, the dim light from the bathroom, felt her pain in a distant way.

She had a headache. Where the hell was she? The room, the bathroom lights on dim. A man....

Lorenzo concentrated harder, and saw himself walking towards her. But as faded as the image was, he didn't know if it were a memory or if it was happening. And if it was, then how? He was here. Not there. He'd damn well know if he were with the woman, and he wasn't.

"Just images I'm getting of her at the house, or at least the room."

"Glamour?" Charles asked.

"Could be. I don't know. I don't know anything anymore." The one thing he did know was that he needed to hurry. It wasn't an option. If he waited too long….

Marcos stood to the side watching him.

He hung up and waited.

Marcos shifted and came to stand next to him. From here the walls of the canyon bit into the ground. This might have been home once upon a time, but he hated this place. She was somewhere near here, he knew that. And he'd damn well find her.

"This isn't good, Lorenzo." Marcos's voice was gruff, probably from all the damn cigarettes the idiot smoked. Not that that mattered to their kind. Normal things didn't kill their kind. Unless a major artery was severed completely and blood was let out--and by another immortal, they rarely died. Of course to make the death certain, silver was always used. Hell, he'd had this life for so long, he'd lost count somewhere after the year one thousand.

"I know," Lorenzo answered him.

"It's not a were. I'd know a were. And this isn't it. This is different. Evil. Plain and simple."

He knew what Charles had told him, what he'd learned since then. "No, it's not a were. He's a demon."

"He? Any particular demon?" Marcos's voice never reflected emotion.

He saw dust clouding in the distance behind a car. Who? Friend or foe?

Then he knew. Darrell and Miss Lilly along with Dena were coming.

Marcos cleared his throat. "Friends, I take it."

Lorenzo saw no reason to confirm. Instead, he leaned back and waited until the SUV pulled to a stop beside them on the desolate dirt road.

The doors shut and Miss Lilly climbed out, Dena helping her. Beads and crystals around her neck chimed, even as her eclectic stick thumped the ground.

"I hate driving. Pain in the ass at my age, but we needed to get here," she said stopping right in front of him.

He glanced at Darrell and Dena. "Thank you for coming."

Miss Lilly waved a hand between them. "Forget them.

We got to hurry. He's trying to weaken her power and he will if he finds a way. For now, I've stalled him."

Lorenzo slowly looked down at her, reigned in his temper and said, "You know where she is?"

Lilly nodded. "Old farm place." She closed her eyes. "Other side of the canyon. You're here on the north side. She's back on the south."

"How do you know?"

"I may be old, I may seem blind, but some things this old woman still knows, skippy. Now get in and drive." With that, she climbed into his Jeep, Marcos helping her this time and climbing into the back.

For one moment, he stood, wondering if she really did know or if he was wasting valuable time. However, he'd known Lilly long enough to know she might seem flighty, might seem eccentric, but she cared and loved Reya and she'd never pull a stunt like this otherwise.

Nodding, he breathed deep, wished Reya safe and climbed into the Jeep. They were going to find her.

Chapter Nine

She awoke, disoriented and tired. The room was dim and she tried to remember. She remembered waking before, her head hurting, and hearing Lorenzo's voice. Reya blinked and looked around. Lo wasn't here.

Stretching, she decided she'd take a shower. Naked, she hurried to the bathroom. Maybe the shower would wash the fog out of her brain. Something niggled at the back of her mind that things weren't right.

Standing, waiting for the water to warm, she studied herself in the mirrors. Still the same, still long, her hair the same, her eyes looked different ... almost sunken as if she'd been ill.

Everything was just as it should be.

When steam rose over the glass door, she climbed inside and breathed a sigh of relief. Probably just a bad dream and its lingering affects.

But then she felt it again ... that whisper that things weren't as they should be. She frowned and reached for her shampoo, the herbal fragrance the same as it always was. She made it herself and used more rosemary than citrus. Lathering it in, she leaned back and let the water beat down on her aching shoulder muscles.

The water hit the medicine bag around her neck. Darn it. She reached up, intent on taking it off, but instead she grasped it.

An image rose in her mind....

"Please, Nybras, no more." She gasped, her vision still grayed.

He was still moving inside her, the smile on his face, "But, Precious, it's so much fun."

She tried to move her chained arms, knowing it was useless. The manacles clanked as they always did.

"Please," she begged.

Instead he moved, his hand tightening again around her neck, squeezing ... squeezing ... until she couldn't breathe. Until she knew she would die. All she saw were his eyes, his

*aqua eyes staring down at her with some twisted version of
love.*

*He released her, she gasped just as he closed his mouth
over hers, taking her breath, robbing her of oxygen.*

*His power swallowed her, sucked her air from her lungs
until again she couldn't breathe.*

*He played with her for minutes, or hours she didn't know.
Tears leaked from her eyes. He kissed them, and when he
straightened, she saw there was blood on his mouth. From
her tears?*

But then she couldn't think as he started his game again.

*"I want to feel you die around me. I love how you do that.
It's not fatal." His chuckle danced between them. "At least
not for you. You're perfect, Precious. I love you."*

*Again his mouth sealed over hers, sucking her very
breath, her very soul and she had no more energy to fight
him.*

Shaking, Reya opened her eyes, her hand still fisted on
the bag. Nybras?

Things around her shimmered…. She closed her eyes,
shook her head.

A sound startled her and she looked out the glass door,
water trickling down this side of the glass. A person,
dressed in jeans and boots, a white shirt walked towards
her.

Lorenzo.

But still her heart slammed in her ribs.

No….

The warning slithered through her.

"Can I join you?" his voice asked.

She saw him drop his shirt, stood silent as he unbuttoned
his jeans. A boot hit the floor, then another. Power rippled
through the air and caressed down her body as gentle as the
water.

Reya took a deep breath, tried to make sense, tried to push
through to her instincts. He was walking towards the door.

For one instant, fear clawed through her, but then the door
swung open and Lorenzo smiled at her.

"Hey. You're looking better."

"Yeah, what the hell happened? I feel like I was run over
by a truck and woke up with fog instead of my brain."

He smiled and leaned his head under the water. Droplets

bounced off his dark hair. She let go of the bag and reached up, brushing her hand through his locks.

"I had the weirdest dream," she muttered, wondering why the fear hadn't left her yet.

The bag weighed, the mark hurt, her ring all but burned. She dropped her hand and looked at him, even as he lowered his head and smiled. Against her lips, he said, "Do you have any idea how much I've missed you?

His lips on hers were soft, not demanding.

But something....

He placed his mouth more firmly over hers, held her tightly, then drew a deep breath, pulling on the air from her lungs.

Her heartbeat slammed in her chest. No!

Aqua eyes.... Sucking the air from her.

She couldn't breathe.

Oh God.

Nybras!

She shoved against him and he only released her mouth, smiling down at her. The smile was on a face she loved.

Rage roared through her, the air shimmered around her. An illusion? A glamour? Her fury whipped out of her, and in that moment, she shattered the shields she hadn't even realized were carefully constructed and bonded with Lorenzo.

No!

He chuckled, against her mouth, the air around them continued to shimmer, shift. He waved his hand and the glamour around them dropped, allowing her to see all that was beneath.

She ripped away from him. She felt the anger clawing up inside her. Her power lashed out at him and he stumbled back.

"No," she hissed.

He smiled.

No, no, please no. She felt the tremors start deep within her. Oh please. Not Nybras. *Lorenzo!*

Blood roared in her ears. She couldn't think, couldn't....

Not Nybras!

Her breath panted. She glanced around the bathroom as the air continued to tremble and the glamour fell, not seamlessly. This was her power, rough, raw and shattering.

Pieces of the glamour fell away only to reveal scattered truths beneath.

He raised a brow and reached for her.

She glared at him.

"Bastard," she muttered. She thought of the words that Lilly had taught her, an ancient chant of protection.

Nybras watched her.

Her mouth moved, but he didn't hear the words. Instead, he felt them. A sharp edged whip lashing out at him.

He licked his lips, tasting her again, reminded again how her essence all but seeped into every fiber of his being. How nothing and no one had given him the same euphoric feelings that she had.

Her breath was rich, dark yet light, full of promise. And something else. Something that hadn't been there before.

It teased, taunted, even as the elusive hint angered.

He'd known the moment she knew. She stiffened, tried to pull away.

He was surprised, but not angered by her spirit. This would be even better than it had been before. This time, robbing her, breaking her down, creating who he wanted from what she was, would surpass their last meetings.

Her eyes chilled him, going cold.

"I like this new you," he said in a low voice, dropping his own glamour.

Her cheeks paled.

"Was it really so bad between us?" he asked, perplexed.

For a moment, she said nothing, then she straightened. "I'm not yours, Nybras. Move. I want out of the shower."

He held her stare, heard her whisper of fear, but her power and ... strength almost drowned it out.

Almost.

Almost wasn't completely. He saw the tremble of her hands, the chills on her damp skin.

He smiled, stepped back out of the shower, and grabbed a towel. This time the bathroom was as he wanted it. A replica of what had been in his fortress, with modern conveniences ... like a shower ... and other amenities.

Candles flickered on the marble vanity. The air swirled with spices and incense, heavy and fragrant.

Arousing.

He dried off, waited. Water hit the tiled floors of the

shower as she slicked it off of her, rinsing her hair. Nybras watched her through the opaque door. The way her long lithe body arched, the way her arms rose, her fingers running through her hair. Next time he'd have her use his soap. He liked it when she smelled of him. He always had.

He held the towel and waited until she finally climbed out. She stood staring at him, anger banked but still in her eyes.

"Here, you'll get cold."

Her body glistened from droplets and rivulets of water. The damn medicine bag and ring still adorned her.

He watched as she dried off, the way her muscles rippled. A sigh escaped. "I've missed you so much, Precious."

"Don't call me that," she said flatly, straightening and grabbing a robe.

"Would you rather I called you Kitty?"

She hissed at him.

He glamoured back into Lorenzo and said, "Or would you rather I call you Reya?"

Her eyes flashed at him and again he felt her wild power swipe at him. This time he stumbled back. "Do not do that. I can see you through the glamour anyway, Nybras. It's a waste of time. And don't call me Reya."

He laughed, straightened, and held his hand out to her. "How about Ree?"

Instead of answering him, she held the bag with her left hand, chanted words in that tongue he'd often heard from her when he'd whittled her down to almost nothing. He wondered if she even realized she did that. It was in the language she'd used when she tried to vanquish him.

"I've rattled you, Precious."

She finished her chant and he felt something come between them. He tried to take a step towards her, but couldn't get closer than two feet.

He raised a brow. "What now? Think that will keep me away?"

Precious simply walked out of the bathroom and into the bedroom. She strode to the closet, pulled open the wide wooden doors, carved just as his had been over two hundred years ago. She shook her head. "Nybras. You can't do this." He watched as she pulled out a pantsuit of dark ruby silk. "One thing I have to give you, you know clothes."

She gave the garments as much attention as she might a pair of cotton shorts. He frowned. They were fine things, for a fine woman. He'd carefully chosen them. "You should be more careful."

Her eyes flashed at him when she raised her head. "You have no control over me."

Is that what she thought? He studied her, saw past her bravado, felt her fear as it caressed him. He smiled. No control over her?

He'd have to show her differently.

Nybras scratched the side of his mouth, smoothed his mustache and goatee. "You know, Precious. You're really not in a position to state that, are you? About who is in control of whom?"

She paused and looked at him. "What do you mean? *I'm* in control of *me*. You have no say over what I do anymore."

He laughed and stepped forward, impressed when she straightened yet didn't step back. Her hair was still wrapped in the towel.

"True," he said, stepping closer. "But it's not just you anymore, is it?"

Her eyes widened, then narrowed. She said nothing.

He stepped closer. Still she held her ground, even as he stood right in front of her. "Precious, Precious, Precious." He shook his head. "When are you going to learn, darling, that you are solely and completely mine?"

Nybras reached up and cupped her face. She pulled back.

"I am solely and completely *mine*, Nybras."

He let his hand move from her face, to caress her throat, felt her stiffen as his hand grazed over her chest, then her torso.

She stopped breathing when he held his hand over her lower abdomen. He tilted his head and studied her eyes. "Just you, Precious?" he whispered.

Anger and hatred flashed in her eyes.

He smiled. "It was one thing that you tried to kill me. Amusing actually and you came very close to succeeding. But you didn't. So here we are." He leaned in, kept his hand over her stomach, and whispered, "Here we are. One big happy family." He brushed a light kiss across her pale cheek.

She didn't move, didn't blink.

Her fear shimmered between them. He decided to stroke it. "While you were sleeping, I thought of how to rid you of the babe."

She jerked back from him. Nybras only stepped closer. "But that was the anger and jealousy. I realize that now." He reached up and carefully unwrapped the towel.

Precious stepped back. "Leave me alone, Nybras. It's not the same. I've changed and people will be looking for me."

He dropped the towel and moved so that she was backed up against the wall. "You mean your cat friend?" He shook his head, tsking. "Really, Precious, what were you thinking? He's hurt you before, do you think he won't again?" Nybras stared into her eyes. "He betrayed you, Precious. Your cat doesn't deserve you."

For a moment, just a moment, he felt her waver, felt his power planting the doubts.

Then she blinked, shook her head and fisted her hand over the damn bag. "Lorenzo and I are mated, Nybras. There is nothing you can do now." She smiled, stepped away and finished dressing. He leaned against the wall and sighed.

"I guess we're going to have to do this the hard way, then?" Anger coursed through him. She wasn't acting right. She was supposed to be happy to see him. Fearful, yes, he wasn't stupid--he expected a bit of fear--but happy. This anger and resentment from her was not to be. She was *his*. His Precious, but things were all wrong.

He waited until she was dressed then motioned for her to follow. When she didn't, he only said, "All I'd have to do is chant a few words, and I could damage, even kill the child you carry. Is that what you want, Precious?"

A tremor moved through her, but she followed.

He waited until they were in the middle of the living room. Right where he needed her to be. He'd installed this just on this eventuality that she might be difficult. "I've a present for you, Precious."

He watched her as she stepped a bit closer, and a bit closer. On the floor was a pentagon, seemingly part of the floor. He smiled. If she only knew.

When she stood in the middle, he held up his hand. "Stop. I want to tell you something, but I want to make certain you're listening first." With that, he reached over and pressed the button he'd installed on the side table.

A loud whoosh slammed down around her. Reya instinctively ducked, covering her head. Metal clanged and clicked. No. She sat huddled on the floor, too afraid to open her eyes, but knew she'd have to. His chuckle danced around her, through her, in her.

Lorenzo. Hurry! Please, God hurry!

And then she felt her husband.

I'm trying, baby. I'm trying. Just hang on. Has he hurt you?

Instead of answering him, she opened her eyes. Her heart slammed into her chest, the bird wanting to be free, but couldn't.

Metal bars obstructed her view, metal bars she'd seen before. No, please no. She looked around. Five sides, just like before, domed just like before, one locked entrance just like before. Fear and anger rushed through her, terror batting back the anger.

She started shaking. Not again. She'd survived Nybras once, she wasn't certain she would ever be able to do that again. Now, now she knew what he was like.

But then, she heard Lilly's voice in her head. *Always remain calm. Chaos and evil often go hand in hand. If you keep your head, you'll find a way out.*

Reya knew, from experience that there was no way out of this cage. She took another deep breath and stared through the bars at him. Nybras, still so handsome, so much what many would dream to be the perfect man. His bald head gleamed in the low lights, his eyes still a brilliant aqua, the dark golden goatee and mustache neatly trimmed on a face that Michelangelo might have used for a model. He wasn't as tall as Lorenzo, not as lanky, but she knew his strength, even though she could look him in the eye at five nine. His muscles were smooth, like gentle waves in an ocean, rolling seamlessly from one to the next.

Perhaps that was what was so terrifying about him. He looked so wonderful, seemed so perfect … until she got to know him. Then his true nature came out. Because of him, she trusted no demon. Nybras was sadistic and enjoyed it, angry if the other participant did not.

She noticed the way his chest moved just a bit faster, even

as he tried to appear calm. The way the light brightened in his eyes and he watched her through the damn cage. She hated the cage, and he knew it.

Anger beat back the fear, yet still she sat. She crossed her legs, sat, and stared back at him. Hoping her voice didn't betray her, she said, "Really, Nybras." She waved her hand at the cage walls. "Couldn't you have come up with something a bit more original? How long have you been using this, anyway? Several centuries? Longer?"

"If it works--" he started.

"You won't get far with me."

He frowned. "I'll get as far as I need to go."

Chapter Ten

"By flying me and this cage through the air all the way back to your lair in Istanbul?"

He pulled out his Amazonite amulet he'd always used to put her in a trance. She snorted. "Sorry, I should probably let you know, that won't work on me. I've taken measures to make certain it won't."

His blond brows beetled. "You're not acting right."

"Aw. Shall I cry? Beg? Quiver in fear?" She felt like it. But that was what he wanted and she knew it. He loved to see her cry, to know that he'd brought her to that point and then be the one that 'fixed' things. No more.

She laid back and yawned. "Don't know what you gave me before, but it's really made me tired."

He sighed. "Battle of wills. Is it any wonder you're the only woman that is perfect for me?"

She clasped her hands together. The thing with Nybras was that sooner or later he caught onto her games.

"If you try to escape I'll make certain the child you carry will never be born."

Her chest tightened. He knew. He knew everything because at one time she trusted him, had even grown to love him. But then he'd shown her what he really was.

Not looking at him, she stared at the top of the cage. "Did you get someone else to make this? Or did you do it yourself?"

He cursed in a language she didn't know but remembered him using before. She watched as the ceiling moved back and a long dark shaft gaped beyond. The smell of earth and cool air hit her full in the face. Where the hell were they? A loud squeak filled the room. She wanted to, but didn't dare move. She could feel him, saw him out of her the corner of her eye standing just to the side of the cage. He always did that before. Just liked to sit and watch her. It messed with her mind, stretched her nerves, and made her wonder what she had done wrong. She now knew, she'd never done a thing wrong. Nybras was just sick and twisted.

Lorenzo....

The squeaking got louder. She wondered what awaited her next. If he wasn't watching, she'd touch her stomach, but she wouldn't now. Wouldn't give him the satisfaction.

Was she really pregnant? She wished she'd tested to learn for certain. She felt different, had taken Lilly's word for it. If she wasn't pregnant, she might be able to beat Nybras as she had before. That was *if* she were *not* pregnant. If she was, she knew from before, there was no way for her to shift.

"Did you at least get scars?" she asked, looking up and to the side from her prone location on the floor of the cage.

His eyes bore into hers, and she read more than his sickness in them. This time there was rage. He unbuttoned the dark blue shirt and pulled the left side of his shirt to the side. It looked as though his skin had been mottled, stitched and seared together. Long slashes ripped from just beneath his throat to his chest. She remembered biting him, remembered the scream of the wind, the tear of skin beneath her claws. But then he'd gone still, the wind died and she'd shifted, digging the keys out of his pants pocket and running for the door. She'd set the room ablaze with the oil lamp and slammed the door shut. Chanting words of old that she still had no idea where they'd come from. If asked, there was no way she could repeat them. Reya had assumed he'd died. She'd run and never looked back. She'd simply kept running all the way back to America, and finally back to New Mexico and years later to Lorenzo.

If pregnant, there would be no shifting into her cat form. She hadn't been able to shift with Little Moon. So what did she do?

Keep your shields against Nybras firmly in place. Call to Lo, and to Lilly.

She looked from her perusal of his scarred perfection to his face. "Bet that pissed you off." She looked back up to the gaping hole in the ceiling that she knew was wide enough for the cage. Something was swinging in the abyss. What?

"If you want me to apologize, Ny," she started, using the nickname he despised. "I should let you know it's not going to happen. My only regret is that I didn't make certain you were dead."

She looked back to him. "Bet that was a turn off to some women huh?"

He smiled, and it held no humor. "If they didn't like it, I made certain they didn't live long enough to complain about another single thing."

* * * *

Lorenzo felt her, could see vague images of bars and the man with the aqua eyes. More than anything he felt her fear, her anger, but wrapped in calm. He frowned.

He had to find her.

He looked at Lilly. "Can I track them using her fear?"

Lilly shook her head and climbed from the vehicle. "Come here, Lorenzo." She pulled something from her pocket. Lorenzo, already out of the truck and leaning against the fender, walked to her.

"Lilly, I really don't have time."

"Shut up. I should have already given this to you. But then things happened before I thought they would. I gave her a medicine bag."

"With what?"

She waved him away. "A bit of this and a bit of that. Worry not. From the same branches and springs of herbs, I also made your bag. From the same crystal, both your stones were born. From the same salt and ash, you both hold. She has your other half and you have hers. That is a powerful connection." Then the strange old woman mumbled something and held the bag out to him. He bent down and she put the leather string around his neck. As soon as it touched him, Reya slammed into him.

Lorenzo staggered under the sharpened senses, under the honed images.

Before things were vague and fuzzy, he closed his eyes and could see much more, the hinges on….

A cage. She was in a damn cage!

"I'm going to kill him," he whispered.

But then he saw more, the memories screaming in her brain, slashed into him. Her chained to a bed, begging, pleading, not breathing. Over and over, the bastard killed her.

The images kept coming, hounding him, slamming him from one side then the other. He didn't realize he was on his knees until Marcos' voice floated down the tunnel of hell he was in.

"Lorenzo! Damn it!" Hands hauled him up. "Get this damn thing off of him now!" Marcos' voice lashed out.

"I can't. It's bound to him, just as it is to her. They become two of the whole."

A hand grabbed his, which he'd fisted on the medicine bag, but he shrugged it off. Tried to pull himself into the here and now. "Son of a bitch," he hissed.

He waited, sniffed and knew this was not the time to drive, not the time to wait and see.

"It's time to hunt," he bit out. "Call them," he said to Marcos.

Marcos' brow rose. "You want me to call the cats?"

Lorenzo stared into those black eyes. "It's getting dark. I want the cats called. This bastard is mine but if I don't take him, I want the pride to rip him to shreds for what he's done to Reya. She's my mate. Carries my child. It's my duty, then the pride's to avenge her."

Marcos nodded. He stepped back, and Lorenzo saw that Darrell and Dena were off to the side, watching silently.

"Is she hurt?" Dena asked.

Rage clawed through him. Lorenzo didn't answer her. Marcos' roar filled the air, bounced off the canyon walls on and on it went.

Soon the area was teeming with cats, shifted and shifting. The wind howled down the canyon. The night promised snow and possibly ice. He could smell it on the wind.

Lorenzo waited. Many were already there, though he wasn't certain how. Charles stepped forward and he wondered how he got there. Charles was still in human form. His grey goatee as neat as always, but the generally teasing eyes were serious. Lorenzo didn't need to ask any questions.

"I contacted The Council. They found out that an Aerial demon whose father was a *djinn* was seen in the area. Goes by the name of Nybras. The Council mentioned that he's wanted in questioning for the murders of mortal, immortal and shifting women."

The rage was iced over with terror. "I'm not going to lose her, Charles."

Charles shook his head. "This is serious, Lorenzo. The Council notified the Keepers' liaison who is sending someone. There are people all over who want to talk to this man, Lo. It's not just you."

Reya's fear and her screaming memories ripped into him. "It is now."

To those present, he thanked them all for coming. "We have to find her. This man is not going to be easy to defeat, but he's harmed and brutalized my mate, who's carrying my child." Even though he didn't want to say it, he did for the liaison present. Wherever the man or men were. "The Keepers want him alive." But he'd be damned if they got him. Nybras was his. He, Marcos and Charles shared a look.

Dena strode up to them. "There is one Keeper here, name's Rhys."

"And?" Marcos asked.

She shot him a look. Instead of answering him, she motioned to a man. He stepped away from an outcropping of rocks. As he got closer, Lorenzo noticed his head was bald, his eyes a wicked green, muscles ripping beneath his long sleeved shirt.

"I'm Rhys. The Keeper. You know what you're doing?" he asked, his voice tinged with Britain.

Keepers were the justice arm of The Council. They kept the balance of power even, kept the peace. They were incredibly powerful beings.

"Yes, I'm saving my wife."

Those green eyes bore into him. "This is a demon, he commands the south winds, he's elusive. He's most vulnerable after either a kill or a transformation. That is when we have to bind him."

"And if we can't bind him?" Lo asked him.

"If you hope to capture him, let alone kill him, he needs to be bound."

Lorenzo looked at the Keeper. Rhys would do what he needed to. Fine, let him. Still looking at him, he said, "He's mine. I'm not letting him leave."

"Powerless is all I've been ordered to do." For a moment, Rhys' bright green eyes bore into him. "Whatever happens to him after I've taken his powers is out of my hands. Though The High Elders want him stopped."

The High Elders? They were a special group who decided on important issues for The Council.

Lorenzo smiled. "Oh, he'll be stopped, don't worry."

For a moment Rhys held his stare, but in the end he only nodded.

With that, Lorenzo threw his head back and shifted into a mountain lion, his clothing falling away, his hands lengthening into pads and claws, his mouth changing shape. Over the centuries he'd become accustomed to the feeling, if not as comfortable with it as he'd have liked.

I'm coming, Ree. Hang on, baby.

* * * *

She kept watching the gaping hole into darkness. A metal cylinder descended then connected with a solid thunk to the top of the cage. Another magnet. She could feel him still watching her. She stayed calm, she looked to the side and asked, "Where to, Ny? We heading to your secret place? Another palace no one's heard of? Or are you so pissed and set on revenge that you'll only take me to hell?"

He smiled, and it held no amusement. Then his power slammed into her and it was as if he reached through the bars and cut off her air.

"You were saying?" he asked, walking closer and closer. She looked into his eyes, the aqua color filling her mind as it always did. Instead, she fisted her hand on the bag and closed her eyes. For one moment, she drew a breath, but then she felt him, whisper soft against her. Her eyes shot open, but there was nothing there.

Fear tickled up her spine. She could sense him, but she couldn't see him. His chuckle danced over her. "Is that fear you're holding back growing stronger?"

She took a deep breath and swiped out with her hand, but air blew past her, around her, against her. His laughter grew stronger until he shimmered and appeared just beside her. "I've missed you," he said.

He said it so … normally. Not with malice, but sincerely. But there was something bent in him. She'd seen it, been part of it and she wanted no part of that madness ever again.

"Nybras," she said.

He stared at her for a long moment. The cage lurched and started to move, as the magnet pulled it upwards.

Magnets often realigned things, powers could dim or become more pronounced. She hoped that the magnets might affect Nybras in the former way instead of the latter.

If his powers were dimmed, she might be able to defeat him.

Then again she wasn't the naïve scared woman she'd been when she'd met him, vulnerable to his lies and deceptions.

The cage rose, swaying in the air. She tried not to think of how far they were climbing.

Instead she carefully kept her walls erected in her mind. Imagining herself behind walls that reached as high as her eyes could see.

He smiled at her as they passed from the lit room beneath up into the black chasm of the shaft. It was dark, the walls not more than inches from the sides of the cage. But they pressed in on her, trapped his power inside the cage with her.

Still sitting, she took a deep breath and imagined herself inside her fortress. Lorenzo would be there soon, she knew. Deeper and deeper into her safe place.

"I will have you. You can hide from me if you wish, but you're mine. No matter if you try to hide on this world, or in your mind, I'll always bring you back to you." His voice whispered hot against her cheek just as the cage lurched again. "Back to me."

Reya blocked him out and concentrated instead on herself, within herself. He could do what he wanted with her, but she would not help him. She would not give him any more. He wanted his perfect mate as he always had.

She, Reya did not belong to him. She was Lorenzo's.

And just his name. She could hear his whisper in her mind, *"I'm coming ... close ... love you...."*

Of course he was coming. The man probably had the entire pride out looking for her. She knew he'd connected with her, had felt him inside her mind as she'd been scared and looking at the damn bars. And considering how staticked their connection had been earlier, she was happy it was this strong now. Comforted.

But what of Lorenzo?

Did he have any idea what they were up against? Did he know this was not Selinna or just another immortal? What if she unwittingly brought him to his death?

Fear blossomed.

Calm down....

Laughter danced in her head and it wasn't Lorenzo's. Who was talking to her? Reya opened her eyes and looked at the face right in front of hers, their noses almost touching.

She didn't jump, didn't flinch, only held her breath.

He smiled at her. "You're very beautiful, but then you always were," he whispered, leaning in and brushing a soft kiss against her lips.

She pulled back, and watched as the corners of his eyes narrowed. "I'll make you want me. You know I can."

She remembered.... She shivered ... there came a point where she'd give him whatever he wanted just so he'd leave her alone, grant her peace, let her breathe....

Then again, she'd finally reached a point, she'd tried to kill him. He'd reduced her to complete animal instincts and stripped away her humanity bit by bit, day by day, piece by piece until she'd finally lashed back.

"My only mistake was in not making certain you were dead."

He leaned in closer, and said, "My mistake was trusting you too much, Precious. I won't make that mistake again."

The cage rocked to a stop and she fell against him.

He laughed.

She shoved against him, wishing more space between them, but knowing it was impossible.

The shack they were in was directly above what must be a mining shaft. Old rusted tools and picks hung on the walls. She glanced around scooted back from him as far as she could. The metal bars of the cage bit into her back.

With another click, and a groan from overhead, the cage walls rose from around her. Reya scrambled to her feet and darted to the doorway of the shed. It was dark, but the cat in her could see the outline of the night around the opening. Just as she reached it, a gust of warm wind slammed into her from behind shoving her through the door. She raised her arms, shielding her face. Pain exploded in her arm and she screamed even as something else scraped along her forehead and cheekbone.

Reya rolled, felt the cold north wind and thought she heard familiar chanting in her head. Her vision wavered but she stood and swayed.

I'm here.

"Precious, Precious, Precious." Nybras stepped through the shattered door and simply stared at her, his aqua eyes glowing until the edges were red. Then wind, hot as fire bit into her flesh, stealing her breath. She gasped, but her lungs burned, her eyes burned.

His laughter danced around her.

Something growled, or someone.

Nybras paused, glanced at her, then back into the night. "Aw. Someone's come to the rescue." Nybras tsked. "You don't deserve her. You betrayed her when she needed you most. She doesn't love you. She's mine."

A growl rumbled across the ground.

Nybras chuckled. "Here, kitty, kitty, kitty."

Fire whirling faster and faster shot up from the ground, hissing over the land.

Angry, she jumped to her feet. "Stop! Stop it, Nybras! Leave him alone."

Nybras hissed at her, his words garbled and serpentine.

She shuddered. "Leave him alone."

He held his hand out to her, and then fisted it.

Pain cramped in her lower belly.

"Don't tell me what to do, Precious. You know I don't like that. And the children witnessed such behavior."

Like they were his?

Rage clawed through her as the pain knifed again.

Roars filled the air.

Nybras grabbed her just as she lashed out at him, all the pain and anger, rage and shame rolled and balled into one. She screamed and focused on Nybras.

He stumbled back, but then he threw up his hands and sucked everything out of her, all her emotions, all her breath, her very soul.

The world went black.

Chapter Eleven

"Nybras!" a voice shouted. His concentration lost, he whirled to see who else was there. He could feel them, slinking through the night, the cats, waiting. Just waiting.

But he would win.

"I am Rhys." The voice was low, deep.

Nybras could have cared less who the bastard was. "And I am Nybras. What do you want?"

A growl rolled through the night and then he saw them. Eyes, hundreds of glowing eyes, like circular mirrors in the night, some tinted red, most were an eerie green-blue. All were staring at him straight on, though moving closer. And closer.

He turned, saw more were at his back.

Circling.

He smiled. He would get out of this. He always did. Chuckling, he leaned down and picked up Precious.

"I don't care who you are." He held her against him, her legs hanging down, her arms limp at her sides, her face near his.

Again the growl clawed through the darkness. A pair of eyes moved one way, then the other, always watching. Waiting. Stalking.

He smiled. "Ah, her cat. Come to get her have you?"

The roar filled the air, filled Nybras' head, bounced around the canyon walls. "Did you know I was her first after you? All those years ago?" The growl rolled across the ground, filled Nybras' chest, but he ignored it and kept on. "She was so easy to comfort. So naïve still, so hopeful, so...." He stared at the eyes that had stopped and stood watching him within the circle of the other cats. "So damn vulnerable." Nybras leaned over and licked her cheek. "And so much fun to *control.*"

The cat crouched low, but the other voice stopped it.

"Me first," Rhys said.

Nybras took a deep breath and called the wind to him. She was limp in his arms. What the hell had happened to her?

He looked down at her, her dark lashes against her cheeks. He barely felt the rise and fall of her chest. For a moment fear fluttered in him. But he knew, if he could get her away, things would be fine. She'd lashed out at him. He hadn't felt emotion like that from her before or since the last time she attacked him and damn near killed him. But this time, he merely reflected the power back onto her.

The warm wind twirled faster and faster, kicking up dust. Roars filled the air. Wings flapped in the dust tunnel he was creating, moans and screams of the damned. Darkness whirled around.

Then another voice, a woman's rose above, chanting. Cold wind slammed into his own heat and pushed it back. He frowned and looked, but he couldn't penetrate the darkness beyond.

Her voice rose louder and louder, pushing against him from all sides. Chills raced over his skin.

He said his own words, calling for his powers to blast the cutting north wind.

But then he heard Rhys' voice and Rhys stepped closer. The voice hissed, serpentine words slithering through the night. And from here, Nybras saw, recognized and *feared.*

Rhys had wings. Black wings with white tips.

A Keeper.

For a moment, just a moment, he tightened his hold on Precious. Rhys walked closer and closer, still hissing.

Nybras carefully set her down. Rage clawed through him. He wanted her, he wanted….

Pain knifed through him from his chest out to his hands. Fire flew from his fingertips, great streaks of white hot orange, sparking hundreds of feet into the dark sky.

He yelled, tried to draw his power back, but it was no use. He knew that. He'd heard the stories.

The Keepers. Always watching, always keeping the damn balance.

He could feel his power flowing out of him faster and faster, screams and gasps filled the air, streaming towards Rhys. The night sky was lit up, glowing in flickering shards of red and yellow.

Then it stopped.

Nybras fell to his knees beside Precious. Rhys walked to him, bent down and picked up Precious.

"No," Nybras whispered, reaching towards her, calling on his wind, on the heat, but nothing happened.

Nothing.

He started to shake. Images of the dead rose in his mind.

Rhys stood and walked away. Just behind him was a cat. A large mountain lion. Rhys didn't stop, only said, "He's all yours."

* * * *

He's all yours.... Damn right the bastard was. Lorenzo watched as Rhys set Reya down beside Lilly who reached her hand out and laid it on Reya's forehead. Lilly met his gaze, smiled and nodded. Relief slid through him, but it was short lived. He turned back and stared at his prey....

He'd seen the way Reya had flown through the air, her scream, then her silence.

Right now, his rage was centered, focused. He circled the stripped demon who knelt in the circle. The bald head rose and those aqua eyes, tainted with madness looked at him from beneath brows. A slow smile started across that mouth.

"I'll always be a part of Precious. She's my precious. You can't change that."

Lorenzo leapt his claws extended, shredding where he swiped. He played for a bit, Nybras' yells only adding to his fury.

The other cats moved closer. He could hear Lilly softly singing a healing chant. He raised his head and looked over the other felines to the woman who now lay near the fire Rhys must have built.

He turned back to Nybras. Time for the kill. He wanted it to last longer, but there were more important things.

Lorenzo swiped out again, catching Nybras across the chest. Nybras fell back, arms flinging to the side and Lorenzo was on him. The smell of his enemy's blood filled his nostrils, soaked his whiskers.

He paused, his teeth just biting into the skin of Nybras' neck. Those aqua eyes locked with his.

"Precio--"

Lorenzo sank his teeth in and snapped Nybras' neck. The bones and cartilage gave way with a satisfying crunch. For just a moment, he wanted what came so naturally to weres.

Instead, he released the man, spit the blood out on the

ground and shifted effortlessly into man.

"Rip him apart. But don't eat of him. I'll kill any who disobey. I won't take the chance of his evil spreading," he growled.

With that he hurried over to the small group near the fire.

Roars and growls filled the air behind him. He didn't care. All he cared about was Reya.

He dropped to his knees beside her. "Baby, baby, open your eyes. Come on." He put his hand on her chest.

His breath froze until he felt the faint flutter.

"Reya?" he asked.

"She's between," Rhys said, his voice devoid of any emotion.

Lorenzo was so happy she was here, here with him the words didn't register at first. He ran his finger over her cheek, over her nose, across her eyes. Then he realized she was wearing different clothing. A silk pantsuit. The anger slammed back into him and he looked back over his shoulder to the cats who were taking turns ripping apart Nybras' remains.

Then the words clicked. Lilly's chanting was getting on his nerves. The old woman bent, placed a fist size amethyst above Reya's head. An amber stone went to the right, a turquoise the left, and jet below Reya's feet.

What the hell? "What do you mean between?"

But it was Lilly who answered. "Our ancestors often spoke of those that walked between worlds, Lorenzo. Souls trapped neither here nor there, neither in darkness or light, life or death. In between."

He shook his head. "I don't understand."

No one said anything. He leaned over Reya, shook her slightly. "Reya. Merria! Answer me. Open your eyes. Open your eyes and look at me, damn it."

But she didn't move.

He couldn't lose her. Not now. Not ever again. They finally had it all. Finally had everything in their grasp. She'd re-claimed to be his. After all this time.

"Please don't leave me, baby. Please," he whispered, leaning closer. His lips brushed hers, and then locked onto her mouth. "Come back to me. Please."

His medicine bag slid down and landed on her chest.

He closed his eyes and kissed her, feeling a pull deep in

his gut. *If she won't come to me, let me go to her.*

* * * *

Reya lay in the soft twilight. It wasn't yet dark, but not daylight. It wasn't cold, or too warm. Her walls here were high.

She remembered Nybras' voice, remembered too the pain in her stomach. She lay back on the cool green grass and looked up at the pallet of sky, bright orange where the sun set changing to a deep periwinkle in the east.

The pain. Then she'd hidden behind her shields.

She wasn't going back out. *If* she could stay here, stay here where it was safe, he couldn't hurt her.

"Come back to me."

Lorenzo….

She opened her eyes and saw him standing above her, with worry in his eyes.

"What are you doing here?" she asked, slightly puzzled. This was her sanctuary. Her safety zone.

He took a deep breath and sat beside her. "You wouldn't come to me, so I came to you."

She frowned. "What does that mean?"

His warm hand cupped her face, his thumb grazing back and forth, back and forth across her mouth. "I was scared today, Ree."

She nodded. "I know so was I."

He took another deep breath. "You should have told me. You should have…." He shook his head again and stared at her. "I don't care about that. I don't. I do, but I think I understand why you didn't tell me."

"You'd have hunted him down to the ends of the earth." She held his wrist, turned her head and kissed his palm.

"I'd have hunted him into hell for what he did to you," he said, his voice low.

She looked into his deep brown eyes. "I want peace, Lorenzo. I just want peace."

He smiled, though sadly. "I do too. But if you stay here, if you leave me now, I can't even try to give it to you."

Her heart fluttered in her chest.

Lorenzo leaned closer and kissed her. The kiss went from soft to coaxing to demanding.

His hand still cupped her face, but now held it more firmly, his fingers lost in the strands of her hair. His other hand ran over her back, up and down, up and down relaxing her until she lay back onto the grass.

"I love you, Reya." He stretched out beside her, letting his fingers dance over the buttons, over her torso, over the waist of her pants.

She wanted this, wanted him. Clothes were quickly discarded until bare flesh met bare flesh.

Reya wanted him. "You...."

He lifted his mouth from hers, staring down into her mouth. She could feel him ready against her. "What?"

She shook her head. "Take him away from me."

For a moment, raw fury shown in his eyes, but then he smiled that sexy smile of his. "With pleasure."

He growled and nipped her neck, then her chest.

The lovemaking was slow, liquid. Not a quick burst of fireworks, spectacular though they could be. No, this was like the rising sun, until finally she crested, light filling every part of her soul, her mind, her heart. In that instant she opened her eyes and looked up into his and knew that this was what was meant to be.

This. Them. Together. She was his mate and no one could ever change that.

Epilogue

Reya looked out of the window at the dusted peak of Taos Mountain, the cup of tea warm in her hands.

She breathed deep the morning air, glad she didn't have to go into the shop today. More and more, she was relying on Charles to take care of the day to day things.

Granted she couldn't always stand being cooped up, but that was okay too.

She closed her eyes and took another deep breath, thankful. Today was a beautiful day. No more secrets, no more fears…. Everything was as it should be.

Arms wrapped around her and pulled her back against a solid male chest. "Why're you up so early?" Lorenzo nuzzled the side of her neck, even as his hands rubbed her ever growing abdomen. "Sun's not even up. Come back to bed."

She didn't turn around. Didn't have to. She knew Lorenzo would always be there for her.

"I dreamed of him again last night," she whispered.

He kissed the side of her head and sighed. "I know."

After the canyon, she'd told him everything, how she'd met Nybras, how she'd fallen for his charm, his … something. She told Lorenzo how she'd almost loved the demon that lured her to a hell of his own making, until she realized there was no rescue, no escape. Until she was forced to act or be killed.

Lorenzo still wondered why she'd hidden this from him, and honestly, there were no easy answers. Fear and shame made strange bed fellows.

"He can't hurt you anymore, baby."

She nodded, turned and smiled back up at him. "I know. You saw to that. You always, in the end, see to me, don't you?"

His brows rose and a soft smile played at the edge of his lips. "You're my mate."

As simple as that.

"I love you," she whispered, turning her attention back to

the window before her.

His arms tightened around her before his hands continued to rub her swollen stomach.

For a moment she gazed across the prairie, almost purple in the early morning light, then turned and looked at the painting hanging on the wall over the mantel. It was a painting of a mother with long dark hair, the pueblo in the back ground, the mountains guarding those below. Children played in the dirt beside the water dappled with sunlight.

Lorenzo had painted it. In this one a boy and a girl were the children and she was the woman.

"You never did tell me why you painted that. Or what you called it."

His hands paused, and she felt his chest rise against her back. Leaning over, he kissed her cheek and said, "I call it *Peace*."

CARNAL INSTINCT

Michelle M Pillow

Dedication:
To Mandy Roth, my other writing half, the pain in my
backside, the ... *ouch!* What'd I say, Mandy?

To Jaycee Clark, I'd like to take this opportunity to ask you
a very important question. You know those cookies I got
from you for Christmas? Got any more and can I get back
on the 'nice' list for next year?

Chapter One

"Oh, like I care how much protein you consume in a day,"
Fiona LaSalle mumbled, glancing up from her clipboard
through the fencing that kept the lion on his side of the
cage. What was she doing here? She didn't belong in a job
that required her to take care of animals. The only pet she'd
ever had was a goldfish when she was five. The poor thing
only lasted a week before she found it floating at the top of
the fishbowl. It was only later that she learned goldfish
don't eat pancakes and powdered sugar.

Fiona sighed, unenthusiastically checking boxes on her
sheet. The bright sun shone overhead, beating down on her
until she could feel rivulets of sweat working their way
down her spine. She'd give anything for a cooling breeze.
The polyester uniform of the Jameson Wild Life Rescue
and Preserve was chafing her delicate skin and the sunshine
was really starting to take its toll on her creamy white

complexion. So much so, she'd found freckles starting on the bridge of her nose that very morning. Fiona hated freckles, but they were the curse of the redhead and both she and her sister had it. Just like their mother, the two LaSalle sisters had dark auburn locks. Their green eyes were from their father.

A long cement clearing made up most of the lion's den and it was populated with only two cats. Mia, the lioness, didn't move. In fact, the female cat always ignored her. The virile male lion was a different story. Almost as if he could understand her, the lion lifted his head and made a grumbling sound. His bushy hairdo shifted as he kept his eerie yellow eyes on her. Fiona shivered. If she didn't know better, she'd say he understood every word she said to him. Every time she came near his cage, he looked at her like that and every time she spoke, he looked at her--studying her so intensely she wondered if he was getting ready to pounce.

Making a few notations on the clipboard, she continued, "They need a 'lazy' check-box and a 'smells funny' one too. And no offense King, not that you would really care anyway, but you've got this so ugly you're cute thing going on. I think it's the hair. Care to tell me how the hell you get it to look that good?"

King lifted his head and shook it slightly, sending his bushy locks rippling. Fiona made a face at the lion. "Show off."

The lion seemed to be smirking at her, its yellow eyes shining. Either that or he was still hungry.

"Great, the sun's starting to get to me," she mumbled, half heartedly looking over the den. The fact she thought a lion could smirk was not a good sign. Seeing King still eyeing her like she was the next piece of meat on the menu, she grumbled, "I know how you get your hair so shiny. It's from basking in the sun all day licking your balls. Guess I'll just have to stick with deep conditioning, won't I?"

Well, she thought, shrugging. *It isn't like he's going to tell anyone I'm being mean to him and it's not like the preserve has security cameras installed. No one will see me teasing the lion.*

Not that it mattered about the cameras, even she wouldn't strike an animal. Verbally goading an obnoxious one was an entirely different story. Besides, King started it--always growling and acting weird whenever she did her rounds.

Okay, she wasn't being completely fair. Her bad mood had nothing to do with the lion staring at her, or the fact that she was wearing polyester, or the fact that she had to work out in the sun. She was mad at herself. However, since berating herself on a daily basis for being a trusting fool had gotten old, she'd taken to venting toward the lion. The way she looked at it, it was good therapy. She got the aggravation out by grumbling at him and no one got hurt by her comments. Besides, there was just something in the way he looked at her, all cocky and knowing.

Fiona took a deep breath. Life really was depressing. Her ex, James, had cleaned her out--bank accounts, trust fund, jewels, cash, furniture, even some of her clothes. What did the man need with her high school prom dress? She didn't even really like the awful pink thing.

He'd even thrown her vibrator in the trash! What kind of man got rid of a woman's vibrator when he was dumping her? Hell, when he was robbing her blind? His lazy ass had spent three months on her couch whining about backaches and all the time he was scheming to take her to the cleaners.

"I'm such a fool," Fiona whispered. She knew she was in a funk, but she couldn't help it. Life really sucked right now. She'd had to go crawling back to her father for help after James left. As if the 'I told you so' wasn't bad enough, she had to get a jobof his choosing before he'd even think about helping her get out of the credit card debt James had run up under her name. Apparently, her ex had applied for every card that came in the mail without telling her. "I am such a fucking idiot."

Feeling feisty and definitely needing to vent today after receiving another bill for nearly six thousand dollars at twenty seven percent interest, Fiona looked at the lion and added, "You're as bad as my ex-boyfriend, you know it? He also had a thing for laying around and pretending to be the boss. From what I remember being said about male lions in elementary school, you're the laziest of the cat breeds." She dropped her voice into a condescending tone as if she were talking to a child. "Aren't you? Yes, you are. You're a lazy little bastard, aren't you? Just like James always bitching about how his back hurt. Oh, oh, poor me, my back hurts."

The lion lowered his head and snorted. He didn't look too amused. Fiona chuckled at him, unable to stay mad. She was taking her bad mood out on a cat, but she couldn't help it. Whatever she said to King wouldn't hurt his feelings.

"Ah, I'm sorry, boy," she mumbled, eyeing the lion. The creature tilted his head and slowly stood. He took a step forward and she lightened her tone. It was the first time he'd ever approached her. "That's not fair to you, is it? I didn't mean it, honest. You are so much better than James. Snakes are better than he is. Horse dung is better than he is. And you're much prettier. You really will have to tell me how you get your hair so silky. I'd make a fortune selling whatever it is to women. Maybe then I'll get out of debt."

When she said 'prettier' the lion snarled as if offended by the girly word, but continued to make his way forward. Fiona clutched the clipboard to her chest and kneeled down to his eye level.

"All I wanted was to be appreciated, you know? And James really seemed to do that." Fiona shook her head, thinking more about the past than looking at the wild beast coming toward her. "He said he believed in me. No one had ever said that to me before but my mother. I just thought if I gave him time and believed in him that he would change, you know, get better." She snorted. "Stupid, huh?"

It had been two months since he left and even some time before that since they'd had sex. Only afterward, did her neighbor confess to the cops that he'd been fucking her as well--apparently with no back problems holding him back. By that point, Fiona could believe just about anything. James was definitely not the man she thought he was. Or maybe he just wasn't the man she'd *hoped* he was.

"I'm tired of being alone. My problem is that I give people the benefit of the doubt--trusting them blindly first only to get hurt in the end." She continued, looking deep into the creature's yellow eyes. They were so calm, almost understanding as they looked at her. She felt herself melt a little. "You know what I think my deal is? I need to get laid. I need to go out tonight after work and screw the first man I come across."

The lion stiffened at her words and she giggled.

"You won't tell anyone, will you, King?" she asked, grinning. "Man, it's been so long and I hate to admit it, but that's one of the things I actually miss about being in a relationship. James was far from being a saint, but he was definitely good in bed. You know what I mean?" The lion growled low in the back of his throat. She took the sound as an answer and continued. "The sex was great, not phenomenal, but really good. It was the only time he didn't seem to be complaining about his back and his fake illness did give me the advantage of always being on top."

All of a sudden, the lion roared viciously. The sound sent chills of dread down her spine, startling her. There was something in the beast's eyes. He was angry. No, not just angry. He was outraged, pissed to the point that he wanted blood. Lunging at her, the lion crashed into the cage. Fiona screamed as the chain link swayed under his great weight. The clipboard dropped from her hands as she struggled to get to her feet. The lion continued to attack the fencing as if he wanted desperately to get at her. She screamed again, loud and long as she ran from the lion's den as fast as her feet would carry her.

* * * *

Fiona looked at the floor in shame before staring desperately at Dr. Eve Matthews from the woman's office door. "I'm really sorry, Dr. Matthews. I didn't mean to scare the kids by running and screaming through the preserve. I promise it won't happen again."

Eve was the veterinarian who ran the preserve with her Russian-born husband, Viktor. They were newly married and in the process of building their dream home on the preserve. Viktor was dark and mysterious and so tragically cute. He was also very much in love with his wife.

The doctor was moving her stuff into her new office--a room cluttered with piles of books and stacks of boxes. It was part of the newer complexes just built by the preserve's new owner, Finn O'Conner. Finn was a friend of her father and it was because of that relationship that she was even considered for this job. Her father wanted her to learn the value of manual labor--or so he said. Fiona knew he just wanted to punish her for striking out on her own against his wishes.

"But please take a moment to listen to my side, doc. I'm

telling you, there's something wrong with King. I go by to do my checks every day and every day he watches me with those ... those intense eyes of his and then today he actually charged the fence. I think he wanted to kill me. I saw death in his eyes. I wouldn't be surprised if he's gotten loose. We should send out a search party for him. There are kids still on the grounds." Fiona took a deep breath, well aware that she sounded like a madwoman. She couldn't help it. Picturing the look on the lion's face gave her chills.

"Actually, the kids have all been taken home. They were too shaken by your performance to stay and finish the tour." Eve took a deep breath. "And I've sent Fletcher out to check on King. He assures me the lion is in his cage, sleeping peacefully."

"Dr. Matthews, please, if you had security cameras installed, you'd know that I--"

"I have no doubt the lion got a little...." Eve paused as if struggling for the right word. "Ah, rowdy, but I can assure you he wasn't trying to kill you. I've had King here for five years. Trust me when I say I know him well. His diet's been changed and he's probably just temperamental because of it. I'm sure that's what you've been noticing."

"I want to change assignments again, please."

Eve studied her, her gaze calm.

"Please, Dr. Matthews, I know I've asked for several changes in assignment, but I swear this time it's...." Fiona paused. Eve quirked a brow. "Please. King's got it out for me. I know it. And didn't you say you didn't want to stress the animals out? If he doesn't like me, doesn't that count as me stressing him out by going by there?"

"Fiona," Eve said, taking another long, deep breath. It was clear the woman was put off by her, but Fiona couldn't help that. They were just different people with very different personalities. This place was Eve's life. To Fiona it was just a job she was forced to endure until her father picked a new one with which to torture her. "You know, working with animals isn't for everyone. There's nothing wrong with that. Now, when I hired you, you said that you didn't scare easily and that you were up to the challenges we face here every day. I gave you a chance, but--"

"No, please," Fiona interjected. She knew what was coming. Eve had the 'I'm so sorry, but I have to fire you' look on her face. Unfortunately, Fiona couldn't blame the woman. "I need this job, Dr. Matthews. I can't lose it. If I lose another job my father will disown me. I'm not complaining. I promise I'm not." She took another deep breath, trying to calm her nerves. "I just want to put in for a transfer to a different section of the preserve. But only if one happens to come up."

"Everyone helps everyone here," Eve said. "You go where you're needed. Now, I already excused you from dealing with tour groups--"

"They asked too many questions I couldn't answer," Fiona interrupted. "I thought it might look bad for the preserve."

And I was tired of looking stupid--being shown up by second graders when it came to big cat knowledge.

"And I excused you from working in the lab," Eve said.

"I already said I'm sorry for fainting. I had no idea there would be that much blood involved."

"It was a surgery," Eve said dryly.

"You know what? Can we just forget I was here? Please." Fiona slowly backed out of the office. She cursed silently to herself, knowing she couldn't lose another job--not after the strings her father had pulled to get it for her. Was it her fault she hadn't found her calling yet? "I'll stay where I'm needed and you won't hear another peep out of me on the subject, okay? And I'll never, ever, ever scream again in the preserve. Even if I'm being eaten alive by one of the tigers. Promise."

Eve sighed and opened her mouth.

"I promise." Fiona drew an X over her heart in the childhood gesture of *really* promising and said, "Cross my heart."

"Fine," Eve said, though she sounded reluctant. "One more chance. Just ... don't get eaten, all right."

Fiona nodded eagerly and hurried out of the office before the woman could change her mind. To herself, she mumbled, "Good going, Fiona. You being a fraidy-cat almost got you fired."

* * * *

"Okay, Cade, what's up?" Eve asked, looking in at the lion. Her husband Viktor was by her side, paying more attention to the way the setting sun reflected off her shoulder length blonde hair than what she was saying. Viktor was a cat shifter--half man, half black panther. Eve was his human turned immortal wife who ran the preserve. The woman had a kind heart and was loved by all the shifters and non-shifting big cats under her care.

Cade let his body shift from lion form so he could stand before Eve and talk with his human voice. He liked spending his days lazing around in the sun at the preserve. Human life was much too complicated for his liking.

Besides, he thought, glancing back at the lioness with whom he shared the cage. *Mia needs me. I can't abandon her now.*

Tan fur rippled into waist length blond hair, automatically blowing forward over his naked chest. Eve averted her eyes. He thought it funny, the way she got embarrassed by their nakedness. After centuries of changing form, all the cat shifters had gotten used to walking around naked. Besides, being half cat kept them trim and lean and most looked damned good in the buff. They had absolutely nothing to hide.

"Howdy, doc," Cade drawled, grinning widely as he crossed over to her. He put his hands on his hips, standing proudly, his cock nestled between his thighs.

"Uh, Cade, do you mind, buddy?" Viktor asked, pointedly. "You're embarrassing my wife."

"Can't help it," Cade laughed. "She's so cute when she's red."

"Cade, get dressed," Eve said, her face turning a darker shade. "Or so help me I'll shave you in cat form just to see if those pretty locks of yours fall off."

Viktor looked down at Eve's blushing face. The pheromones he was emitting were potent enough for the whole preserve to smell. His voice dipped and his voice became husky. "Yeah, she is cute, isn't she?"

"Eh, come on," Cade grumbled, waving his hand in the air in a feeble attempt to get rid of the pheromones. "Give us bachelors a break, would you?"

"One of the girls who works for us says that King's been intimidating her," Eve interrupted their teasing. Viktor chuckled lightly, but kept quiet. "Care to tell me why you're harassing the help?"

"Oh, her." Cade frowned and crossed over to the small

cave. He was still angry when he thought about the woman telling him how she'd slept with another man. Pushing on a fabricated rock, he waited for a secret compartment to open. The preserve was closed and he felt like getting out of the cage. Taking the clothes he found inside the compartment, he pulled on a T-shirt. Tight blue jeans were soon to follow.

"Yeah, her," Eve said, tapping her foot. "Care to explain?"

"I hope you fired her." He shook his head. That woman was annoying as hell, putting him down one minute as if she actually knew him and then talking about fucking another guy the next. It didn't help that just seeing her walk near his cage made his body tight with desire. Everything about her was a distraction. His cock twitched, wanting to rise to full length. He was glad he'd dressed, not wanting Viktor to mistake the reaction for Eve. Eve was beautiful, but she was also very much taken. Catshifters respected each other's territory.

"Well, no, I didn't," Eve said. Cade wondered at the relief he felt at her statement. "I know Fiona is a handful, but Finn's been insistent that we keep her on. He says it's a matter of great importance and the truth is I have nowhere else to put her. I've tried everything. She can't cook so the small café's out, she's useless in the lab and all the other cats aren't as patient as I know you can be. I put her in this section because I thought you'd be nice to her."

"Vik, tell your wife to turn off the flattery and batting eyelashes," Cade said, even as he felt himself softening to Eve's dilemma. She really was a good person and he hated to see her so upset--especially in her so recently delicate condition. "You should talk to Finn and tell him her attitude is all wrong for this place."

"I will," Eve promised, "just as soon as he gets back from Europe. So, can you do me a favor and put up with her until then? Please? For me, Cade?"

"Well..." He hesitated, his resolve crumbling. Damn, but he was weak when it came to his female friends. "Okay, I'll stop harassing her." He paused, giving a meaningful look down to her flat belly. "But only if you name the baby you're carrying after me."

Eve looked confused and Cade knew Viktor hadn't told

her yet. She turned to her husband in surprise. Viktor shot him a look of slight annoyance, but Cade didn't care as he gave an insolent grin. With a light jump, he hopped over the tall fence with ease and strolled down the path. As he walked away, he heard Viktor say, "I was going to tell you, my love, but there wasn't time. It just happened this morning."

Chapter Two

Cade shifted his motorcycle into gear. Riding was almost as nice as running free on all fours through an open plain. He loved the feel of the wind in his long hair, the freedom of the cool night as he rode through the countryside. Only tonight, he wasn't headed to the countryside. He was going into town.

For some reason, he was drawn to find some female companionship. Shifting his hips, he suppressed a growl. His cock was so hard that he could barely straddle the big bike. He knew damned well who the reason was, even if he hated to admit it.

Fiona. Her name was Fiona. He hadn't known until he heard Eve say it. The woman didn't wear a nametag like the rest of the staff at the preserve. It didn't stop him from staring at her shirt though, especially her round breasts.

Cade liked aggravating the woman, because she aggravated him. Unfortunately, it wasn't just his temper that she provoked, but his libido. Every time he was near her, he'd smell her sweet perfume and it was all he could do not to shift and throw her up against the chain-link fence just to fuck her delicate little body until neither of them could walk straight. She was so tiny, with wide green eyes and beautiful auburn hair. Oh, and her breasts. Man, they would fill his hands to overflowing. She had dark, round nipples too. He knew because he'd splashed her one hot day when she'd taken off her work shirt. The damp white undershirt had molded very nicely to her upper body.

He growled, loud and long into the wind as he sped up, hunching forward on the bike. His stomach was tight with pent up need. Already he could smell her in his head. He was going to find her tonight and he was going to purge the aggravating woman from his system so he could think straight.

Damn those green eyes of hers!

Mm, and her mouth. Cade forced the motorcycle to go faster until he soared over the dark pavement. That woman had the kind of full lips a man paid big bucks to have wrapped around his cock. Damn, but he wanted to fuck her sweet little mouth. Already he could picture it in his head-- had been picturing it since first seeing her at the preserve.

Hell, while he was at it, he might as well fuck her firm little ass, too. No reason to leave any part of the woman untried. The carnal instinct inside him was strong and bursting to get out. He'd suppressed his animalistic human nature for too long and it was suddenly letting loose with a vengeance.

"Fiona," he whispered, knowing that tonight was about so much more than sex. This was his future. Their future. He was a cat, used to trusting instinct. And every instinct told him he'd found the one. His mate. Fiona.

He didn't want to admit it, but there it was. Fiona was his mate.

When desire was this hot, there was only one way to cool it. He needed to feed the flames until they were spent. Only then would the fire burn itself out. Only then would she belong completely to him. Cade took a deep breath. He only hoped she felt the same way.

* * * *

Fiona sat alone in the corner booth, eating her grilled chicken salad. Sighing, she thought, *I really need to get out of this depression...*

Almost regretfully she thought about work. Her father had really picked a doozey of a job for her this time and she'd have to do it until he told her where to go next. He was punishing her for leaving his fold in the first place. Fredrick LaSalle had wanted her to marry the right man, get the right house, have the right babies. When she didn't do it, forsaking his desires to live her own life, he'd been livid. Crawling back to him hadn't been easy, but she had no choice. It was either she lived up to her responsibilities and paid for her mistakes by honoring her 'debt' to creditors, or she declared bankruptcy and took the easy way out.

Fiona was not the kind of girl to take the easy way out. Besides, doing things this way was also a form of self-punishment. She'd been such a fool for trusting James!

Taking a sip of water, Fiona forgot the salad and slumped down in her seat, losing her appetite. What she needed was a diversion. She needed a man--some drifter coming through town who wouldn't be averse to having a one-night stand. She hadn't been lying when she told King that she needed to get laid. Her pussy ached with need, even more so now that she didn't have an eligible partner with whom to slake her desire.

Apparently the lion didn't think it was such a good idea. Good thing she didn't need his approval to go through with her plan. She'd always been a sexually charged person, but since starting at the preserve, her lust had gotten worse. It was probably just a coincidence, but it didn't make her life any more tolerable. Unfortunately, she needed a willing candidate and she had no clue where to get one.

Just then, like a sign from above, a single headlight shone into the restaurant's front window as a motorcycle came to a stop. Her heart nearly exploded in her chest as the rider cut the engine. The light shut off and, in the soft glow of the streetlamps, she saw a man like no other. He had incredibly chiseled features, a broad muscular body, and long blond hair that flowed to his waist.

Her eyes traveled down over his body as he lifted a leg over the bike. He was trim, fit, lean. Tight denim hugged his thick thighs and outlined his perfect hips. Now this was what she needed. A man that looked this good would definitely know how to treat a woman in bed. Heck, at this point Fiona would gladly let him take her anywhere, just so long as he took her.

Feeling slightly reckless and knowing she had little to lose at this point in her life, she met the man's eyes boldly as he stepped into the restaurant. His wide frame seemed to fill up the tiny dining area and his vivid green gaze found her instantly. When he looked directly at her, it was as if the whole world faded away. Lightning pierced her soul at his attention, making her shake all the way down to her toes. He didn't move for a long time, appearing just as stunned as she was.

Carnal, primitive fire had never consumed her like it did when she looked at him. A silent understanding seemed to pass between them. Fiona reached blindly for her purse to find her wallet. The man stepped toward her, his chin lowering some as he neared. There was something very predatory in his gaze, the primal fire of a hunter on the prowl. Her heart sped in her chest, thundering in her ears.

This was insanity, but she didn't care. She'd prayed for a gift like this.

He stopped at her table and glanced over her. Men like this just didn't exist, did they? Everything about him radiated potent male. His eyes flickered to her hand still stuck in her purse. A slow grin curled the side of his face as he reached behind his back and pulled out his wallet. Without looking, he grabbed a bill and tossed it down on the table. Then, he offered her his hand.

Fiona gripped her purse, shaking slightly as she slipped her fingers into his warm ones. He turned, leading her from the restaurant. Her eyes drifted down to the tight fit of his jeans. The denim hugged his perfect ass. Everything but the man was a blur and inside her body every nerve seemed to whisper, *This is meant to be. Go with him. Be with him.*

He led her out the door to his motorcycle and let go of her hand to climb on. Fiona watched, wondering what she should do. His large thighs straddled the seat and she swallowed to see the obvious bulge of his cock pressing against his jeans. Unless he stuffed his crotch with a sock or something, the man was incredibly well-hung.

"Where are we going?" she asked, trying to come to her senses, trying to ignore the pull he had on her. The strange, animal magnetism was too potent to disregard. It was like part of her soul knew this man, knew that she'd be okay with him. Strange thoughts whispered in her head.

Go with him.

Be with him.

He's yours. Claim him.

"For a ride," he answered, his tone husky. His silky voice was almost as gorgeous as he was. A brow arched on his chiseled face. "Why? You got somewhere else to be?"

"No," she answered, before she could think to stop herself. Why did she say that? Why was she even out here? This was crazy!

Claim him.

"Worried, then?" There was challenge in his words, but also a light teasing. When he looked at her in such a way, he became so familiar. A nagging thought pulled at the back of her mind, but she couldn't quite place where she would've seen him before.

Yeah, in your dreams, silly. Now go and claim him!

Fiona smiled as she looked deep into his green eyes. He had kind eyes, soft and affectionate. She trusted those eyes. Regrettably, she wasn't so sure she had the best judgment. She had trusted James, after all.

This is a mistake. Don't trust your instinct. He's a stranger. This is crazy.

Fiona opened her mouth to politely thank him for the offer and decline, but the breeze pushed his masculine scent over her and she got a deep whiff of it instead. It was like he emitted a pheromone she couldn't resist. Instantly, her body numbed and all she could think about was having sex with the delicious man in front of her. Nothing else mattered but the need building in her stomach. Her nipples budded against her shirt, begging to be freed.

A soft moan passed her lips. Slowly, she climbed on the back of the bike and put her purse between them to keep her sex from rubbing up against his firm butt. Just the idea of it made cream gather between her thighs, dampening her panties even more.

Fiona didn't care. She couldn't resist, didn't even think to try. Every fiber inside her body told her that this was right. This was the man she was meant to be with.

"No, I'm not worried, but you should be," she said, answering his question, her tone husky as she slipped her arms around his firm waist. The man chuckled softly. His heat soaked into her as did his delicious smell. Wantonly, she pushed her chest along his back. Her breasts instantly swelled at the contact, sending fire through her blood. His long, gorgeous hair was crushed between them, lifting to tickle her bare arms. The man glanced over his shoulder and grinned, his expression saying he knew exactly what her reaction to him was.

"Do you believe in fate?" she asked, not knowing where the question came from. She never would've said that out loud to a man. It sounded so girly.

"I believe in destiny," he answered, moving to turn the key. The bike roared to life, vibrating between her thighs. It took all her willpower not to wiggle against the tight leather seat until she orgasmed.

"Then let's go." Fiona held him tighter. Maybe she had met him before in a dream. Or maybe she was just a fool.

He nodded once, not turning back around as he revved the

engine. Laying her head on his back, Fiona hugged him tightly and took a deep breath. Again the smell of him invaded her with its heady lust.

Oh, yeah. This is definitely the only place I have to be.

* * * *

Cade couldn't believe that Fiona had followed him from the restaurant without question. Part of him was angry that she'd merely walk off with a stranger without so much as asking his name. Another part of him was elated that he didn't have to waste time trying to convince her to go with him. His cock hurt too badly for him to be charming and smooth at the moment. If he had to seduce her later, fine, but right now he needed release.

Feeling her arms tighten around his waist as he purposefully sped up the motorcycle, he decided to be mad at her later. Besides, it was quite possible she felt and understood their destiny just as he had. She did ask about fate, after all. Was that her way of saying she knew and she accepted him as her mate? Cade gave a small smile. He'd have thought mating would be a lot more difficult than a couple of sentences.

This whole thing might turn out easier than he first pictured. The way her thighs curved around the back of his made his cock lurch to be free of his jeans. Maybe her aggravated behavior at the preserve was because she'd been waiting for him to shift and make a move. It wasn't completely unheard of for humans to know of his kind and accept it. Maybe Fiona knew he was a shifter. Though, he wasn't about to shift and find out until she said something first. Her small body felt too good pressed along his back and it had been way too long since he'd been with a woman. He didn't want to scare her away.

I'll show you who's lazy, he thought, remembering her words to him at the preserve. The idea held no malice, just pure intention. *When I'm done with you, you won't be able to walk and hopefully neither will I.*

There was just something about her that made him forget every thought in his head. He looked at her and all he understood was desire. She wasn't his normal type--sure, pretty was his type and she was way beyond pretty--but she knew nothing about animals, or at least about big cats. By the way she walked and acted at the preserve, she was a little on the prissy side. Cade was an outdoorsy type of guy, which wasn't too surprising being that he was a shifter. He liked camping, hunting and hiking. He'd bet his right testicle that the preserve was the closest Fiona had ever been to the wilderness.

Despite these superficial differences, he'd wanted her from the first moment. The little look of fascination she sometimes got when she watched them was adorable and he could tell by her gentle movements that she was kind hearted under her wounded exterior. Cade would've loved to have met James, just so he could kick the man's ass for hurting her.

The pull between them was strong. It invaded him to the point that he actually waited for her to walk by his cage. His eyes took in every movement of her body when she was near and he thought about her when she was gone. The restaurant was the first time he'd looked at her with his human eyes, but the attraction between them could've set the room on fire. She'd felt it too. He could smell that she did. Her longing was a fragrant scent in his head--calling to him, urging him to ride faster. He did, slipping her away into the night.

Knowing he couldn't hold his desires back much longer, Cade finally slowed the bike and turned onto a narrow dirt road. Fiona purred like a kitten, rubbing her face along his back. He knew she was too far gone to even worry about where he was taking her. The pheromones he was giving off probably had her nearing the throes of passion. Good thing the pheromones only affected his destined mate or the whole restaurant would've rushed him.

* * * *

Fiona took a deep breath of air as the man pulled the motorcycle to a stop in front of a lake. The dirt road stretched along the banks and the night sky reflected off the glassy water. She climbed off the back of his bike as he cut the engine.

Now that they were stopped, she began to shake. It was peaceful around the water and only the hum of insects filled the air. They really were isolated out here in the country. He got off the bike and turned to her. His body was large, easily towering over her slighter form. She felt small, delicate, weak next to him.

What am I doing here? I must have been insane to get on this man's bike.

The green in his eyes seemed to glow in the moonlight as he stared at her--confident in himself. Fiona shivered. There was nothing sexier than a confident man and the hint of danger only added to her arousal.

"I'm Fiona," she said, realizing she didn't know what to call him. He stepped forward, his hand brushing along her cheek.

"Cade."

As the soft word passed his lips, he leaned in, opening his mouth to hers in an instantly deep kiss. She'd never felt so much passion in another person as she did when Cade thrust his tongue into her mouth. He explored her depths, groaning into her as if he couldn't get enough. His hands slid down her arms, only to pull her shirt up.

Fiona couldn't reason beyond the feel of him. A carnal instinct welled inside her, forcing her to succumb to an animalistic side she didn't know she had. Cade's smell overwhelmed her, driving her passions to the boiling point. Part of her felt as if she really knew him in her soul--on a very base level. Before she realized what was happening, he broke the kiss just long enough to yank her shirt over her head. He then tore her bra free with a mighty rip.

Cade stood, staring at her breasts as they both gasped for breath. Then, his movements purposeful, he reached forward, watching her reaction as he touched her breast. He weighed the globe in his palm before flicking a thumb over the nipple. A shockwave hit her stomach and she leaned into him, wanting more.

She gasped as his long hair tickled her flesh, surrounding her as the breeze pushed over them. Cupping her breasts with his warm palms, he again kissed her. His tongue teased her mouth, until she was so crazy for him that she aggressively sucked it between her teeth.

"Ah, kitten, you taste so good," he moaned into her mouth.

Cade tore his lips from hers only to lean over and smother his face in her chest, groaning and breathing deeply as he pinched her nipples. She couldn't pull away--not that she wanted to. Fiona gasped, forced to take a step back at his forceful persistence.

A low growl sounded in the back of his throat. It was seductive, yet raw and possessive. His hands slid to her hips, stopping her from backing away as he sucked a nipple into his mouth. Cade was so strong, holding her captive as he did wickedly delightful things to her breasts. Primitive grunts sounded in the back of his throat as if he would devour her whole.

Yes. Oh, yes....

Fiona ran her hands through his beautiful locks, letting him work his magic on her skin. She was so caught up in the pleasure of his mouth that she was surprised when she felt the cool night air caressing her naked butt. He'd quickly worked the pants and underwear from her hips. The warmth of his palms made her shiver in delight as he grabbed her ass and kneaded the cheeks hard. The movement parted the folds of her sex, but the breeze could do nothing to cool the wet heat that built there.

Cade moved his hand to her sex and slipped a finger up into her tight folds. He watched her carefully, his voice dipping as he said, "Ah, no wonder I can't keep my hands off you. You're in heat."

In heat?

She tried not to giggle and failed. That was an interesting way of saying her pussy was wet for him. At the sound of her laugh, he thrust his finger up deeper. Instantly, the sound became a weak moan.

"I can't wait to feel your tight body wrapped around my cock."

Fiona barely heard him through the blood rushing in her head. When he spoke she got the barest trace of an accent, but she couldn't make out what kind.

Southern, perhaps? Definitely not deep south, but....

His calloused thumb flicked over her clit and she forgot all about placing his accent. When he touched her like that, she could barely stay standing. Fiona grabbed his arms, disappointed to realize that he was still wearing all his clothes. She'd been so busy letting him have his way with her that she hadn't even tried to undress him.

"Cade," she moaned, pulling at his T-shirt. "Please, baby. I want to feel you--*ahh*."

He wiggled his finger inside her with expert precision, hitting the sweet spot buried within. Her hands gripped his shirt, unable to find the strength to pull it off. A tiny orgasm exploded inside her.

"Ah, yeah, that's it. You're so hot, aren't you, kitten?" His voice soothed as he continued to work his hand along her pussy. Her muscles clamped around him and he only groaned louder. "Your smell has been driving me crazy. I want to claim you so badly."

Fiona merely whimpered as he pushed the sweet spot harder, fingering it in a steady rhythm.

"You're primed for me, aren't you? Your body knows me, doesn't it?"

It was true, every word. The lure of his body had pulled her to him since she first saw the bike stop in front of the restaurant. Strange as it sounded, their coming together felt like fate. She could no longer avoid this moment than she could live without breathing.

He thumbed her clit and growled, "Doesn't it?"

"Yes!" she gasped, grasping his strong arms for support. His forceful nature excited her.

"Mm, that's a good little kitten," he coaxed, sounding very much the dominant male. He pulled his hand from her sex and she thought she would die if he didn't put it back.

"Oh, please, don't stop," Fiona begged. Instantly, she reached for his cock, curious to see if the giant bulge was really all him or just stuffing. Feeling the unmistakably hot outline of his shaft through the denim, she trembled. It was all him.

She rubbed his arousal as he worked around her to free it from his jeans. He didn't wear underwear and as soon as he pulled the zipper down, his shaft sprang forward into her hand. She gasped. His cock grew in her palm now that it was free from the confines. Instantly, she let go.

"It's, ah...." She tried to step back. The man was ridiculously huge. Too huge. Monstrous!

"Your sweet pussy's going to feel so good and tight on me, kitten," he said, his eyes continuing to glow in the moonlight as he stroked himself. The orbs mesmerized her and she stopped her retreat. "But first I want to feel those lips of yours sucking me until I cum in your mouth. When I do, I want to watch you drink me down. I'm going to lay claim to every inch of you."

Fiona found herself nodding weakly in agreement.

Whatever you want, Cade.

She watched his fist swallow up the thick head of his shaft only to pump over the length. Even as she feared his great size, she couldn't completely fight the euphoric pull of his pheromones as they wrapped around her. Fiona told her legs to run, so she could get away from him and think. They didn't listen.

"What's happening?" she whispered. "Who are you?"

"I'm the man you've been waiting for."

"How...?" Fiona shook her head, trying to clear the fog. Here she was standing naked by a lake in the middle of nowhere.

"Fate."

Fiona's lids fell heavily over her eyes and she moaned as passion continued to well within her.

"Get on your knees for me," he said, his tone commanding and imploring at the same time. He was cocky and confident. She found it an incredibly sexy combination. Everything about this man was pure Alpha male and she found herself willingly obeying.

She eyed the thick shaft as she pulled the jeans lower on his hips. He threw the shirt from his head, breathing hard in anticipation. Muscles dominated every inch of his chest and waist. Fiona smiled and peeked up at him from her place on the ground, feeling very catlike as she licked her bottom lip. He groaned, his body tensing visibly at the gesture. Fiona's smile widened and she had the insane urge to dominate the Alpha.

Oh, yeah, you go ahead and think you're in control. We'll see who claims who.

Purring, she licked the tip of his shaft. The smell of him only seemed to grow stronger at the brief touch. The purr turned into a moan. She licked him again, slowly sucking the tip between her lips. Suctioning her mouth, she pulled lightly. Salty pre-cum moistened her lips as she slid off.

So good....

Grabbing his cock, she stroked its long length and sucked the tip deeper. Cade thrust, surprising her as he hit the back of her throat with his thick length, nearly gagging her with his great size. She fisted her hands, squeezing him tighter as she mindlessly began kissing and nibbling the hard length. Fiona took him as deep as she could as she practically devoured his hard shaft. She'd never tasted anything like it.

"Ah, damn, kitten," he panted for breath. "I'm going to ... *ahh!*"

The words never made it out. His cock twitched a second before releasing a hot stream of cum down her throat. It was delicious and she drank down every tasty drop. When he pulled her off him, she expected him to be tamed. She was wrong. His large shaft stayed completely erect and the fire in his eyes burned hotter. He fell to his knees before her and grabbed her hips. With surprising strength, he spun her around and had her on her hands and knees before she could think to protest.

Cade positioned his body behind hers and reached a hand between her legs, sliding his fingers along her wet sex from behind. Water lapped the shore from the lake and the breeze did nothing to cool her ardor. The taste of him in her mouth only strengthened her need for him. She was crazed, mindless, and she needed him to release her.

She dug her fingers into the moist dirt road, not caring that they were technically out in the open where anyone coming by would see them. It only added to the forbidden danger of what she was doing. Fiona never took herself for such a wild, primitive lover, but with him she couldn't seem to help herself. The carnal need overrode anything else.

She looked down just as Cade flipped over on his back. He positioned his head between her thighs and pulled her hips down so she was smothering his face. Fiona tried to let him breathe, but he only growled, pulling tighter. His tongue delved into her pussy, lapping up her cream as if she were a delicacy. He nibbled her clit, sucked it, licked it. Soon she was wiggling against his mouth, needing to find climax. Her pussy worked along his chin.

Cade groaned and didn't let her pull away as he rubbed her body's moisture all over his lower face. When the tension inside her body was to the snapping point, he released her hips and was poised behind her with lightening speed. She wiggled, disappointed that he'd stopped before she reached her climax against his wonderful lips.

But, as teeth grazed her ass, she knew he only had more pleasure in store for her. Hands spread her thighs wider and she felt a tongue licking along her slit. A finger trailed from her pussy, dragging her cream to the tight rosette buried in her soft cheeks. She tensed as he probed her. When he'd said he was going to claim her, she never imagined he'd go there--to a place no man had ever touched her. There was no time for second thoughts or embarrassment. It felt too good.

Cade's moans of approval only grew as he pushed his finger inside her anus. He wiggled his finger in small circles, hitting nerve endings she never realized she had. His touch stayed light and gentle on her ass as he rubbed his cock along her wet slit. Fiona's body jerked, her pussy still sensitive from his intimate kisses.

Ah, yeah, fuck me like an animal. Just like this. Claim me.

Fiona pushed back, curious to feel his enormous length prying her open. She needed this, needed to be fucked so badly it hurt. She wanted to feel his big cock pumping its release inside her.

"Ah, Cade!"

* * * *

Cade couldn't believe his luck in finding the passionate woman before him. Her taste was on his mouth, driving him wild. He wanted to roar, to shift, to let the cat in him out to play. But, he knew it was too soon. Humans didn't know his kind existed and they really didn't mate for life on the first 'technical' date--if that's what this could be called.

Cade had dated a lot in his time, but he'd never had a woman as hot as she was. Fiona was a wildcat, secure in her passions. Her body pressed back in offering, her body stretching before him. It was a gift he wouldn't refuse. Pushing forward, he pried her tight body open with his cock. He held his breath. Her pussy fisted his shaft to the point he nearly exploded.

He wasn't sure her tiny little body would take all of him, but when she didn't protest, he kept going. It was too much. With a growl, he slammed into her, fitting himself to the hilt. She gasped, her body tightening on him as her muscles adjusted to his size. Cade didn't have to move. Just feeling her muscles contract to fit him was pleasure enough.

However, Fiona had different ideas. She pulled forward, only to thrust herself back onto him. He gasped when she did it again and again, urging him to take her. The animal in him wanted to play and he couldn't stop himself as he grabbed her hips. With a wild jerk he roughly rode her willing body, sliding her over his cock.

Her body bucked as he pumped his hips and watched her firm little ass. Cade wished he could hold back, fight the orgasm building inside him, but it was no use. His body needed another release and it was going to take it whether he was ready or not. This time he couldn't hold anything back. The second her body clamped in release, he let loose, filling her with a hot jet of his cum.

"Cade," she cried, his name heaven on her lips. She moaned, shaking in her intense pleasure.

Cade didn't move, as he stayed buried deep. He felt the beginning connection stirring between them. Fiona was marked as his woman.

Chapter Three

Fiona couldn't keep the smile off her face, as she made her rounds at the preserve. After their session by the lake, Cade had driven her home. She wanted to talk to him, but it seemed silly to make small talk after what they'd just done. There was also something very sexy about holding him silently on the back of his bike.

On her front porch, he gently kissed her and then rode off into the early morning hours. Part of her was sad to think he was riding out of her life forever. He'd just have to be her little secret--a wild thing she'd done one night, something to fuel her lonely fantasies. She was tired, but her body still sung in the aftermath of so much pleasure that she wasn't about to complain about lack of sleep.

Walking past the cougar, she frowned. The animal was watching her, his yellowed eyes narrowed as he sniffed the air. At almost every cage she passed by, the animals within did the same--especially the males. She frowned, lifting her arm to quickly smell herself. She'd taken a shower and put on the same lotion she always wore.

"Huh," she said, flipping a page on her clipboard to make a notation. Documenting wasn't a fun job, but it beat cleaning cages. Seeing a worker making his way cautiously into the cougar's area, she gave a slight wave. The man nodded his head, but didn't return the gesture. The animal was new and really feisty. It scared easily and Fiona backed away slowly so as not to startle it while the preserve worker was in there.

Taking a path, she found herself skipping the tigers to go to the lions' den. For some reason, she wanted to go see King. It was strange, considering the day before he'd lunged at her. Finding him on top his usual rock, his head lazily resting on his paws, she hesitated.

King sniffed, before raising his head to look at her. For a moment, he just stared. Then, hopping down, he lowered his head and walked forward. Fiona glanced around and made her way guardedly to the cage.

"Are you still mad at me?" she asked, her voice shaking.

King shook his head as if he could understand her. Fiona couldn't help but laugh. There was something different about him--more relaxed. Maybe it was her. Her whole body was numb from her night with Cade. Her only regret was that he had ridden off into the sunset--not that she wanted a relationship with him, but a repeat performance would've been welcomed.

"You didn't happen to tell all the other cats what I told you yesterday, did you?" she asked, thinking of how all the cats looked at her funny.

He nodded once. Fiona laughed. It was as if he was really answering her.

"Shame on you, King," she scolded playfully as she moved to mark her clipboard. "Can't you keep a secret?"

He nodded again.

"Hmm, we'll see." Fiona answered, marking a few more boxes on her form. When she'd finished, she said, "Oh, all right. I have to tell someone and I guess you're as close to a confidant as I'm going to get. I met someone last night."

The lion tilted his head. Was it just her, or did it look like he was waiting to hear about it? Who was she to turn away a willing ear? Fiona smiled. It wasn't as if she could tell anyone else. Cade would have to be her secret--hers and King's. Besides, she was under her father's thumb for the time being and she knew he'd be livid if he caught wind of her wanton actions. Proper young ladies just didn't ride off on the back of stranger's motorcycles.

"His name is Cade and I know I'll never see him again, but last night ... *oooh!*" She shivered just thinking about it. "It was wonderful. I've never done anything like it and I probably won't again, but it was just what the doctor ordered. He was so ... so wild, untamed, passionate. Mm, my body is still sore from...."

Fiona blushed. The lion growled low in his throat.

"To tell you the truth, King, I'm actually glad I won't see him again. You know, I don't really need the complication of a man right now and he would definitely be too much of a distraction." As she said the words, Fiona wondered if she was trying to convince King or herself. Even now, with her insides stiff from his claiming, she wanted him again. "Besides, my father called this morning and he has this colleague of his he wants me to start seeing. The man's probably a bore if he works with my dad. I guess I don't really have a choice, do I?"

King's head lowered and his eyes narrowed. Fiona quickly backed away, recognizing the look. "Whoa, easy there, fella. Don't get edgy, I'm going." She gave a nervous laugh. "You're not much for long conversations, are you, boy?"

King continued to glare at her as she made her way back toward the tigers. What was wrong with him? Was he just unstable? Maybe he'd been caged up too long. It was kind of sad seeing all the animals stuck in cages. Fiona kept a steady eye on the lion. When she finally turned the corner, she took a deep breath, glad the lion didn't charge the fence again.

* * * *

Cade paced the den, angry beyond belief.
How could she? She is mine! MINE!

Fiona planned on going out on a date, did she? With one of her father's rich buddies. Yeah, he knew all about her rich 'daddy.' That morning, before going back to his cage, he'd stopped by to see Eve. She'd filled him in on Fiona's background, but only after he begged her for nearly fifteen minutes and then resorted to whining. Viktor had merely stood behind his wife grinning like a fool. If he hadn't been in such a great mood, he would've decked the man for laughing at him.

But Cade wasn't laughing now. With the rage forming in the pit of his stomach, he'd be able to tear someone to shreds in the blink of an eye. And he planned on starting with Fiona's date.

* * * *

Fiona smiled at Joe Gutterman, doing her best to look interested in what he had to say. He worked with her father and, according to him, was an 'indispensable asset to the team.' He was cute, with a nice body and an easy smile, even if it was a tad on the smarmy side. His dark brown hair was cut short, slicked back in a style that befitted his business suit--or a used car salesman. When she looked into his blue eyes she imagined green ones, and when she heard him speak she remembered the lower, husky tone of Cade's voice.

It was crazy to miss a man after just a one-night stand, wasn't it?

Mm, Cade....

"...dropped the account. Oh, man, it was classic. I can't wait to see that in the interoffice memo," Joe said, laughing heartily.

Fiona blinked in surprise, realizing she'd been about to fantasize about her motorcycle man while she was supposed to be pretending to listen to Joe. She nodded at his expectant look and chuckled politely, but hadn't heard a word the man said. All he talked about was work, just like her father. In fact, the man reminded her so much of her father that it was a little unnerving.

No wonder dad likes him.

Ugh, no wonder I don't.

The restaurant he brought her to was nice, not New York five star nice, but pleasant enough. Music played overhead, light guitars and harps. Joe had ordered for the both of them. Why men believed that was a romantic gesture on the first date was beyond her. Her father didn't even try to order for her when they were out--which wasn't often. Joe didn't even know what she liked--proven by the escargot now in front of her.

Ick, snails!

She pushed one of the little things around on her plate, refusing to put it into her mouth. Did Joe actually think she'd be impressed by a man 'sophisticated' enough to eat slimy mollusks? She would've preferred a greasy cheeseburger and french fries, but a free meal was a free meal and a broke girl couldn't be too picky. Poking a snail with her fork, she shivered.

Okay, maybe I should just starve.

"I must admit, I was a little surprised when Mr. LaSalle asked me to take out one of his daughters. I haven't seen pictures of you around the office and was actually scared you'd turn out to be...." Joe's words trailed off.

"Fat?" Fiona filled in for him dryly, arching a brow. How superficial could this man be? "Ugly? Hideous?"

"Well, yeah," Joe said, laughing louder.

Ugh, did I just think that he was passably cute a minute ago? Listen, buddy boy, can we skip the flirting and get right back to you talking about you and your boring job?

"Something wrong?" Joe asked.

Fiona shook her head, tapped her throat as she took a hurried drink. Choking slightly, she said, "Ah, no, just something in my throat."

It was a boldfaced lie, but her father would be really upset if this date didn't go well and she really couldn't afford to be cut off. She looked at the man, forcing her smile to widen. It was easy after the years of practice she'd had under the guidance of her socialite mother.

Damn you, James, for putting me in this situation.

"Ah, who am I kidding?" she mumbled. "I did this to myself."

"Excuse me?" Joe asked. "Did you say something?"

"Who? Me?" Fiona forced a fake laugh. "No, I didn't say anything."

Joe's eyes narrowed and he turned to his plate. It was all she could do not to lose her water as he popped another snail into his mouth.

* * * *

Cade watched Fiona's head tip back on her shoulders as she laughed at something the asshole in a suit was saying. Just being this close to her made his cock itch to claim her and seeing her smile at someone else made the animal in him want to stake his claim right there in the restaurant-- right after he ripped the man's throat from his weak little neck.

Clenching his hands into fists, he pushed past the very worried looking maître d' and headed straight for Fiona's table. The Alpha in him wanted to show her who was boss, who her mate was. Did last night mean nothing to her? The man in him was hurt that she could forget him so easily.

The second she saw him, he knew. Her face paled and her wide eyes rounded in shock. A waiter charged him and he thrust out his hand, knocking the insolent man back into a table. Cade didn't break stride. Fiona gasped, shooting to her feet.

"Cade?" she asked. Her voice was weak, but somehow he heard it through the blood rushing in his head. He turned to glare at the man she was with and drew up his fists. Fiona gasped and grabbed his arm. "Cade, no! Joe, stay back."

"Hey, man, easy," Joe said, backing away.

"You think you can just date my woman and I'm going to

let you?" Cade yelled.

"What?" Fiona asked, her jaw dropping in shock when he looked at her to make sure she was out of harm's way before any fighting started.

"Hey, listen, man," Joe said, backing away like a coward. Cade's lips snarled at the man. He reeked of weakness and cheap cologne. "She's just my boss' hard-up daughter. The girl means nothing to me."

"Hey!" Fiona said, sounding irritated. She charged forward and Cade automatically grabbed her arm and pulled her back to safety.

"I'll deal with you later," Cade told her with a growl.

"Wait, deal with me?" Fiona asked, her voice rising. "Who the hell do you think you are, buddy boy? I'm not yours to deal with."

"I'm the man that fucked you last night," Cade answered, just as angry. Her words broke his concentration and that brief second was all her date needed to slip closer to the door.

"Hey, I don't want in the middle of this." Joe backed away, holding out his hands. When he was by the door, he took off running.

Fiona made a weak noise, stopping Cade from following the man outside. He turned to her, suddenly realizing what it was he'd said to her. She looked mortified. Glancing around the silent restaurant, she sniffed back tears and pushed past him, unable to look anyone in the eye as she ran for the door.

"Ah, damn it! Fiona, wait," he called.

Without thinking, Cade grabbed his wallet and threw cash down on the table. He was used to paying for damages after his temper flared and the gesture was automatic. Following Fiona outside, he caught her scent easily. She was halfway down the block when he found her.

"Wait," he commanded, jogging after her. "We're not done here. You have some explaining to do."

"What?" Hands on hips, she turned back and charged him. Taking her purse, she whipped it violently at his face. Cade grinned, watching her breasts bounce under the tight little black dress she wore. The handbag glanced over his shoulder, striking him hard but not hurting. "Are you psycho? What do you think you're doing?"

"Hey, I wasn't the one having a date," he said.

"What?" Fiona asked in openmouthed surprise, shaking her head. She pressed her lips into a harsh line and looked confused. As if she lacked anything better to do, she hit him again with her purse, swinging it hard. The bag glanced off his arm, not hurting him in the least. "Get away from me, psycho."

"Fiona," he warned. What was wrong with her? One minute she gets on the back of his bike like she knows what's between them, the next she's pissed when he proved his dominance as her mate? It made no sense.

Taking a deep breath, Cade had to remind himself that things were different in human form than in cat. In the cat world it was simple.

"I forget. I'm sorry," he said, doing his best to explain and calm her at the same time. "Things are not so complex in the wild."

"The wild?" she asked, backing away from him.

"Where I'm from," he rushed, doing his best to remember she didn't know about who he was. It was just so hard to concentrate on his words when his body recognized her scent and wanted to claim her again and again. His cock pressed against his jeans. He'd worn looser denim, but it didn't help. His erection still hurt with the need to be freed. "Where I come from, it's not so complicated. If you are hungry, you eat. If you are tired, you sleep. If you are threatened, you fight."

"And just where do you come from?" she demanded.

Cade frowned. "Ah...."

"Yeah?"

"Texas," he said weakly.

"Texas," she repeated in disbelief. "Things are less complicated in Texas?"

"Yes," he answered, debating on whether or not he should tell her the whole truth--or perhaps show her. He glanced around the busy street. A few people had come out of the restaurant and were watching them with interest. He lowered his voice. "And, if you love, you mate for all eternity."

"Okay." The words sounded forced and she edged away from him. "I'm not sure how they do things down south, but here you can't act like a Neanderthal. We had a nice time. That's all. I'm sorry if you thought it meant more than it did, but we didn't even talk--"

"Miss, are you all right? Do we need to call the cops?" someone yelled.

Cade growled, ready to roar at the gathered crowd until they went away.

"I'm fine," Fiona said, only to add in a softer tone. "I am fine, aren't I? You're not going to pull anything weird, are you?"

"I would never hurt you, kitten." Cade tried to control the volatile combination of rage and desire running rampant in him.

"Listen, Cade, I know we made love, but that doesn't mean we're an item. It was just sex--really good, hot sex."

Okay, why did he want to strangle her for saying it like that? Her tone all condescending and worried. She took another step back and he tilted his head to the side, watching her. He felt the shift coming, the animal inside him wanting to take over.

"You're mine," he said, knowing that he sounded like a caveman about to hit her over the head with a club.

"I'm no man's."

"What about your father? Weren't you dating his golden boy in there? Do you honestly think that a passionless little worm like that could make you happy? I felt the passion in you. I know what you like. I know what your body needs." He lowered his voice, taking advantage of her stunned hesitance to close the distance. Reaching for her face, he cupped her cheek. Her skin was so soft, so sweet. He couldn't resist as he leaned in to kiss her. Her eyelids grew heavy as his mouth brushed along hers. He took it slow, making her bring her mouth to his. Lightly running his tongue over the seam of her lips, he waited.

To his great surprise, Fiona pulled back. "Stay away from me, Cade. We are *not* a couple. I don't even know you."

"But--"

"No."

He watched her walk away. What the hell? How could she not feel the attraction? He smelled her desire for him. She was his woman, his mate and soon she'd be his wife. There was no turning back. He loved her. It wasn't logical or reasonable, it just was. He'd seen her and his heart just knew. She was his.

Frowning he stormed after her, feeling a shallow victory in the fact that he'd ruined her date with daddy's golden boy. As he passed the restaurant he growled, letting his eyes shift to yellow as he stared at the crowd. They gasped in unison and he stalked off to the sound of them shuffling to get back inside the building.

What on earth do I have to do to make her know she's mine? Pee on her damn leg?

Chapter Four

Fiona marched down the darkened street. Joe had picked her up at her apartment, so now that Cade had chased her date away, she didn't have a ride. And since she was broke, she couldn't call a cab. She'd have to walk the half mile home.

"Stupid ... overbearing...." she mumbled, cursing Cade.

"You didn't seem to mind last night, kitten," Cade answered, his voice tinged with anger. She stopped. He was so stealthy, she hadn't heard him approach. Glancing over her shoulder, she caught sight of his handsome face in the streetlight.

"Don't call me kitten," she hissed. "You have no right to be so controlling of me."

"Can you honestly say you like that man?" Cade asked, drawing closer to her. Fiona gripped her purse.

"It's not a matter of what I think," she said. "It's what my father wanted."

"Do you always do what daddy says?"

"Shut up," she growled, hating her situation. Her life was out of her control and she couldn't do anything about it. Seeing Cade, she knew that part of the thrill of their night together had been because she'd chosen to be reckless. So help her, he was still damned sexy and her body wanted her to be reckless again. His possessive show in the restaurant turned her on, even if she'd have preferred he didn't tell the whole city that they'd fucked the night before. "You know nothing about anything in my life. And stop following me!"

"Mm, well," his voice dipped, causing a ripple of pleasure to run up her spine, "if you'll recall, kitten, I know a few things about some things."

His hot gaze picked up the light, seeming to glow, as he purposefully looked over her body, lingering in all the right spots. She shivered. Cream pooled in between her thighs and her flesh tingled with desire for him. With just a look he could get her hotter than anyone she'd ever known.

"Damn," he murmured, coming so close their chests

touched. He touched her cheek. "I love your smell when you're aroused, kitten. I've been thinking of you all day."

"What have you been thinking?" she asked, knowing she should push him away. Fiona couldn't do it. He was a possessive, borderline psycho, and yet she couldn't resist. Maybe she was a glutton for punishment in choosing the wrong kind of man. Though, when she looked into his green eyes, she instinctively knew he wasn't like James. His smell wafted over her, as potent as before. Her body pulsed, each nerve taut with anticipation of being claimed.

"How much my cock aches to be buried inside you again. Of how tight you were around me." Cade's chest skimmed her nipples through their clothing as he took a deep breath. "Of how I want to fuck you and keep fucking you until you can't walk." Fiona's knees weakened and she nearly collapsed. Cade caught her and held her up. Chuckling, he said, "Or perhaps longer."

Fiona blushed. What was it about him that made her forget reason and sanity? Looking over his tight body, she knew the answer. She bit her lip, her mouth watering to taste him again, to drink down his release.

"Where?" she sighed, glancing around. Besides the restaurant down the street, most of the businesses were closed.

Cade grinned, rocking his hips into her as he touched her waist and held her close. "How picky are you tonight?"

Fiona felt the heat rising under her skin. Cade's fingers worked along her black dress. "There's an alley over there."

Cade chucked. "Mm, I like you eager for me."

Taking her hand, he led her into the darkness. Instantly, he pressed her up against the wall. She couldn't see into the alley, but could make out the bricks at her back and the hard pavement under her feet. The light framed the entrance to the street so they could see out, but no one looking in could see them.

His mouth pressed against hers as he made love to her against the cool wall. Their hard breathing mingled as they kissed, his tongue warring with hers in passion. Their bodies were a frenzy of hands and hurried caresses. Cade pulled up her skirt as she fumbled with his zipper. Urgency overcame them and before she knew it, Fiona was lifted up against the wall. Her legs dangled along his waist as he held her by her thighs. She wrapped her arms around his neck.

His cock brushed her wet slit. Her body jerked in anticipation of that first thrust. Cade's mouth unexpectedly lightened on hers.

"Tell me this is what you want," he whispered and for a moment, she thought to see his hot eyes glowing like a cat's from the darkness.

"Yes," she answered just as softly, running her hands over his bulging muscles. He was so strong, holding her as if she weighed nothing. "This is what I want."

His hips pressed into her, claiming her gently. Even after being together the night before, her body needed to stretch to fit him. He rocked, keeping a slow, easy pace.

"Ah, Cade," she moaned, taking deep breaths. It was almost too much. His body felt too good and his cock was pressing along her sweet spot.

"That's it, kitten, come for me." He nibbled along her neck. "Ah, your tight body feels so good. I'm going to fuck you all night. I want you so bad."

How could she hold off when his gruff voice was so persistent, so naughtily sexy as he continued to whisper dirty little words in her ear? Just as she almost came, he slowed his pace, keeping her on the edge of release. Cade growled in the back of his throat.

"Oh, please ... please ... please," she groaned with each thrust. "Faster, please, faster."

An unearthly roar sounded, just like the wild cats at the preserve, as he began to pump hard and fast. His eyes glinted in the night, the yellow orbs glowing with an inhuman light. Fiona was shaken by the noise and the look in his eyes. She was about to push him away when an intense orgasm took over. Gasping, she came so hard she could barely breathe. The pleasure ripped through her body, hitting every nerve until it buzzed with warmth.

For a long moment, she stayed pinned against the wall, unable to move. Weakly, she hit Cade's shoulder, her only defense. The sound of his growl echoed in her head. Humans didn't make that kind of noise--at least not that she knew of. And his eyes....

"What...?" she asked, when she could finally manage to

speak. His body slipped from hers. "...are you?"

His breathing only deepened, coming out in harsh pants. It was a primal, dangerous sound.

"What are you doing to me?" Fiona pushed him again. Her panties were torn off. She didn't remember him doing it. Her skirt fell around her thighs. "I lose my mind when I'm around you. It's your smell ... but there's ... more than...."

Fiona shook her head, slipping past him as she stumbled her way from the darkness into the light.

"I don't know what you are, Cade," she whispered, "but I want you to leave me alone. Do you understand? Stop whatever it is you're doing to me. Get out of my head. I don't want you there."

Fiona turned, running toward the street. Glancing over her shoulder, she was glad when he didn't try to stop her.

Get out of my heart, Cade. I can't be in love with you.

* * * *

"How exactly did you explain it to her?" Viktor asked, glancing sideways from where he lounged on his back in the long, open field. Grasses rolled all around them in the breeze, blocking out the distance from their place on the ground.

Cade didn't answer. He couldn't. Insects hummed and white clouds drifted overhead. The south field spread out around them and even in human form they didn't mind being so close to nature. In fact, they preferred it.

"You didn't explain it to her, did you?" Viktor laughed, turning his eyes back to the blade of grass he twined in his fingers.

Cade snarled in Viktor's direction. His friend really wasn't helping his bad mood. Viktor only laughed harder, completely unaffected by the dark sound.

"What?" Cade demanded. He hadn't known Viktor a long time, but they'd become fast friends. Just like in mating, their instinct also told them who they could befriend and who they could trust. "I knew it the first moment I saw her. She should have as well."

"What? When she first saw you as the lion she knew as King? You really expect her to fall in love with a cat?" Viktor shook his head. "Man, for someone so smart, you really don't know too much about women."

"What do you expect me to say? Hey, kitten, wanna see me change shape?" Cade rolled his eyes. "Please. She'd go runnin' for the hills."

"And you'd enjoy chasing her." Viktor smirked.

Cade gave a small laugh at that. "Yeah, I would, too."

"If she really is your mate like you say, you're going to have to tell her sometime."

"Can we just get her to accept me as a man before we work on me as a lion?" Cade took a deep breath. This whole wooing a mate thing wasn't going as easy as he'd first expected. Sure, he'd gotten her marked, but what good was it if plain humans couldn't sense the mark and if she herself didn't accept or want it?

"Yeah, that's probably a good plan." Viktor nodded. "Let me make sure I've got this straight. So, you both had dinner and then you mated."

"Ah." Cade grimaced.

"What? You didn't mate?"

"We didn't have dinner. The first time, she was eating. There was an understanding when I walked through the door and looked at her. I paid. She got up and followed me. Then, we mated. The second time, she was eating with that man I told you about. Ah, I'm pretty sure I paid again. She was upset but then we reached an understanding. Then, we mated ... again." Cade sighed, his body heating with the memory of it. It had been two days since he'd interrupted her date and he hadn't seen Fiona since. She'd been off work and he missed her terribly. Short of stalking her, he knew there was no way but to wait until she had another shift if he wanted to see her. Not that he hadn't done just a little bit of stalking. He was part cat, after all, and it was in his nature to guard what was his.

"But you did talk first," Viktor insisted.

"Um, not really. The second time there was some yelling. Damn, she has a fiery temper." Cade nodded in approval.

"Then afterwards you talked?"

"No, not really."

"What did happen afterwards?" Viktor sighed, concentrating on the blade of grass in his hands.

"The first time I took her home." Cade frowned. "The second time she took herself home. Why? What are you getting at? I told you we had an understanding. No words were needed."

"You have been in the wild more than I realized," Viktor said. "This isn't a one-night stand. You have to tell her how you feel. You have to romance her. You have to listen to her when she talks."

"I did listen. Her pheromones have been in my head and her body language said she wanted me--"

Viktor's laughter cut him off. "Uh, yeah, you do realize she's not a catshifter, don't you? Women need actual words. I swear, you've been hanging with Mia too much."

"There is nothing between Mia and me. She's just a friend. You know we don't mate with cats," Cade defended.

"Whoa, someone's a little touchy."

Yeah, because I have a mate and a hard on and the two are not on speaking terms.

"Besides," Cade said. "Eve can sense you just fine. Why should my mate be any different?"

"Yeah, now she can, but it wasn't always like that. That bond had to grow. Listen, if you want my advice, go to Fiona. Be charming, attentive, but most importantly try and keep your hands off her." Viktor smirked, as if really enjoying himself at Cade's expense. "And tell her how you feel. If she really is your mate then she'll accept what you are."

"Thanks, Dr. Vik," he drawled.

"Now, on to actual business," Viktor said. "Some of the shifters have said they sense a new scent on the premises, but they can't tell if it's shifter or just a wild cat. Eve doesn't have any new arrivals or incomings listed. If it's a shifter, it's possibly just a tramp. If it's a cat, someone could've dropped it off on preserve property and run, leaving us to take care of it. Unfortunately, that happens a lot. Humans take wild cats as pets and then wonder why they can't handle them or why they turn on their owners."

Cade sighed. He knew all about the tendencies of humans. It was why Mia was so messed up. Her last owner had beaten her senseless. She'd grown up in captivity and didn't know what a real lioness was supposed to be like. "I'll see what I can find out."

"Thanks," Viktor said. "I'll start in the north section tonight. Eve's worried about the animal spreading disease to the rest of the cat population or even attacking one of the workers. Can't say I blame her."

"Yeah," Cade agreed. "Tell Eve not to worry. Her new preserve security team is on the case."

"She'll worry anyway." Viktor chuckled, rolling up to stand. He reached down to help Cade. "It's what wives do."

* * * *

"Fiona, darling!"

Fiona smiled at the enthusiastic greeting her mother gave her as she came through her parents' front door. The woman had dark hair and pale, ageless skin. She always thought her mother looked like a fragile porcelain doll. Her pretty wardrobe certainly attested to the image.

The old Gregorian- style mansion sat high on a hill, overlooking the town below on one side and a long stretch of forest on the other. There was about seventy acres total, including the forest and a small stream in the woods. Six of those acres were the old gardens in the back. Several paths wound through them and Fiona had explored them often as a child with her older sister, Darcy.

The house was several thousand square feet with well over sixty-five separate rooms. A large marble staircase stretched before the front door in the reception area. The craftsmanship of the surrounding woodwork was just amazing--from paneling to some of the house's original furniture. There were also some outbuildings, including an old coach house from the late nineteenth century that had been converted into a garage that housed her father's classic cars. She used to tell Darcy that the 1950 Chevy Fastback Sedan was their long lost brother. The way their father babied the thing was borderline ridiculous.

To anyone looking in, she'd lived a fairy tale life. But it was all glitter and mirages. What couldn't be seen were the security systems and the hidden guards who monitored every movement. Though handy when it came to cheating at hide and go seek, it was more than annoying when they were teenagers just trying to live a normal life. In the LaSalle household, normal really wasn't a part of the everyday routine. Just walking in the front door made Fiona feel suffocated. It was why she'd left. Darcy had stayed, making them their father's favorite.

"Mom," Fiona said, giving the woman a genuine hug.

Teresa LaSalle could be a little flighty and was a hopeless socialite, but she had a kind heart and giving nature. Since she'd never really had a job, she spent most of her time volunteering and holding benefits for a local hospital, Mercy. "Oh, I've missed you!"

"Well, if you'd come home more often...." her father said behind her.

Fiona stiffened as her mother let go. She turned to her father and nodded, not greeting him as enthusiastically as she had Teresa. "Dad."

"Hmm." He thrust a newspaper under his arm and looked her over. "You've lost weight."

"Starving will do that to you," Fiona quipped.

"Don't be so dramatic," Fredrick answered, his face blank.

"Oh, darling, if you need to eat you should just come home," Teresa said, looking helplessly at her husband.

"Don't worry about her, my love," Fredrick said. "She's exaggerating."

At her father's meaningful look, she said, "Yeah, I'm just in a foul mood. Ignore me. I'm eating plenty."

Teresa smiled, completely put at ease. She was so trusting, Fiona almost felt bad that she and her father took advantage of her nature like they did--even if it was for her mother's own peace of mind.

"So, Fiona, Joe tells me your date was interrupted," Frederick said. Fiona cringed.

"Well, I'll just leave you two alone to talk," Teresa said, backing out of the reception hall. She looked uncomfortable at the sudden strained vibe in the room. Fiona wasn't surprised by the woman's retreat. Her mother had never been really strong when it came to her father. "Fiona, darling, come have tea with me when you're finished. I've missed you so much and I miss our little talks. I want to hear all about your work at the wildlife rescue place. I think it's so great that you volunteer there."

"It's a job, Mom," Fiona answered, raising a brow in her father's direction. He grimaced back.

"Oh, well, I didn't realize. Still, I'd love to hear all about it." Teresa smiled, unfazed.

"Sure, Mom," Fiona said.

When Teresa was gone, Fredrick motioned his daughter

to follow him. She did so, going past the marble staircase to the door at the end of the reception hall. It was her father's office. Thick fur rugs lined the floor before a giant dark wood fireplace. Bookshelves were built so high a ladder had to be used to reach the top. Darcy had spent her entire life trying to read through the collection. Fiona hadn't touched a one--except those which were required of her growing up.

"Is Darcy still in Europe?" Fiona asked, moving to an oversized leather chair before her father's desk. She didn't know why she felt the need to make small talk with him. As if delaying the inevitable conversation would make it easier in the long run.

Her father threw the paper on the thick piece of oak furniture and took a seat behind the desk. He studied her for a moment before nodding. "Yes, she is. Last I heard she was touring Tuscany."

Lucky her.

"Oh." Fiona knew she sounded unenthused. She glanced around the office, feeling very much like a little girl about to be yelled at. There was just something about her childhood home that made her forget every independence she'd learned as an adult.

"So, who's this mystery man of yours?" Fredrick asked, leaning back in his chair, arms crossed.

Fiona didn't answer.

"Joe told me everything, but I'd like to hear it from you."

Fiona tried to read her father's face, but it was impassable. It was what made him such a great businessman. Unfortunately, she'd been trapped like this before. It was his way of getting her to confess things he didn't know and confirm the things he did. Only question was, how much did he know?

"His name is Cade," Fiona said. "He's just a friend."

"He stormed in and declared you were his woman," Fredrick stated bluntly. "I'd say this Cade believes you're more than friends. Wonder what gave him that impression?"

"I'm not sure," Fiona said.

"Hmm."

"We only had one date."

"Mm." Her father's eyes narrowed.

Fiona took a deep breath, knowing she was about to start babbling and confess everything--well, not *everything.* "He's, ah, very nice."

"I'm sure," Fredrick said. Fiona was glad when he continued, saving her from embarrassing herself with a full confession of having had a one-night stand with a complete stranger. "Tell me, is it serious?"

"No."

"Hmm."

She really hated when her father hummed like that. "Are we done? Mother's expecting me for tea."

A slow smile curled the side of her father's mouth. "You know, dear, someday you'll understand my position."

And someday, daddy dear, you might understand that your life is not mine. I want freedom. I want my own life. I like sleeping without guards pacing the halls. I like going and doing what I want without having a 'family schedule' to check in on first.

Fiona only nodded as she stood. Her body stiff, she walked out of his office in search of her mother in the back gardens for afternoon tea. The day was warm, but not so hot that it was uncomfortable. The back gardens were a little overgrown, but that only added to their rustic charm. Shrubs spilled over onto the pathways, creating hidden nooks that were perfect for escaping the nosy security guards.

Fiona had actually lost her virginity to her high school sweetheart in the back section of trees. It had been a horribly disappointing experience which only turned to a mortifying one when she was discovered sneaking back in by one of the guards. The jerk security director had called her father down. As if the dreadful sexual experience wasn't bad enough, her father's disappointed look had topped the evening off. It was that night when she knew she would never stay under her father's thumb. Several years later, she'd moved out of his house and never looked back-- until James' betrayal forced her to.

"How was it?" her mother asked, glancing over her fine china cup. A small smile alighted on her lips as she studied her daughter. "Did he mention James?"

"Ahhh," Fiona answered, the sound caught between a sigh and a groan. "Actually, he didn't, which is surprising."

"Mm, that's good. I told him if he did, he'd be kicked out of our bedroom for a week."

"Ugh, Mom." Fiona rolled her eyes, only to stop and add, "Hey, why only a week?"

Her mother laughed. "Trust me, dear, that's punishment enough."

Replaying her groan, she repeated, "Ugh, Mom!"

Teresa smiled. "You know the problem is you're just as stubborn as he is. When you get together, it's a wonder either of you talk about anything productive. It's like watching two bulls about to charge each other."

Fiona laughed, taking an iron seat across from her mother. The cushion underneath her was soft, contrasting the hard wrought iron at her back. An umbrella shaded the patio set. Automatically, Teresa leaned forward to pour her daughter a cup of tea. Fiona took it, adjusting her body to sit like a lady--a habit drilled into her head by her mother while growing up.

"Mm," Fiona nodded, taking a sip of the hot brew. "My favorite. Just a hint of the hot stuff."

Her mother winked. "It's like I told you, dear, what men don't know, won't hurt them. We women are allowed our little secrets."

Fiona smiled. Her mother was cleverer than she sometimes gave her credit for.

"Besides, how do you think the tradition of afternoon teas has lasted so long?" Teresa laughed softly.

"Mom, can I ask you something?"

"A question that starts like that can't be good." Teresa set down her tea, instantly serious.

"Why'd you marry Dad?" Fiona always wondered how her parents got together. They never talked about it, except to say they met when they were young and fell instantly and madly in love. The fact that the hardheaded Fredrick still openly called his wife 'my love' after decades of marriage said a lot.

"Because I love him," her mother answered. Fiona frowned slightly. Teresa took a deep breath. "Because the first moment I saw him I knew we were meant to be together. I just looked at him and I knew."

"Just like that? And you've had no regrets?" Fiona thought of Cade. He'd been in her head, but she didn't know what to do about it. At night, she dreamed of him, her body so hot she barely had to touch herself to orgasm. During the day, she caught herself searching the crowds for him. He wasn't there, at least not that she saw. Sometimes she thought she felt him watching her, but if he was he never approached.

"Well, we've had our share of fights to be sure, but I have no regrets," Teresa said. Fiona quirked a brow, wondering what her mother would consider a 'fight.' The mild-mannered woman hadn't lifted her voice a day in her life. Teresa laughed. "What? We have."

"Oh, really." Fiona smirked. "When?"

"The last time was the day you moved out, Ms. Smarty Pants, if you must know."

Fiona wiped the look off her face. "Anyway, as you were saying, you love him and have no regrets."

"You tend to make things so complicated, just like your father." Teresa shook her head and picked up her tea. "Sometimes, darling, life is what you want it to be. The women on our side of the family can feel our soul mates. It's an instinct inside us, a pull we can't ignore. If you think you've found him, then why fight it? Life can be so short and so cruel. You have to grab the things you know you want and just hold tight no matter the cost. And, if you find your soul mate, then you grab onto him and never let go."

"And if he doesn't feel the same?"

"If he's your soul mate, he will."

Fiona studied her mother. "You're deeper than you let on, you know."

"What?" Teresa winked. "Did you think all I knew how to do was throw parties?"

She didn't answer.

Teresa sighed, motioning her hand to the side. "Now, tell me what you think of my new lilies. Aren't they beautiful? I just love lilies."

Fiona dutifully turned her head, knowing her mother was ending the serious conversation. She eyed the pretty little white buds and nodded. Lily of the Valley was one of her favorites and her mother had always had a way with flowers. "Yeah, they really are beautiful."

Chapter Five

Cade ran through the dark fields on all fours searching for the intruder. He'd picked up an unfamiliar scent about an hour before and the stronger the smell got, the more sure he became that the cat was a male shifter. And the way his gut clenched assured him that the shifter was up to no good. Besides, had he been friendly, the man would've shown respect and introduced himself to those at the preserve. It was simple etiquette to say hello before coming into someone's home and Jameson Wild life Rescue and Preserve was home to many.

Slowing his pace as he neared the tree line, he sniffed. He was getting closer to the man's hideout. Cade crouched on all fours, silently moving into the dark woods. His cat eyes saw easily in the night, but he knew the shifter he tracked would most likely see him with just as little effort.

Cade tensed, ready to pounce. His ears twitched in warning and his hair stood on end. A low growl sounded in the woods, near some dense brush close to the path.

"What do you want?" an old voice yelled, after a long silence. "Leave me be."

The cat had shifted to his human form. Cade did the same, keeping his senses keenly alert for an ambush.

"I said leave me be," the man repeated. "I'm not doing anything wrong. Go away."

"You're on private property, shifter," Cade said.

"You know where I am?"

"Show yourself," Cade demanded. An old man appeared from behind a tree, standing as naked as the day he was born. Instantly, Cade saw his white eyes. The man was blind. His guard relaxed some, but an uneasy feeling still resided in the pit of his stomach. In his centuries of living, he'd never met an old shifter. And, over time, the man's body should've been able to restore his eyesight. Something was unmistakably wrong with this situation. "Who are you?"

"Name's Ricard." The man shook as he leaned against the

tree for support. He hardly looked able to support his own weight, let alone do anyone harm. Cade kept a keen eye on him, but relaxed his guard some as he felt no immediate danger. "Are you the shifter who's been stalking me?"

"My name's Cade," Cade answered. He too was naked after shifting, but barely paid it any mind.

"Nice to meet you, Cade," the man said. "I didn't mean to trespass. I don't always know where I am. I haven't seen anyone for months."

"You're at the Jameson Wild Life Rescue and Preserve." Cade took a slow step forward as Ricard reached out a hand. He took it, shaking it before hooking it onto his elbow to lead the man out of the trees toward the clearing.

"Then I made it," the man said, giving a great sigh. His body seemed to relax with what could only be relief. "I wasn't sure. When no one picked me up, I assumed I'd gotten lost. Word has it there's a lady here who takes in strays."

Yep, that would be Eve all right.

Cade chuckled at the thought. It was no wonder that her generosity had gotten around the shifter world as well as the humans. Just as she took in strays left behind by human pet owners, it would seem she'd now become an infirmary and homeless shelter to down and out shifters.

Eyeing the man, he still didn't feel right about him. There was definitely something off to the whole situation. But, what could he do? He couldn't leave Ricard to wander the woods unwatched and Eve wouldn't be happy if he even thought about turning him out of the preserve. The woman really did have a soft heart.

Though, she'd probably punish me by putting the birth control back into my food.

Cade suppressed another chuckle. The extra hormones had made him feel a little edgy at times. She'd added it in all the shifter's food. It wasn't intentional. Eve didn't know that they were shifters at the time and had thought she was keeping them from reproducing with the female cats. The female cats certainly didn't hold any appeal to them.

"Come on," Cade said, as they made the south field. "You look hungry. Let's get you something to eat and have Dr. Matthews check you out. The facility is about a mile from here. Are you up to the walk?"

"Mind if we shift first?" Ricard asked. "I tend to do better in my old age when I shift."

Cade let go of him, letting the form of the lion instantly wash over his skin. When the fur covered every inch of him, he growled low in his throat. The old man was slower to shift, but soon he took the shape of a tiger. His orange and black fur looked ragged and dull, and he had to take hard, deep breaths.

They began walking, taking a slow pace to accommodate Ricard's weakness. The tiger was exceedingly thin and, being that he was blind, Cade assumed that he didn't hunt very well.

Strange, he thought. *Very strange, indeed.*

* * * *

"He was discovered along the south section last night," Eve said, pointing at the tiger in the laboratory's new arrival cage.

Fiona nodded, eyeing the mangy tiger. The animal's head was turned toward the far wall and he didn't move to look at them. Eve studied the animal and Fiona took a moment to study her. The doctor had never spent time with her on her work shift before and Fiona thought it odd that she would do so now. They weren't really doing anything, just talking shop.

Eve really loved her job. It was clear in every word and every movement. She lived for this place. Fiona wished she could feel half as much for something in her life. She thought of Cade and shivered.

The sterile building was nearly empty except for a few interns checking on the sick cats. A baby cougar was in one cage and the lioness, Mia, was in another. Eve had told her that Mia had a cyst on her back that was causing her pain. They'd just discovered it that morning and had her in to do tests.

"Is he sick?" Fiona asked, turning her attention back to the mangy tiger.

The tiger whipped around at the sound of her voice. His white eyes stared blindly in their direction and his head tilted to the side.

"Huh," Eve mused, kneeling down to get on the tiger's level. "That's the first he's moved all morning. I think he likes your voice."

Fiona didn't move, not liking the sensation that washed over her at the tiger's attention. "I should probably get to work."

Eve blinked, looking up. She stood and nodded. "Actually, I wanted to ask you to spend some time with King today. He's been a little down and I think some company will actually help him."

Fiona wondered at the request. Eve gave a small smile as she said the words.

"All right," Fiona agreed at last. "You just want me to sit by his cage today?"

"Pretty much. Just talk to him, let him hear your voice so he knows he's not alone."

"Okay." The word was slow coming and Fiona nodded. Suddenly, it sounded like just what she needed. She wanted to see the lion, even if he was temperamental half the time. "He's not sick or anything, is he?"

The tiger growled low in his throat. Eve glanced at him before saying, "No. Just depressed about Mia, I think."

Depressed? Lions get depressed? Fiona had never thought about it before, but she supposed it could happen. Mia was his wife of sorts, wasn't she? He probably did miss his partner.

"I'm on it," Fiona said, turning to go to King's cage.

"Thank you!" Eve called as she walked out of the laboratory.

It was a short walk through the preserve, but she found herself hurrying to see King. She had a lot on her mind and the lion was the perfect sounding board to get it all out.

* * * *

Cade watched Fiona as she talked to 'King.' She blushed as she spoke of him, whispering through the chain-link fence about what had gone on between them. The sunlight outlined her slender body as she sat on the ground, haloing her auburn hair to perfection.

It was interesting to hear about their experiences from her viewpoint and he couldn't help noticing the unguarded, dreamy smile that crossed her face or shone from her green eyes whenever she said his name…

Cade.

"Mm, enough about me," Fiona said, setting her head against the fence. It was the closest she'd ever come to him in shifted form. He made no sudden moves, not wanting to scare her. She'd already seen enough displays of King's temper, but Cade couldn't help it. Whenever she spoke of herself with another man he saw blood. "How are you holding up?"

He sighed softly. If only he could shift without her freaking out on him and tell her how he was. He'd been miserable without her, so lost and lonely.

"It must be hard not having your wife with you," she said, eyeing her hands.

What? She knew?

Cade pushed up on his front paws. Fiona pushed away from the fence at his movement.

"I mean, you and Mia have been together a long time, huh? You must really miss her."

Mia? She thinks I'm married to Mia?

Cade didn't know whether to roar or try to laugh.

"I wish I had someone like you worrying over me," Fiona said, sighing wistfully.

You do, kitten.

"Oh, listen to me, babbling on about Cade. I hardly know him. He's arrogant, possessive and probably a stalker. I wouldn't be surprised if he rode into town fresh out of a mental institute. I know I belong in one for even going with him. I just couldn't seem to stop myself. I saw him and I was compelled to follow him. You know, he had this smell to him. It drives me wild. I don't think its cologne, per se, because he doesn't appear to wear any, but it's great."

She likes my smell.

Cade grinned.

But, she also thinks I escaped from an insane asylum.

His grin fell.

"Want to know a secret? Something I haven't told anyone?" she asked him, her voice dropping as she looked into his eyes. He longed to pull her into his chest and hold her. "I think I'm in--"

"Cade!"

Cade tensed. It was Eve and she sounded hysterical. He stood up. Eve would never yell for him in the middle of the day unless it was an emergency. Fiona looked at him in confusion before standing.

"Cade!" Eve screamed as she ran straight for his cage.

Blood dotted her white lab coat and she looked pale. Stumbling slightly as she saw Fiona, she didn't stop.

"Dr. Mat--?" Fiona began.

"Cade," Eve said, looking down at him, her breath coming out in hard pants. "I need you. It's…"

"Cade?" Fiona whispered. They both ignored her.

"…it's Viktor," Eve gasped. "And Mia. The tiger. He got loose and--"

"What's happened?" Fiona asked, sounding slightly hysterical. Cade was torn between comforting her and helping Eve--who was obviously distraught. "Did something happen?"

Not given much of a choice, Cade glanced at Fiona and began to shift. Time seemed to slow as he transformed. Fiona paled, her expression of horror burning into him. He could see her tremble.

"Cade?" Fiona whispered.

"Fiona--" Cade reached for her, but she jerked further away.

"Cade, I'm sorry, but I need you. Viktor's hurt. Ricard jumped him and Mia got loose and tried to help him, but--"

"I'm coming," Cade said. Eve took off her lab coat as he leapt over the fence.

"Ah!" Fiona cried, falling to the ground.

Eve threw the lab coat at him as he landed. Glancing at Fiona, he said, "I can explain. Don't go."

"Uh," she whimpered, trembling on the ground.

"Cade!" Eve insisted.

Torn, he took off into a sprint.

* * * *

Fiona didn't move as Cade ran off into the distance, tugging the white lab coat over his arms. Eve turned to her.

"Fiona, I…" she hesitated, as she stepped backward in the direction of the lab. Her words hurried, she added, "I know this looks strange, but I promise it's all right. Just … just get into the staff lounge and stay there. This is all under control. There's nothing to worry about."

Eve took off running, following to where Cade had disappeared. For a long moment, Fiona couldn't move as she stared after them.

"King?" she whispered. "Cade?"

No, it can't be.

Cade?

Fiona pushed to her feet, not knowing what to do. Cade was a lion? He was King? She looked at the cage. All this time, she'd been telling him her secrets. Oh, and today! All the stuff she'd said about having sex with him, of never having felt so much and never having had such pleasures.

Torn between mortification and fear, Fiona glanced around the preserve, hugging her arms around her waist. If Cade was a cat-man, were there others? Her co-workers? Were they like Cade? Eve? Her husband, Viktor?

"I have to get out of here," she whispered, talking to herself. The sound of her own voice brought her no comfort. Shaking, she tried to make her way to the employee lounge to get her car keys. There was no way she was staying at the preserve now that she knew what was here.

Grateful that it was still early evening, she kept moving, scanning around her as she walked. Then, out of nowhere, a voice came from behind her.

"Fiona, what a surprise."

James?

She tensed, suddenly nauseous.

"What? Is that any way to greet the love of your life?" James said. She would've known his deep timbre anywhere.

"You're not," she whispered. Her mind tried to process everything that was happening. Cats turning into men. James at the preserve.

"Tsk, tsk, tsk, Fiona," James' breath fanned her neck. She couldn't run. This had to be a bad dream. "I thought I meant more to you than that. Had I known your taste ran toward shifters, I'd have shown myself to you long ago."

"What?" At that she did pull away and spin around. Backing up, she shook her head. "I don't believe you."

James grinned and arched a brow. He wore a white lab coat much like the one Eve had given Cade when he turned. His eyes glowed, turning from brown to green. Other than that, he looked just as she remembered him--handsome, youthful.

"What are you? What is going on? What do you want?"

"Sweetheart, don't get so dramatic on me." James frowned and said, as if talking to a child, "Take a deep breath. Try to relax."

"You took everything from me. Don't call me sweetheart!" Fiona continued to stumble away.

"I am sorry about that, but you see, you refused to marry me and I had to get your money somehow."

"James, please, just go away."

He came for her, drawing nearer. His movements were confident and he didn't walk as he once had--like his back was no longer hurt.

As if it had ever been...

"What are you?" she demanded.

"A shifter. I turn into a tiger. Would you like to see?" His eyes again flashed, gleaming yellow.

"That was you ... Ricard. You're Ricard." Fiona tensed. "What did you do, James? Did you kill someone? What did you do?!"

"Easy, turtledove," he crooned. "Take it easy. I only killed the lioness. You see, I needed her blood. Call it my own personal fountain of youth. The others just got in my way."

"Was she a...?"

"Shifter? No. Shifter blood doesn't work. Only cat blood."

"Are you going to kill me?" Fiona hated herself for asking, but she couldn't stop the question from escaping her lips. Insanely, she thought of Cade. Would he come for her? Did she want him to? Was one shifter better than another? In her heart, she already knew the answer. Cade might not have told her everything, but he wasn't as bad as James.

"Mm, probably not, my darling."

Fiona shivered, hating the pet names. When he said it, they sounded like insults.

"Or, is it kitten now?" James surged forward with so much speed, she screamed in fright, only to find he was upon her before she could blink. His hand shot over her mouth, pressing tight to her lips until she was forced to breathe from her nose. Her heart thundered in her head. She never imagined he would strike so fast. "Isn't that what he calls you? Kitten?"

Fiona shook her head, trying to talk, but his hand muffled her words. His eyes flashed with a supernatural light.

"I saw you, kitten," he spat. "I watched you spread your legs for him like a whore. Did you like him fucking you? Was his cock so much more than mine? Did he make your sweet body come?"

He's crazy! Cade! Help!

She struggled to be set free, but James merely slipped his hand from her to replace it with his lips. He kissed her hard, as if he'd expected her to respond to him. When she pushed her lips tight, refusing him entrance, he growled.

"What? My kiss not good enough for you?" he spat. Thrusting his hips to her stomach, he let her feel his erection. She imagined he was naked under the lab coat. "My cock not good enough anymore? It was plenty good enough when you used to ride me every night."

"James, stop--" It had hardly been every night.

"I'll show you, you bitch." His eyes were wild, almost insane as he studied her face and pressed a finger along the seam of her mouth hard. "I want you to act for me like you did for him. I want you get on your knees for me and suck me like you did him. Then you're going to beg me to fuck you like an animal. Yeah, yeah…"

"No," she began. He shook her hard. "We can't. Not here. Someone will see. Please, James."

As if coming from an impassioned haze, he glanced around the open section of the preserve. "You're right."

He took a deep breath and Fiona wondered if she'd made a mistake. Now she had no idea where he'd take her. At least here, someone might come and help her. But, she just couldn't force herself to give him a blowjob. She didn't want him anymore, realized she'd never wanted him. She'd just been lonely and looking for something James could never give her.

"Come on," he ordered, jerking her arm and making her walk with him. "I know a place that's perfect."

Cade, Fiona thought. *Please, help me.*

Chapter Six

Cade pressed his hand to Mia's throat. It had been slit open with a claw in such a way she would've died instantly. Rage and sorrow ripped through him. Mia didn't have much of a chance in this life. After five years at the preserve, she'd only started to relax around humans. It was his presence alone that kept her calm. If he would've left, she would've gone berserk on the staff and would've had to be put down. So he'd stayed with her, because she needed him. And, when she needed him most, he'd let her down.

"She saved my life," Viktor said, coughing, "and Eve's."

Cade fought back tears and nodded once to indicate he heard him. His fists clenched over the lioness' chest. They were covered with blood. Viktor had a slashed chest, but would live. Unlike Mia, he had the ability to heal himself.

"Cade," Eve whispered. "Please. We have to find Ricard."

Cade's head snapped up, his eyes glowing hot. The murderer was still out there.

Fiona.

His heart dropped. Fiona was still out there as well.

"Fiona," Cade growled, turning toward the door mid-shift. His blood-stained paws hit the floor and he took off running, the white lab coat fluttering behind him. He picked up the man's scent and his stomach clenched as he ran back toward his cage. That's where he'd left Fiona.

Please let her have run off. Please let her have listened to us.

Cade skidded to a stop as he caught her scent. The smell was light, but he detected fear in it. Was it from seeing him shift? Or was it Ricard?

Oh, kitten, please be safe. I can't lose you too. I can't lose you. I can't lose you...

* * * *

Fiona trembled as James pulled her through the preserve to a part she'd never been to--the forest. Her feet stumbled as she was dragged over a rope bridge. Wild grasses grew, rolling in the evening breeze, caressed by the orange light of dusk. The planked walk was sturdy, but seeing the creek flowing beneath her feet made her dizzy. James stopped, sniffing the air.

"We're alone," he said, his tone lowering with meaning as he glanced over her body.

"James, let me go." Fiona tried to pull her arm from his grasp, but claws as sharp as knives grew from his fingertips. They pressed into her skin, drawing blood. It beaded on her uniform shirt.

"I hated to leave you, Fiona," he confessed, his eyes glowing. "You were so good to me." He smiled, caressing her cheek. "Taking care of me, feeding me. Mm, and fulfilling my needs."

"Yeah, while you took advantage of me!" she yelled. It was foolish to piss him off, but she couldn't help herself. She was so angry with him for what he'd done to her. "You took everything I had!"

"It killed me to hurt you," he soothed, pulling her to his chest and patting down her hair. "I know you're mad at me, but I didn't have a choice. Once I was better, I was going to come back for you."

"What makes you think I'd take you back?" she demanded.

James stiffened. When he pulled back to study her, his eyes were hard.

"You would have," he stated with confidence. He jerked her close once more. His tone softer, he gripped her tight. "You would have."

Fiona's eyes filled with tears and she blinked them back. This wasn't the James she knew--this wild-eyed man. But then again, had she ever really known him?

His hands rolled down her spine and she bit back a sob. James moved to study her. She blinked harder, but couldn't hide her fear from him. He frowned.

"It's him, isn't it? It's your lion."

Fiona didn't answer. The overhead light flickered on him as the sun started to set. It cast an eerie light over his features, contrasting them.

"I watched you," James said, his tone accusing as his face contorted. "I watched you fuck him."

"James." Fiona shook her head. "Please."

Please, Cade.

"I bet you're thinking of him even now, aren't you?" He lightly touched her jaw. When she didn't answer, he stuck a clawed finger under her chin. "Aren't you?!"

"Only because you keep mentioning him," she ground out. It was a lie.

"Get on your knees," James ordered. "Do to me what you did to him."

Fiona took his moment of distraction to run. She almost made it to the end of the bridge before he pounced on her back. Growling, she felt his claws ripping into her flesh.

"Ah!" she cried, as the white hot pain tore her flesh.

James roared, as she wiggled to be free. A paw swiped the side of her head, not ripping the flesh, but knocking her momentarily senseless as she rolled on the planked wood. Her arm struck a post and she heard the babbling creek underneath her. Staying on her back, she groaned. James snarled and she watched in terror as a large tiger bared his sharp white teeth.

"James," she whispered, her body sore. She struggled to sit up. Pain shot through her back and blood flowed freely from her wounds. Fiona wanted to cry out, to do something, anything to get him to stop but she couldn't. She knew she was losing too much blood and didn't want to think about the damage James had already done.

Suddenly, out of the darkening forest, a lion leapt through the air, roaring as he struck the tiger in the side. James fell. The lion looked at her and she saw a flash of familiar green in the yellow depths.

Cade?

"Cade." Groaning, she fought to get up. She fell back on the wood, too weak to try again. Wet, sticky warmth flooded her back. She was bleeding badly. Her head spun, but she couldn't take her eyes away as she watched Cade square off with the tiger. James slashed with his paw and Cade ducked only to counterattack with a strike to the tiger's head.

Cade's feline body moved with precision, graceful and fierce at the same time, each movement fluid and perfect. James' style was rougher, as he mindlessly and viciously hacked and growled.

James drew blood as he struck Cade's shoulder. Fiona moaned, frightened, as the tiger tried to bite at his neck. He drew back, looking as if he was unable to bite through Cade's thicker mane.

Cade leapt into the air, his body stretching out. The tiger went down. Cade's mouth gripped James neck. Blood bathed them both as James weakened almost instantly. A gurgling sounded in the back of his throat. Breathing hard, Cade withdrew. His cat eyes found her.

Fiona's vision was dimming fast. Her head swam even as her heart soared. Cade had won. He lived. His body shifted back to human form. She saw him crawling for her, his body dripping wet with James' blood. His fingers reaching for her was the last thing she saw before passing out.

"Fiona, kitten, hold on…"

* * * *

Cade paced the laboratory as Eve stitched up Fiona's back. She might have been a vet, but in her line of work she'd seen Fiona's type of injuries before.

"Shouldn't we get her to a hospital?" Eve asked, for about the fifteenth time in three minutes.

"Finn's on his way with a doctor," Viktor assured her. "You're doing fine, sweetheart. Besides, Fiona's not the same as other women anymore. She's like you. She's special. Regular doctors don't know how to deal with it."

"She looks pale," Cade said, rubbing his hands against his temples. They were still covered in blood.

"She's always been pale," said a stranger's voice. "Just like her mother."

Cade turned to the doorway. Finn stood with an older gentleman. The man had Fiona's green eyes but darker hair.

"Finn," Cade said, nodding.

"This is Fredrick LaSalle," Finn said to the curious stares. "Fiona's father."

"Where's the doctor?" Cade demanded, worried.

"She won't need one," Fredrick said before glancing at Eve. "Dr. Matthews, I presume?"

Eve nodded.

"Thank you for taking care of my girl." Fredrick instantly went to where his daughter lay stomach down on the operating table. He stroked back her hair. "I was afraid this might happen with that bastard."

"Who?" Viktor asked. "Ricard?"

"James Ricard Hamilton," Finn said. "He was part of a small group of men who believed they could harness the power of the cat."

"A man made shifter?" Cade asked, not taking his eyes off Fiona. "There's no such thing."

"In the 1930s a group of scientists found a way," Fredrick said, standing. "They called it the Feline Project. Only two men survived. One was fine, taking to the shifting. The other, Dr. Hamilton, took partially. Whereas the first subject lived as an immortal, James Hamilton's transformation was different. He aged like a man, but could shift into cat. Though, eventually, his cat body began to show the age his human one did. As the years passed, he discovered that the way to keep himself young was to drink the blood of pure blood cats--those who didn't shift."

"Mia," Cade whispered.

Fredrick frowned in confusion and glanced around.

"A lioness here that was attacked by Hamilton," Viktor answered his silent question.

"I've been trying to track him down for years," Fredrick said. "He went mad in his pursuit, needing more and more blood to sustain his youth. Then, when I discovered he was dating my daughter, I knew I had to act. Only I found out too late. I wanted to give her independence." Fredrick touched his daughter's cheek as Eve finished stitching the woman's wounds. "I hoped that James robbing her blind was the end of it. I see now I was wrong."

"And why send her here to work?" Eve asked.

"To make sure she was protected," Finn answered. "Fredrick is an old friend and he came to me for help."

"There's one more of these guys out there," Cade said, his lips tight. His heart ached for Mia, but he knew she'd moved on to a better place. This world had never really been for her. She was better off. But that didn't stop him from missing her terribly. Seeing Fiona laying on the table, he took a deep breath. He loved her and he would be damned if he'd lose her like he did Mia.

"Oh, you don't have to worry about him," Finn said, laughing slightly.

"And why's that? What's to stop him from coming here someday?" Viktor demanded.

"Because that man," Fredrick paused, looking Cade in the

eye, "is me."

* * * *

Fiona moaned. Her body no longer felt ravaged by pain and fever and she was glad when she could breathe without her lungs feeling as if they were on fire. Opening her eyes, she got a flash of Cade's naked body covered in blood. The memory of that moment had haunted her dreams, holding her in its delirious throes. Sitting up, her body weak, she glanced around. She was in her childhood bedroom.

How'd I get here? Dad? Cade?

Feeling her waist, she discovered bandages were wrapped tightly around her midsection. She pulled off her shirt and slowly began to pull them back as she crossed over to a mirror. Pajama pants hugged her narrow waist.

"What in the...?" she mumbled as her body was revealed. There wasn't a scratch on it. Even her back, which she vividly remembered being ripped to shreds, was completely healed. There weren't even any scars. In fact, she felt great--strong, alive, powerful.

She looked at her reflection closely. Her body looked tighter, as if she'd spent every day for a year in a gym. Slipping her pants from her hips, she found her legs were just as toned.

Nervous, she pulled the pajama pants back up and got her shirt. As she pulled it over her head, she heard someone approaching. She watched the door, expecting it to open. It didn't. The sound of footsteps got louder and louder until she was forced to cover her ears. The latch moved and she smelled her father before he even entered.

"Dad," she whispered, part in acknowledgement, part in confusion.

"You're awake," he said, smiling.

"What's happened? I..." Her head twitched as she heard more footsteps approaching. They stopped and walked the other way. A servant, maybe?

"Fiona, darling, please try and listen to me," Fredrick said.

Her eyes darted to him and she frowned. Had he been talking? She'd been so busy listening for more footsteps.

"I said, you're changing. All you're feeling is normal." Fredrick held out his hand and stepped closer.

"Ch-changing?" Her voice was hoarse with apprehension

and she cleared her throat. "What do you mean changing?"

"I should have told you a long time ago, but I never knew if my burden would be yours as well. When you were born, you and your sister, neither one of you showed signs of it. After a time, I thought maybe my altered genes had stayed with me."

"Altered genes? What are you talking about, Dad? Signs of what?" Fiona lifted her chin, eyeing her father carefully. She saw every subtle shift of his features like never before.

"I've been in the lab, but all I can determine is the near death experience has triggered a dormant part of you. Your body wanted to survive and so my genes kicked in and became active."

"What genes? What lab? You don't have a lab. You're a businessman." Fiona shook her head. What was going on here? Was her father mental? Was she? Did she get transported to some alternate universe where nothing made sense?

"Shifter genes. And I'm a businessman now. I was a scientist, long ago, years before I even met your mother."

Fiona...?

The sound penetrated her brain, making her stiffen. "Cade?"

"What?" her father asked.

"Sorry, nothing, you were saying?"

"A group of us discovered a rare genetic disposition that created shifters--cats in particular. We worked for the government and had unlimited funding. Basically, we manipulated our own DNA to become shifters. For most it backfired. James and I were the only survivors."

"James," Fiona whispered, hit with a vivid memory of blood covered hands. "Cade killed him."

"It's for the best, darling," her father soothed.

Fiona? Can you hear me? Is that you?

"What?" She frowned, glancing around. *Cade?*

"It's probably just some maids talking in the other room. You'll get used to blocking it out. Your survival instincts have kicked in and you'll need some time to adjust." Her father stepped closer. "Cade saved your life."

"He was King. He's a lion." She studied her hands. They looked the same. Taking a deep breath, she was calmer than she would've imagined being at such a surreal time.

Though, thinking back, there were things about her father that made sense with this sort of explanation. He never got sick. Once, on her fifth birthday, he'd fallen and broken his leg. She'd seen the bone. A week later she remembered him at a ball. It was all better.

"That's why we never get sick," Fiona said. "Not once have I had the flu."

"Yes." He nodded.

"What am I? What are you?"

"We're a mix. We have immortality, enhanced senses, but we can't shift. At least, I can't and assume the same for you."

"But, James shifted. I saw him."

"His body reacted differently than mine. He got the ability to change at great pain to himself, but not the immortality."

Fiona's head spun. She took a deep breath, doing her best to accept all her father said with grace and poise. It was hard though.

Fiona, are you there?

She heard Cade's voice but was just sure it was her imagination.

"What is it?" her father asked, a hopeful expression on his face.

"Nothing," she lied. "It's nothing."

"Do you hear something? Someone?"

"What do you mean?" Fiona scratched the back of her head.

"Just, well, I hear your mother in my head and I thought ... well, Cade seemed really shaken when Dr. Matthews was stitching up your back."

Fiona took a deep breath. Cade was King. She'd told King everything, confessed her feelings for him without censure. She'd told that lion everything--how Cade made her feel, how he gave her the best sex of her life. How could she possibly face him after that?

"No," she answered. Her stomach growled and she walked toward the door. "We barely know each other."

"But--"

"I'm starved," Fiona said, placing a hand on his shoulder. It was nice not feeling the usual tension between them. "Let's go raid the kitchen. I know where mom hides the cheesecake."

* * * *

Fiona smiled at her sister. It was so great to have Darcy home. Biting into a piece of cold chicken, she swung her legs as she sat on the kitchen counter.

"So, meet anyone special in Italy?" Fiona asked, eyeing her sister. Darcy blushed. "Oh my! You did!"

The two sisters were nearly identical--from their red hair and green eyes--only Darcy's hair was a mess of curls compared to Fiona's straighter locks.

"Well, yeah...." Darcy grinned and then rolled her eyes in embarrassment.

"So, Darcy got herself a little Italian action, did she?" Fiona teased.

"Actually, he's American," Darcy admitted before jumping up and down and giving a small squeal of excitement.

"Do tell."

"I think you know him. Finn O'Conner? He owns the Jameson Wild Life Rescue and Preserve."

"Ugh, you're dating my boss?" Fiona teased, before stopping to think. Actually, Mr. O'Conner wouldn't be her boss anymore, since she had no intention of going back to the preserve.

"No, he doesn't even know I like him," Darcy admitted, her expression shy. "I never got the nerve to tell him. Anyway, I want to hear about you. I overheard Daddy talking to someone on the phone. Something about Fiona and Cade? Hmm?"

Fiona felt the blood draining from her face. She set her chicken aside and pushed the plate away, losing appetite. Hopping off the counter, she washed her hands under the facet and said, so Darcy couldn't see her expression, "I don't know."

"What don't you know?" Darcy asked. Fiona didn't answer. How could she? Every part of her missed Cade. It was insanity, but it was like her soul just knew him. "Sis? Talk to me."

"I think I love him." It was strange to admit the words out loud, but how could she stop them? She never lied to Darcy. "But, I hardly know him."

"Mom always tells me that when you meet the one, you just know." Darcy brushed back Fiona's hair and rested her head on her shoulder. "If you love him, then what's the problem? Who cares if you don't know him?"

"What if he doesn't feel the same way?"

"Have you asked him?"

"No."

"Have you told him how you feel?"

Damn your logic, Darcy!

Fiona frowned. "No."

"Well, then I think you know what you need to do." Patting her shoulder, Darcy left Fiona alone in the kitchen.

Chapter Seven

Fiona's stomach was a bunch of nerves. She took a deep breath, forcing her legs to walk up the slight incline that would lead her to the lion's den and to Cade. She didn't know where else to look for him and was a little scared of seeing Eve and Viktor after all that had happened.

Were they shifters too? Were the other caged animals?

She stopped walking, worried about what he'd say. The sundress she wore was on loan from Darcy--a dress for good luck she'd bought while she was in Italy. The blue and cream floral print set off the red in her hair. Clutching a bouquet of daisies, she studied them.

Was it stupid to buy a man flowers? Especially a man like Cade?

"You're just going to thank him for saving your life. That's all. See what he does and go from there. Just go and thank him." Fiona's feet refused to take another step.

Maybe I should just tell him. Cade, I love you. No, I can't say it like that.

She bit her lip in thought, trying to organize her words in her mind.

Okay, Cade, I know we haven't known each other long, but I think I'm in love with you. I love you. Do you think you could love me? Do you think that there is a chance for us after a few explosive dates and an embarrassing tell-all confession when I thought you were a lion? Is it crazy that I think I know you? That I hear you in my head and that I want to always hear you in my head? I want to spend the rest of my life with you. I love you. I want to bear you children and grow old. Wait, no, not grow old. I'm immortal now and won't do that, but the children part would be nice. I can't shift, so maybe you'd consider living in a house and not in a cage. I don't know....

Fiona let loose a self-depreciating groan. "That's the stupidest thing ever."

"Really? Because I was just thinking that it was about the sweetest." Cade's warm tone washed over her and she spun around in surprise. He wore a loose T-shirt and tight blue jeans. Seeing that his body was already aroused almost made her blush, if not for the fact that her body was reacting to him in the exact same way. His eyes roamed over her in appreciation before stopping on the flowers. "Are those for me?"

"Ah." She glanced down and this time she did blush. "Yeah. Is that stupid? Buying a man flowers?"

He smiled, shaking his head in denial. "Not at all."

The brush of his hand against her cheek was like heaven. She'd missed him so much.

"I missed you, too," he said.

Are you in my head?

He grinned and nodded.

Yes, she heard him answer. *We're connected.*

"And," he continued out loud, "for the record, you're not crazy. However, if you are, well then I'm crazy too. I've loved you since the first moment you walked by my cage. I just saw you and knew that you would be my mate."

"You did?" Fiona was so overwhelmed with emotion, she didn't know whether to laugh or cry. She started doing both. "Really?"

Cade leaned over and kissed her lightly, brushing his lips over her eyelids. "Really."

"I was so scared you would think I was nuts. I'm sorry I freaked out on you," she said.

"You were under a lot of stress. I can't imagine seeing a shifter for the first time was easy for you."

She laughed. "No, not really. But, I'm okay now."

"I'm glad." He cupped her face, brushing his lips to hers. Suddenly, he stopped and pulled back. "I'm sorry. Viktor told me I needed to just listen to you and not touch you."

Fiona frowned. Huh? "Why in the world would he say that?"

Not touch her? Why? If he didn't she might explode with the need building rapidly between her thighs. Cream nearly poured out of her at just the thought of Cade making love to her.

"Well, because as a cat, I act on my instincts and as a human you need me to--"

"Ah, I see," Fiona giggled, lowering her voice into a soft purr. "You see, sweetie, I happen to be part cat myself and

I like a man who acts on instinct."

"You do?"

"Mm, yeah, definitely." She licked her lips, liking the way his eyes darted down to watch. His pupils flashed with an inner fire, filling with yellow light. "Especially when you act on your more carnal instincts."

A low rumbling growl sounded in the back of his throat, like a lion stalking his prey. Fiona dropped the flowers and grinned, backing up. She instinctively knew he would chase her and that he would get pleasure from the hunt. Her heart pounded in excitement and she wasn't scared.

Running toward the den, she darted to the right to a small enclosure of trees. It wasn't the most private, but it would have to do. It wasn't like the preserve was open at this late hour anyway. Secretly, she'd hoped for the best and knew her body would demand his attentions, should he be willing to give them.

Glancing over her shoulder, she saw Cade was gaining on her. She had no doubt he could've overtaken her at any time, but she enjoyed the game. Fiona ran faster.

Cade caught her just as she made the small enclosure. He roughly pulled her body along his hard frame, letting her feel the full extent of his cock pressing along her butt. Warm lips met her neck, licking a fiery trail to her ear.

Fiona trembled all the way to her toes. "I love the way you make me feel."

"I love feeling you," he whispered back, nipping at her neck with a dark, seductive chuckle. The dangerous thrill of his sharp teeth grazed her delicate flesh.

The breeze picked up, shaking the leaves overhead. Turning, she backed up against a tree, hidden from the walkway. Slowly, she worked the buttons along the front of her sundress free, exposing her lacy white bra. When she looked into his eyes, she felt him inside her. His voice was in her head, whispering seductive words, urging her to continue. His emotions were her own. At first, she'd thought that they were hers alone, but now realized that she'd always felt him inside her--from that moment he walked into the restaurant. Their instincts took them where her mind had been reluctant to go.

"I love you," he whispered, grabbing her face and kissing her so passionately she couldn't breathe.

"This is so crazy," she panted when he let up. "I never believed in love at first sight, but it happened when I first saw you. I love you, too."

He grinned, a look of intense pleasure on his face. He nipped playfully at her mouth a few times. His hands glided up to her breasts, kneading them trough the lacy material. The bra clasped in front and it didn't take him long to unlatch it.

Cade slowly kneeled before her, worshiping her body with his lips. He kissed her breasts, sucking a taut nipple between his teeth. She heard his pleasure echoing in her head.

Mm, I love your breasts...

You make me so hard...

I can't get enough of you...

Keeping his warm palms cupped over her chest, he continued down. She hadn't unbuttoned her dress all the way, but he merely worked around it, licking and kissing her stomach. Groaning, she grabbed his beautiful hair and pushed him down. Cade chuckled and slid his hands down her sides to lift her dress. He pulled the skirt over his head and instantly jerked the lacy panties from her hips.

Fiona gasped, grabbing onto the tree behind her head as his mouth brushed over her pussy. His wet tongue probed her slit, licking at her cream.

Yes, she thought. *More! Don't stop.*

Delicious, he responded.

His teeth grazed her clit, as he pulled the cheeks of her ass slightly apart. Fiona let go of the tree only to massage her breasts, tweaking the nipples as Cade's mouth worked against her. It felt so good she didn't want the sensations to end.

"Ah," she cried softly, trying to keep from screaming at the top of her lungs. *Mm, Cade, don't stop. I love you. Please don't stop.*

His answering chuckle vibrated along her body, causing a torrent of cream to flood his mouth as she came hard. Her legs weakened and she would've fallen if not for his hold on her hips. When he pulled her skirt from his head, he had a victorious grin on his devilishly handsome face. "You like that, kitten?"

"Mm-hmm." Fiona clutched his shoulders.

"I have something else you might like better," he murmured. Cade kissed her, letting her taste herself on his tongue. It was highly erotic and it only turned her on more to sense how he enjoyed her pleasure in it.

Fiona blindly worked at his waistband, eager to free his hard cock. His hands were everywhere at once on her body, rubbing and pulling and massaging until she couldn't open her eyes. Sensations flooded her blood, pumping vigorously though her. She'd never get enough of this man.

"I'll never get enough of you either, kitten," he said.

Fiona groaned, freeing his arousal. Grabbing it, she massaged the thick length, working her hand enthusiastically over the shaft. Animalistic noises sounded in the back of his throat and his eyes lit with the yellow fire of a shift. The wild cat inside him only excited her more.

Cade growled low in his throat and lifted her off the ground. Wildly, he worked himself between her thighs, thrust up into her slick depths with rough intensity. He called out as he sank all the way into her depths, stretching her tight sheath wide to fit him. Holding her up with his strong arms, he pumped into her.

Fiona matched his untamed rhythm, taking all of him-- heart, soul and body. Her life would never be the same, but that was a good thing. It would be better, because she'd have Cade.

They climaxed in unison, their bodies exploding with intense pleasure. Fiona never felt so complete in her life. Cade held her close, buried deep, as the tremors wracked through them, only to subside into a mind-numbing aftermath. For a long time they didn't move, locked together in a tight embrace.

"I want to make love to you every day for the rest of our lives," Cade said, breathing hard. He lightly kissed her throat.

"Just the day?" She pretended to pout before giggling. "I'd kind of hoped for nights, as well."

"Whatever you demand of me, kitten, is yours." He moaned, again kissing her neck before letting her legs fall to the ground. His body slid from hers as he stroked her hair from her face. Sweat made the locks stick to her. Glancing down, she saw his long hair was also stuck to her- -the blond locks clinging to her breasts.

"You really have to tell me how you get your hair so healthy," she said, picking the strands off her flesh and studying them.

"Basking in the sun," he answered. His voice lowered as he repeated her words back to her. "And licking my balls."

"Oh!" Fiona hit his arms. "I'm sorry for that. I was just in a bad mood. If I knew you could understand me, I never would have said that."

"I know." Cade winked, looking audaciously wicked. "But, also had you known, you wouldn't have told me all that stuff about my cock being the biggest you'd ever had and me being such a wonderful lover."

"Ah! I never said yours was the biggest." Fiona felt her cheeks flame.

"Um, yeah you did. Trust me." His grin widened as he nodded emphatically.

She laughed, feeling lighthearted and free. Hugging him close, she asked, "So, you never answered me about the cage thing. You won't expect me to live in there with you, will you?"

"No, no cages. I only stayed in the den because of Mia."

Fiona suddenly turned serious. "I'm sorry about Mia. I know you were with her--"

"Mia was a friend," he said. Fiona believed him without question. "I did love her, but I mostly felt sorry for her. She had a rough life."

"So what will we do? I'm sorry to say I'm flat broke. James took everything I had."

"I don't care about money," Cade said. "But we also don't have to worry about it. Having lived so long, I've tucked a little nest egg away."

Fiona laughed. "So where will we go? What will we do with ourselves?" Seeing his gaze dart down to her breasts in meaning, she rolled her eyes. "God help me, I love your one track mind."

"Technically, I'm the head of security here at the preserve. Finn's offered repeatedly to let me build a house next to Eve and Viktor. It's what I'd prefer. We do a lot of good here for both cats and shifters alike."

"Uh, I've been meaning to ask about that. Are there a lot of shifters living here?"

"Just about half the population." Cade kissed her lightly.

"So, what do you think? Do you think you could be happy here?"

Fiona glanced around. "I think I could be happy anywhere, as long as I am with you. And, as long as you're all willing to teach me what I need to know to be of some use. I really do want to help, but the truth is I don't know much about caring for animals."

Cade nipped at her neck. "Put your hand between my thighs and I'll teach you how."

"Ah! Cade!" Fiona tried to hold the appalled look, but ended up laughing. "I meant me helping out at the Preserve. I don't know what to do, not really."

"I know," Cade chuckled. "Eve had to make up that fake checklist just to give you something to keep you busy."

"Ah!" Fiona's cheeks flamed.

"Don't worry, kitten, I'll teach you everything you need to know. We do have an eternity."

"Hmm." Fiona wrapped her arms around his neck. "It doesn't feel long enough, but I guess it will have to do."

Cade kissed her and there were no more words as he slowly made love to her again and again, long after the moon rose high over the preserve.

THE END

To learn more about Michelle M Pillow's other titles or the Instinct Series (part of the Ghost Cat Anthologies), please visit her website (www.michellepillow.com).

Best Intentions 2:
DANCE OF SOULS
Mandy M. Roth

Chapter One

Mason Blackwolf sat in the back booth of the bar he'd
stopped at on his way home and watched the patrons
closely. His ever vigilant eye had picked up on a number of
oddities in the bar. Nothing that would send him running
but enough that Mason knew to be on his guard. He sat
there, peeling the label off his beer, wadding the moistened
paper into tiny balls and depositing them into the ashtray.
He took another swig of the dark amber substance, savoring
its rich brew but wishing it was stronger than it was.

Why his best friend, Brayen, and his grandfather,
Running Elk, had sent him on a wild goose chase was a
mystery to him. They had to have known that the rogue
werewolf pack in Virginia had been captured and brought
to justice. Everyone else seemed to know. They'd come
just shy of laughing in Mason's face when he arrived. Why
the hell did they still send him? Sure, a vacation was nice
but even he had to admit that he missed being home.

He hated to fly and had opted to drive instead. If the gods
had intended him to fly, they'd have made him a werebird
of some sort, not a werewolf. With a ridiculous amount of
miles under his belt, Mason was ready to climb in his own
bed and not look back. Unfortunately, he had a distance to
travel before that could happen. The need to stretch his legs
and relax had been great. The pull to this particular place
had been all consuming--bordering on obsessive. He'd
given into it and stopped. Now, he just had to figure out
why.

Mason looked around, doing his best to put his finger on the problem. The smell of whiskey filled the air, coating it like a thin blanket of gasoline, no doubt as ignitable as the tempers of the occupants.

Nothing in the bar seemed out of the ordinary. It was the same run of the mill, clean place with a gritty clientele he was used to. Though, his normal hang-out didn't have humans roaming about it. This one did. That didn't surprise him. Ninety-nine point nine percent of the places Mason went when he wasn't home had them in it.

A row of pool tables flanked one side of the bar while a long bar ran the length of the other side. Tables filled the area in between and in his darkened back corner, sat several booths. The place wasn't bad. It wasn't extraordinary either. Mason couldn't understand why he'd had the urge to stop here.

"Come on, baby. Give daddy some of that sweet ass," a drunk called out from a table full of men.

Mason watched the brunette waitress who had caught his eye earlier as she did her best to ignore the heckling that had been going on since he'd first arrived. The bartender seemed to be leery about the group of men that had pushed several tables together and were taking up a large portion of the center of the bar. If he had any clue what the hell the guys truly were, he'd have kicked their asses out long ago.

With a rifle loaded with silver bullets in his hands no less.

The music, pumping out of a jukebox up near the stage, varied from country to classic rock. It served to drown out some of the ruckus. Unfortunately, not enough to give Mason the peace he so desperately sought. Was it too much to ask for a break? Apparently so.

"Jeanie, you okay?" the bartender asked as he served an older man at the bar a beer.

Of course she's not all right. The woman is being harassed by shifters, jackass!

The woman nodded as she went to collect dirty glasses and empty bottles from the table full of rowdy men. "I'm fine."

"Yes, you certainly are fine," a man with short, sandy brown hair said as he reached out and grabbed her ass. "Mmm, come on, sugar."

She pushed away from him and scurried towards the bar.

Mason groaned as he set his beer down. As much as he wanted to enjoy his time off, he wasn't about to let a woman be manhandled by a group of drunken assholes. Shifters or not. The fact they were supernaturals only meant he could fight them head on and not have to hold as much back.

It'd be a real shame to kill one of these assholes. He snorted. *A real shame.*

The bartender put his palms down on the bar top and glared at the group of men. It was clear to see the man would attempt to protect his waitress; he was just playing it smart--avoiding a conflict if at all possible. It's what Mason had been trying to do but suspected his attempts were in vain. He smiled.

Oh, well, kicking the shit out of someone will help me sleep better.

The door to the bar opened and Mason's heart stopped for a fraction of a second as his gaze ran over the most beautiful creature he'd ever seen. The woman had to be at least five-eight and at six foot two he liked to avoid having to bend nonstop to kiss them if at all possible. She'd work just fine.

The low-rise, boot-cut jeans she had on caught his attention immediately. Her toned abdomen showed, revealing a silver bellybutton ring. It was perfect. She was perfect. Gathering her up in his arms and spending the remainder of the night and most of the next day fucking her senseless chased his homesick blues away, replacing them with a rather optimistic outlook.

Long, shiny blonde hair stopped just before the small of her back. It was hair that a man would pay money just to be allowed the opportunity to run his fingers through and see it fanned out on the bed while sliding in and out of her. The very thought made Mason's dick hard.

She smiled, making her classically beautiful face even more appealing. Her high cheekbones, narrow, slightly upturned nose and full rose-colored lips made his body throb with need. As his cock began to dig painfully into his black jeans, he instantly regretted not shacking up with the last hottie he'd crossed paths with. She'd been easy on the eyes and more than willing to have some fun but he felt compelled to get on the road and head home. That wasn't something he normally passed on.

The bizarre urge to get on the road and head home had stayed with him and gotten stronger and stronger until he'd neared here. He'd given in to the compulsion to pull off, find a bite to eat and grab a beer. Somehow, he'd ended up here. It wasn't as though the bar was close to the highway. No. Mason had driven a good distance off course before stopping. It wasn't like he even had a choice. Something here had called to him. If he was right, it was the blonde.

"Hot damn," the man at the table full of assholes said. "Take a look at the legs on that one. The rack isn't bad either. How you doin', sugar?"

Instantly, Mason found himself fighting the beast within, doing his best to keep the wolf caged. The urge to kill every one of the men for daring to look in the woman's direction was so strong it shocked him. He clenched his fist, digging tiny crescent-shaped wounds into the palm of his hand and not caring in the least.

Jeanie went to the blonde quickly and Mason made sure he utilized every ounce of his supernatural gifts. First up, his ultrasensitive hearing. "Chan, you're here! Ohmygod, I can't believe it. When did you get in? Hey, I thought you weren't coming until ten."

The blonde smiled and his stomach did a flip-flop. If her flashing her pearly whites had that effect on him, he was screwed. Hopefully, in the literal sense if he played his cards right.

The blonde winked at her friend. "Hon, it's eleven now. Don't worry. I thought I'd head down and see if you needed a lift home or a little help?"

Her voice was every bit as smooth and sexy as she was. The need to hear her whispering sweet nothings in his ear while he fucked her left Mason fighting the urge to run to her and toss her over his shoulder. Fucking her was definitely something he would be doing before he left for home.

"Chandra Holbeck, are you telling me that you actually drove here for once?" Jeanie asked, sounding shocked.

Chandra. Chan. Mason let the name roll around in his head, taking more pleasure from it than he should.

Fuck, even her name makes me horny.

She laughed. He cupped his erection, praying for relief.

When she spoke, she offered no such thing. "Uhh, please, Jeanie. You know me better than that. I didn't drive. I walked. It's gorgeous out. I can't get enough of the fresh mountain air."

Mason wanted to jump up and shout at her for being stupid enough to walk around at night, alone with shifters frequenting the area--drunken ones at that. Somehow, he managed to hold back. It wasn't easy. Maybe the beast within him wanted to be fucking her tonight as bad as the man so it didn't want to risk the opportunity by opening his mouth and inserting his foot.

Oh, we are so getting a piece of that tonight, my friend.

The woman slipped the jean jacket she had on off, leaving her in a tiny red fitted tee shirt. The cream-colored swells of her breasts showed due to the deep V-cut of it. Never before had Mason wanted to cover a sexy woman's body but now he did. Wrapping her in a blanket and taking her home to peel back the layers and unwrap the prize inside in privacy was all he wanted to do. None of these men deserved to look upon her. She was special.

Special? What the hell am I thinking? She's just another piece of ass.

Even as the words entered his mind, Mason knew they were a lie. She was more than just a piece of ass--way more and that scared him. Thankfully, the very idea of having his dick sinking into her lush body more than turned him on. It managed to set him on the verge of a full-shift and with his position as alpha male and right hand to Brayen, the guardian of the wolves, that was something that didn't happen to him. He was stronger than that. Or so he'd thought. The blonde before him challenged that at an alarming rate.

Chandra glanced around the room, seeming to soak it all in with a childlike wonderment that made Mason smile. "Man, I missed this place. It's packed." Her brow creased. "Bertin, where's Diane?"

The bartender shifted awkwardly. "She never showed up for work and I haven't been able to get her by phone," Bertin said, sounding anything but pleased. "It's good to have you home, Chan. The place wasn't the same without you."

Something passed over Chandra's face. She walked

quickly to the bartender, slid her arm around his waist and sent spikes of jealousy ramming through Mason's body. "If you're worried about Diane, which I can tell you are, go look for her. I'll take care of things here while you're gone. And it's good to see you too, Bertin."

He wouldn't dare leave two women alone to run this bar with those assholes here.

Bertin nodded. "Okay, I'll be back as soon as I can. You sure you'll be okay?"

What? Mason had to fight not to fall out of the booth from sheer shock. There was no way in hell any man in his right mind would leave two women with the likes of the characters in the bar. The man was clearly insane.

Chandra did a rather long, sensual blink that had Mason's entire body reacting to it as if it were hard-core porn. If she could do that to him with no more than a look, imagine what she could do with a touch. The very idea left his cock throbbing.

"Go on, we'll be fine. I promise," she said softly.

Bertin smiled and Mason considered ripping his head off and pinning it to a dartboard. He's noticed several of them on the wall nearest the pool tables on his way in. They'd work nicely.

"Thanks, Chan. Keep an eye on the big group. They're a bit rambunctious tonight. Jeanie is nervous dealing with them and I think they know it."

A bit rambunctious? They're psychotic.

Chandra nodded and patted Bertin's shoulder as she walked behind the bar to pick up where he'd left off. Bertin hesitated just a moment before turning and glancing directly at Mason. Their gazes locked. The slight nod the bartender gave him had Mason wondering what the hell was going on. Had the man sensed that Mason wasn't human? Did he know Mason could and would protect the women at all costs? How could that be? Mason wasn't even positive about what was going on--why the need to protect the blonde especially was so great. How the hell could some stranger hold the key?

All he knew for sure was if one of those assholes so much as sneezed in the blonde's direction, it would be the last thing he ever did. Mason raked his gaze over them, coming close to daring them to try something. He felt like fucking the blonde until one of them passed out. Considering his legendary stamina, Mason had little fear he'd be the first one to fall asleep.

"Jeanie, how about something a little more upbeat? I really don't want to hear some guy sing about losing his wife, job, dog and pickup truck tonight. It's depressing," Chandra said, as she leaned forward and put her hand over the older man's at the bar. "Hey, Grandpa. How are you doing tonight? You're not getting yourself into any trouble, are you? I've been worried sick that you'd go causing an uproar while I was gone."

Grandpa?

Jeanie headed towards the jukebox quickly and selected a new sequence of songs. The first one that came on was about a young girl having issues fighting the moonlight. Mason couldn't help but smile. Being a werewolf left him having roughly the same problem, though he'd never once thought to write a song about it.

"Yeah, Grandpa," the man who had been hassling Jeanie mocked as he lifted his beer in the air. "Have you been a good boy tonight?"

The old man glanced over his shoulder but said nothing to the group. He simply stared at them with a look that would have been intimidating if it wasn't coming from a man who looked to be pushing ninety.

I'm not exactly a spring chicken. Thank the gods I don't look my age.

"Damn, Fisk, that looked like a challenge to me," a buzz-cut blond said. He sat next to the one called Fisk and grinned from ear to ear.

Mason could no longer hold back. He eased forward in his seat, ready and willing to kill something. If he was lucky it would be a table full of assholes. After he was done with them, he'd take Chandra, get a room, and spend the night fucking her brains out.

His brashness made him cringe. Someone, even thinking about her in terms like that, sickened him. *You don't make love to women, idiot. You fuck them. Get over the self-imposed guilt trip.*

He locked gazes with the old man at the bar and an unseen force slammed into him. It stole his breath. Mason tried to stand, only to find himself pinned to his seat.

What the hell?

* * * *

Chandra glanced at her great-grandfather and shook her head. The man was mischief in the making. Regardless of what he was doing, he seemed to get himself and everyone around him in a jam at a moment's notice. Normally, they were good-natured predicaments that left all included laughing with a string of stories to tell. This didn't feel good-natured in the least. "Way to egg them on, Papa. You just want to watch me kick the crap out of them. You get some sort of sick joy out of me leveling big guys."

Grandpa winked. She laughed. The man would never change. He'd never once backed down from a fight and never would. It was part of who he was, his charm, and she loved him for him that.

"Is that true, old man?" a large man with short light brown hair said as he stood in the middle of the large group Bertin had warned her about. "Are you challenging me?"

"Whoohoo, Fisk, give 'em hell," another man called out, his speech slightly slurred. "Be careful, he might have a cane."

Laughter sounded from all directions.

Yeah, real funny.

Fisk glanced in Jeanie's direction and a slow smile splayed over his face. Chandra wasn't about to allow anything to happen to her friend. "Hey, Jeanie, we're out of lemons. Could you run in the back and find some more? And whatever you do, don't leave me in charge of slicing them again. I'll take a finger off or something."

Jeanie eyed the table full of men cautiously as she headed towards the back. "Call me if you need *anything*, Chan."

It was so very like Jeanie to think she could help. In truth, she'd only be in the way.

Chandra wrinkled her nose. "Take your time. I'll be fine. I could run the place with my eyes closed. It's a side effect from having spent my life growing up here," she said, winking at her grandfather. It was his bar.

The smile that moved over Jeanie's face was priceless. "Yeah, you may have grown up here but you've seen other places, Chan. You've gone away. I've never been off this mountain and probably never will."

It broke Chandra's heart to hear her best friend speaking

the truth. At the rate she was going, Jeanie never would see anywhere else. It was safer for an unmated female werepanther to stay close to her family and protectors.

"Jeanie, I only left to study, nothing earth shattering."

"Did you meet new people? Do new things? See beautiful places?" Jeanie asked, as a faraway look came over her face.

Nodding, Chandra put her hand out to her friend. "Remember the dance I taught you when I got back?"

"The one that some Indian Shaman taught you?"

Chandra sighed. "Native American, but yeah, that one. You learned it right away. I bet you can still do it. I haven't done it since the last time I was home and showed it to you."

Jeanie beamed and Chandra knew her friend had practiced it daily. She'd heard the rhythmic sound that seemed to accompany it as she'd walked past her friend's house many times. Plus, Wesley had told her about it each time they spoke. He was good about keeping her up-to-date on her friends.

As Jeanie took her hand, Chandra smiled and winked at her grandfather. He winked back and the music changed suddenly. It was laced in chants, drums and some sort of a wind instrument she couldn't place. "Would you look at that? The darn thing must have known we wanted to dance."

Jeanie's eyes lit and she twisted a bit, never catching on that Grandpa had used his magik to make the music change to a song that didn't even exist in the jukebox. "Do you think it really works? Do you think it will bring your," she glanced around the bar nervously, "one true love to you? Your mate?"

It was hard for Chandra to not be envious of Jeanie in that area. Jeanie had a mate out there somewhere. A man who would love only her. In theory, so did Chandra but it wasn't very likely she'd ever find him. No. Mr. Wonderful wasn't beating down her door. "Yes, it'll work for you."

"I've been doing it for months and he hasn't shown up yet, hon. And why did you leave out it working for you, too?" Jeanie pressed her lips together. "Hmm?"

"Because," Chandra said, beginning to move her feet to the steps the Shaman had taught her. "Well, you know why.

I'm not like you, Jeanie. I don't think I'm like anyone." She began to sway her hips just enough to look provocative. Jeanie laughed. Chandra shrugged. "Hey, I know it doesn't belong there but it feels like it should. Doesn't it?"

Grandpa laughed. "What else does it feel as though you should be doing right now, Chan?"

"Honestly?"

He nodded and she didn't hold back. She knew she didn't have to. "It feels like I should be doing this outside under the light of the full moon, around a fire with sleeping bags laid out."

"Why do you need sleeping bags?" Jeanie asked, dancing along with her.

Chandra laughed. "On the off chance Mr. Right would show it would be nice not to have to lie in the dirt."

Jeanie giggled and then stared at Grandpa. "She is so much like you, Gildas, that at times it scares me."

"Thank you. She is more like me than even she wishes to acknowledge." Grandpa focused on her with a twinkle in his eye. He was up to something. That much was clear. That was his look of mischief. "Does it feel like you should be doing anything else, Chan?"

Chandra glanced towards the back corner of the bar and began to move her hips even more. Her breath caught as her inner thighs tightened. Suddenly, the air around her felt sexually charged and it wasn't her power that was causing it. It was someone else's. Someone in the back of the bar. The urge to seek out the owner of the power was great.

Fisk picked then to interrupt. "Hey, Pops, I asked you a question. Are you challenging me?"

Jeanie stilled and cast Chandra a wary look. Not wanting her friend exposed to any more violence than she'd already been, Chandra motioned for her to head to the back. "How about those lemons?"

Nodding, Jeanie ran off, knowing that she'd only be underfoot if something big went down. It took years for Chandra to get her friend to understand it was better to be out of the way than hurt while trying to help. Still, Jeanie often tried to voice her need to lend a hand.

Movement from the table full of men caught her attention. Taking a deep, calming breath, Chandra hoped that it wouldn't come to what she knew it would--someone dying.

She moved out from behind the bar and headed straight for the table full of rowdy men. "Anyone need a refill?"

The one called Fisk narrowed his blue eyes on her, making her stomach twist and her blood run cold. "Oh, sugar, I want to fill something all right." He licked his lips. "She's tall, blonde and staring at me from hazel eyes, wanting me to fill her so full of my cum she can't walk straight."

Chandra bit back a laugh. "I'm sorry, but was that a yes on a beer or a no?"

"Where did your friend go?" Fisk asked, glancing towards the back room.

Far away from you.

"Beer? Yes? No? Going once, going twice...?" She didn't give in to him, in hopes he'd lose interest and just go before Bertin got back or any more men she knew showed up. It would be a blood bath. One she didn't want to see happen.

Fisk snickered. "You're scared. I can smell it."

She shrugged. "I'm a little concerned. I'll admit it."

The men all got equally smarmy smiles on their faces as they stared up at her like she was a piece of meat. If she wasn't careful, that was exactly what she'd end up being. She knew exactly what these men were--not human. Neither was she. Fisk tipped his head and eyed her up. "Are you scared of me?"

Grandpa laughed and Chandra cringed. The man caused her more grief at times but she loved him dearly and knew that he always had an ulterior motive that was for the best. At the moment, it was a bit hard to understand why he would provoke these men but she trusted him.

"What's so funny, old man?"

"Nothing," Chandra said quickly, doing her best to head things off but wanting desperately to smash the man's face for talking to her grandfather that way. "Yes, I'm afraid of you. Happy?"

Now, shut up and leave.

"Chan, do not lie to the boy. Tell him the truth that you are afraid *for* him--for them all."

Great, Grandpa, why don't you go ahead and throw the first punch? Save time, get right to the fight.

Grandpa chuckled. "If one more comment is made that is not acceptable in regards to a woman, I will, young one. I will. And if you are thinking of batting your eyelashes and calling me Papa to get me to stop, it will work but it will not work on the one who watches now. His need to see you safe will outweigh his better judgment. Trust me when I say you do not want him revealed to the others, Chandra."

Whatever her grandfather was trying to tell her, it was big and she knew better than to not trust him. His insight was unrivaled. *Any suggestions?*

He chuckled again. "Yes. I believe they have no respect for women and should. Perhaps it is time they learned a valuable life lesson."

That's what she was afraid he'd say. She thrust her thoughts out at her grandfather. *And the other, the one who is watching me? What should I do about him?*

"I will see to it he is kept in line. Though, you will have to be the one to calm him down when all is said and done."

I knew you'd say that, too.

"Because you know me well."

The men at the table exchanged confused looks. "The old man is talking to himself. Put the old bastard out his misery, Fisk. He's insane."

Fisk raked his cold gaze over her. "First, I'm gonna teach the blonde a lesson and then I'll teach the old man one. Women shouldn't walk around looking that good unless they want to be fucked."

Chandra felt her grandfather's power move past her fast, heading towards the back corner of the bar. She tried to follow it with her gaze, to see who this mysterious man watching her was but Fisk picked that moment to appear in front of her. Her slight distraction had cost her valuable time and she'd completely missed his approach.

He took a deep breath and laughed. "Ahh, nothing smells better than a scared human. Unless she's soaked with my cum that is."

"Chan," her grandfather warned. "Handle him or I will."

"Papa." She batted her eyes.

Grandpa sighed, never one who was able to resist her when she pulled out the use of the word papa. "Fine. Handle him or I will set the other free. He wished greatly to use a man's head for dart practice only a moment ago. I do think that would be a sight to see."

Chandra glanced at her grandfather. "Huh?"

He winked.

Oh, he's up to something all right.

Knowing that he was dangerously close to stepping in and that the pard, or rather, rest of the group of cat shifters, would sense if he did, Chandra nodded. "I've got it, Grandpa. Keep the other back."

The men all laughed. "Sounds like she's not scared of you at all, Fisk. You gonna let a chick get away with that attitude?"

Reaching out, Fisk stroked her cheek. His hand smelled of blood and it sickened her. As he began to run his finger down her neck, Chandra took a step back, turned and put some distance between her and him. "What have you done? You smell like blood. Who did you hurt?"

"Aren't you a fast human?" Fisk smiled, flashing a set of very inhuman teeth. She gasped, not expecting him to slip into a partial shift as soon as he did. He laughed, letting his teeth return to normal. "Aww, who is afraid of the big bad wolf?"

Chandra continued to back up, wanting to draw Fisk away from the safety of his friends. It would make it so much easier if she didn't have to worry about them attacking instantly, too. She was good but even she had her limits. They didn't know that though and she planned on keeping it that way.

"That's it, run. It only makes me want to pin you under me and fuck you even more."

Backing up, Chandra bumped into a table. Getting stuck in one place wasn't high on her list either. Fisk reached for her and she twisted to the side, only to find him snatching her around the waist. He lifted her off her feet and licked her ear.

"Looks like your hero isn't willing to risk it," Fisk said, pressing his mouth to her.

"My hero?"

I have a hero? News to me.

Fisk seized hold of the back of her hair and held it firm, directing her attention forward. "Yeah, the big tough lookin' human sitting there glaring at me like he wants to slit my throat but not moving a muscle to help you."

Chandra knew instantly it was the mysterious man her grandfather had been talking about. When her gaze flickered over him her breath hitched. His olive complexion, dark brown eyes, thick black lashes and head of chin-length, almost-black hair demanded her attention. Looking away wasn't an option but staring could cost him his life. Still, she found herself letting her gaze trace the hard lines of his face. It would have been too square if it wasn't for his pronounced chin with the slightest of dimples on it.

The all black ensemble he wore, consisting of a snug fitting short-sleeved shirt, jeans and boots screamed badass. The fiery look in his eyes made her hike that assumption up to deadly instantly. There had to be a reason her grandfather was holding him in place, blocking his ability to help. Grandpa had also gone as far as to warn her she wouldn't want the mysterious man revealed to the others. It was clear to see he was straining, fighting her grandfather's hold and that meant he was strong. Stronger than a human for sure.

"Is that your boyfriend, sugar?" Fisk laughed. "How about we have a little fun with him, see how much pain he can take and then make him watch as we do the same to you?"

The mysterious man's muscles all bulged, showing off the fact he was solid, steely perfection. As hard as Chandra tried to fight her body's natural response to him, she couldn't. Her inner thighs moistened as her nipples hardened. The very thought of him wrapping those large arms around her made her pussy quiver in delight.

Fisk took a deep breath. "The idea of me being in you is making you hot, bitch. Will killing your little boyfriend make you even wetter?" He pulled harder on her hair. "Thuc, come handle the bitch's boyfriend."

Chandra's natural instincts kicked in, waking her from her odd fascination with the man in the corner. "No."

"Excuse me?" Fisk asked, sounding floored she would dare to challenge him.

"I said, no. You and your friends will not lay a hand on him." She took a deep breath, preparing herself to do what needed to be done. "Leave now or I can't help you when they come and trust me, buster, they will come."

He laughed hysterically. "We aren't scared of a bunch of humans. Damnit, Thuc, I told you to get your sorry ass over here and handle this punk who keeps glaring at me."

Chandra called upon her gifts, letting them run over her, igniting the skills she carried deep within but rarely used to defend others. No, that was generally left up to Wesley and the rest of the men of the pard. She glanced down at the mysterious man before her and could almost feel the rage radiating off him. She winked and he jolted, looking as though she'd struck him upside the head. Some of the rage eased from his eyes and Chandra realized that she'd taken him by surprise. He didn't seem like a man to be caught off guard.

"Tell me, bitch, is he your boyfriend? Is he the man you run home to, spread your legs and beg for more?" Fisk asked.

She'd completely forgotten he had hold of her and that shocked her. Gathering her wits about her, Chandra accidentally let power out. It went straight for the man her grandfather was pinning to his seat. It eased over him and she could sense his shock. So far, she'd managed to surprise him at least twice in one night. Somehow, she didn't think that was the norm.

"If I'm lucky enough, he will be the man I wrap my legs around tonight." It came out before she could stop it. She wasn't sure who was more taken aback out of the three of them. From the look on the mysterious man's face, she was going to have to go with him.

Fisk lifted her higher. "Oh, I'm going to love drilling into you while I make him watch. Though, how you could want a weakling like him when you've got me is fucked up. He'll die a slow death just because he's not man enough to warrant a fast one."

Chandra merely tipped her head and kept her voice even, unimpressed by Fisk's threats. "Walk away now or risk not leaving this mountain."

"Bitch, you got a lot of spirit in you."

"You have no idea how many spirits I have," she said, feeling the rising of the spirits that came to her often. They sensed the disturbance and would no doubt come to guide her. "And, Fisk, they aren't too happy about the situation."

"They?"

She didn't answer. Drawing her legs up to her chest, she changed her weight distribution, catching Fisk off guard.

He dropped her and she fell to the ground.

Not wasting any time, Chandra kicked out hard, letting the sole of her boot come into contact with his groin. She rolled to her feet and stood in a fighting stance. Fisk clutched himself and growled at her. "You have no idea what you're messing with, bitch."

"A guy with his testicles receding would be my first guess but hey, I've been wrong before," she said, sinking lower in her stance, ready and willing to incapacitate him if need be. Anything would be better than letting Ferran and his men get their hands on him. They'd kill him. She'd just leave him permanently maimed.

The hate in Fisk's eyes told her he wasn't about to give up but she had to offer him the out. "You need to leave peacefully now because I won't hold back anymore."

"Pfft, humans." Fisk glanced back at his buddies and let out a choked laugh sound. "Come play with your food, boys. We might as well make her run from us. There's nothing like a good chase."

They tried to stand, each straining with the effort. "We're stuck. Something's holding us to our seat," Thuc said, desperately trying to rise.

Fisk took another deep breath. "I smell magik." He eyed Chandra up carefully. "Is it you? Are you hiding something from me? You're not like us. What are you?"

"Leave now." There was no way she was going into an in-depth discussion about who or what she was with Fisk. The moron wouldn't grasp the concept anyways.

He snorted. "Or what, witch? You'll hold my men in their seats while I have my way with you and then gut you in front of your little boyfriend?"

Chandra couldn't help but laugh. "I dare you to find something *little* on him. I'm betting you can't. Mmm, I hope he gives me the chance to play later. I'm sure I'll be happy with *all* I discover." She winked and then smiled wide.

"He'll be dead," Fisk said, glaring at her.

"No, he won't."

Fisk snorted. "What makes you so sure? You gonna use that magik you got holdin' my men in place to protect him?"

"That's not my magik, asshole," she said, rolling her eyes.

"If it was, you'd be dead already. I gave you your chance to leave. You didn't take it."

"Do you have any idea what we are?" Fisk asked, licking his lips slowly, baring his wolf teeth once more.

Chandra rolled her eyes. "Grandpa, this hardly seems fair. He's all big and scary with huge teeth and I'm just me. I'm so envious. His muscles are bigger than mine, too. This just doesn't seem right. How can I teach him to respect women like this?"

Grandpa let out a soft laugh and nodded his head. "I suppose you are right. I am sorry, Chan. I still view you as a little girl, not the woman you have become."

Fisk looked confused, just the way she liked her opponent to be.

"I shall even the odds, Chan," Grandpa said, lifting his magik enough to free three more men from the table Fisk had been at. They looked as confused as Fisk.

"Oh, come on. I can take them. Just let them all go."

She sensed the mysterious man behind her straining even harder to be free. He probably thought she was crazy.

Fisk and his men laughed. "Sugar, consider yourself fucked."

He lunged at her. This time Chandra didn't hold back. She struck out hard, thrusting him backwards. Two of his friends charged at her. Dropping low, she waited until one dove at her before rising fast and driving her shoulder into his stomach. He flipped backwards with ease, gasping as he went. She couldn't hide her smirk.

The other man swung out hard, narrowly missing her gut as she sidestepped and countered his strike, delivering a direct hit to his neck. The man dropped quickly and rolled away.

Fisk flipped in midair, landed on his feet and put his hands out to his sides. Long claws emerged from them as his eyes began to swirl with black. "Surprise, the big bad wolf is ready to have some fun."

Fisk charged at her and she kicked out again, this time catching his chin. He slashed out at her. Chandra pulled her head back rapidly as his claws swept past her, so close she could feel the wind they generated. He tried it again and Chandra grabbed his wrist, twisted it hard taking him to his knees. She stomped on his other wrist, holding it to the floor as she snapped his arm with ease. He struggled for breath as she pressed his clawed hand to his throat and held tight.

"No, Fisk, you're wrong. I'm not the one who is fucked here." Chandra could almost feel his intentions. She laughed at the man's stupidity. "Go ahead, do a complete shift and try to bite me. You should probably think about the fact I'm holding your hand and pressing on a point that will not allow you to retract those nasty lil' things you tried to gut me with so you'll be slitting your own throat if you do shift fully or move too much."

It was easy to see the question in his eyes. He didn't believe her. "Go ahead. Retract them if you think you can," she said, daring him.

The hand that was still pinned beneath her boot returned to normal but the one she held to his throat didn't. His eyes widened. "How? What are you? You're not a shifter. What...?"

"I'm someone who offered you a chance to walk away, to save you and your friends' lives but you didn't take it."

They never take it.

The other men moved towards her and she shook her head. "Unless you really want him dead and me pissed, I'd turn around and leave. I suggest you hurry before...."

The door to the bar opened and Chandra knew it was too late for the men. Ferran entered slowly, eyeing up the men at the large table before setting his sights on her. He shook his head. "Tsk, tsk, Chan, such a bad girl showing up in town, not coming to see me and then saving all the fun of killing werewolves for yourself. You know how much I love doing that. Every last one of them should be wiped off the face of the earth."

He pressed his hands together and brought them to his lips. "Oh wait, knowing you, you're trying to do what you can to keep the peace. That's always what you try to do, right? Make us all just get along."

She didn't answer. There was no point. Ferran knew her well enough to know he was right. Chandra didn't need to confirm that for him.

He arched a light brown brow and smiled at what he saw. The situation didn't look good. "How's that working out for you, darlin'?"

"He agreed to take his people and leave, Ferran. He swore to me he'd just go. No one needs to die tonight."

Fisk started to say something and Chandra pressed his clawed hand to his throat more. He shut up.

Ferran shook his head slightly. His spiked light brown hair barely moved as he locked his blue eyes on her. "Now, Chan, you know I can't let them go. You know how we feel about that type of filth around here."

She swallowed hard. "Ferran, he swore to go and not return. No one has to die. No more blood needs to be shed. Enough people have died already. The cycle needs to be broken."

"Chan, I do my best to keep my patience with you, to try to keep in mind you aren't like us--that you don't have an inborn need to kill and to protect but you wear my patience down. When I find you clearly in a position you were left to defend yourself, I have to wonder if your opinion even matters here." He took a few steps in. "He had every intention of spreading his filthy seed, of creating more of them with our women, didn't he?"

Chandra shook her head no but stayed silent.

"Jeanie!" Ferran called out.

Jeanie came rushing out from the back room and stalled when she saw what was going on. "Ferran?"

"Little sister, kindly tell me if these men were planning on doing something they shouldn't. Something that involves taking privileges with you and with Chan."

"I am not one of your women, Ferran," Chandra said, giving him a hard look.

He narrowed his gaze. "Says you. One little bite and you will be. You'll be claimed."

"It doesn't work like that for me, Ferran, and you know it." In truth, it did if the person doing the biting was her true mate. Ferran was not. He didn't seem to understand that though.

Shaking his head, Ferran laughed. "And what makes you so sure, Chandra? How do you know that when you're accepting my seed and I sink my teeth into your tender skin, you won't find yourself claimed?"

Standing tall, Chandra smiled. "I know because you will never sink anything into me *again*, Ferran."

"Again," he licked his lower lip, "don't remind me I

missed my chance, Chandra, or I might forget I'm a gentleman."

"I'll be sure to remember for the both of us."

Ferran put his hand out towards Jeanie. "Answer me, little sister. Did these men want to take liberties with either of you?"

Chandra watched as Jeanie glanced towards her, obviously looking for an answer. Ferran stroked her cheek and smiled. "Don't look to her for guidance, Jeanie. I'm asking you." Ferran put his head against hers and huffed. "You don't have to answer. I already know. I could smell their lust when I entered. Go finish what you were doing. I trust you were a good girl."

"Stop talking to her like she's a child, Ferran." It sickened Chandra how Ferran treated Jeanie.

Ferran smiled. "In my eyes, she will always be a child. Now, you, Chan, you are altogether different. So much younger than me but it doesn't bother me. Why is that? How can I feel for you when, according to you, you aren't even one of our women?" He walked towards her and slowed when he neared her grandfather. Chandra stiffened, unsure what Ferran might try.

"Gildas, old friend, it's good to see you out and enjoying yourself." Ferran put his hand on her grandfather's shoulder and Chandra held her breath. "Do you think that granddaughter of yours will ever stop her humanitarian efforts or is she a lost cause?"

"Oh," Grandpa said, not seeming the least bit concerned that a man who teetered on the edge of sanity had hold of him. "I think she'll stop."

Like hell I will.

Ferran patted her grandfather before walking towards her. He glanced at the jukebox and tipped his head. "Gildas, I find it odd that you'd have the red man's music playing in your bar."

"Red man?" Chandra asked, disgusted at Ferran's derogatory term but not surprised by it in the least. "Even you can't be that big of an ass. I could make kitty jokes to bring you down a notch or ten. You know what they say about throwing stones, Ferran."

"What?" He grinned, no doubt fully aware of the fact he was pissing her off. "Do you have a stance on the red men, the Indians, as well? I don't know why I'm surprised. You seem to have a stance on almost everything. It's so very human of you, Chan. Your obsession with ancient religions, peace and harmony is sickening."

"Then why hasn't it managed to repulse you enough to leave?" she asked, knowing she was pushing her luck with him but not caring. Someone had to stand up to the man while Wesley, her brother, was away.

Ferran put his hand out and motioned around at nothing in particular. "Because, I'm next in line to rule the pard, Chandra. Why would I give that up?"

"Do you really believe what you're saying? Do you really think you'll lead anything?"

"Yes, Chan, I do and so should you." He took another step towards her. "I can't promise to go easy on you when I do take over. I think you have quite a few things to learn. First and foremost, you need to learn to respect me."

"Respect is earned," she bit out. Holding her tongue wasn't an option at this point. "Do something that shows me you're more than you've let on so far and I might start, but until then, you will not gain respect. You rule through fear. That's not the making of a great man, Ferran. It's the start of their downfall."

Clapping, he tipped his head to her. "Ever the one to speak your mind in the most poetic of ways. I adore that about you, to a point."

"You weren't always this way. I can remember a time that you didn't hate like you do now." Glancing at the floor, Chandra sighed. "I can remember a time when you had more than my respect, Ferran. You had my love. What happened to you?"

"Well, finding one's parents, friends and neighbors slaughtered at the hand of werewolves tends to harden a heart, Chandra. And finding one's soon-to-be wife beaten, full of claw marks and on the verge of dying doesn't ever help. Having her wake with no hate for the species responsible, still every bit as concerned about peace as before it happened kills all rational thought." He gave her a knowing look that left emotions she didn't want to have flooding her. "Did you also try to reason with your attackers that night, Chan? Before the wolf-pieces-of-shit ripped you from *our* bed, did you try negotiating? Or did you go willingly?"

Chandra stiffened, careful to keep her hold on Fisk's hand. Her voice shook as she spoke, "I-I tried to stop them, Ferran. You, of all people, know I did."

"They didn't care about reasoning out our differences, Chandra. They didn't care that they slaughtered innocent women and children--that they attacked a guardian. That's what you are, isn't it? It's what you spent so many years hiding from me and it's why you left to 'study' isn't it?"

She didn't answer. What was the point? He didn't want the truth.

Ferran shrugged. "It doesn't matter, Chandra. You don't have to confess your secrets out loud. I know enough to know that the wolves didn't show you an ounce of mercy, did they?"

"No," she said, not wanting to remember that day.

He nodded. "And they came in such numbers you and your *gifts* couldn't hold them back. How is it you don't fear a repeat of that happening? How can you want to do anything but kill every last werewolf you run across, Chan?"

"I was nineteen when they attacked, Ferran. I didn't know what I do now. I didn't fully understand things."

"And disappearing in the middle of the night to travel the world helped you to better understand them, Chan?" he asked, his voice strained. It was obvious he still hurt from her leaving but she didn't have a choice.

"The call came and I had to answer, Ferran. If Wesley summoned you and you didn't answer there would be hell to pay. It was the same for me. They called and I had to go. I had to learn about who and what I am." Licking her lower lip, Chandra focused on anything but the tears that wanted to come. "My time away helped me to see that the wolves aren't all that way, Ferran. Just like every one of your kind aren't ruthless killers hell-bent on wiping out an entire race of the gods' creatures. They have bad apples, too. We all do."

You're one of them.

Fury showed on his face as he struck his chest. "They ripped you from our bed, Chan! They came in and plucked a sleeping young woman, someone who refused to kill an insect even, from her bed and they forced you to watch as they slaughtered others. As they tried to...." He stopped and swallowed hard.

Chandra bent her head down, not wanting to remember what Ferran was going to force her to think about. It was a nightmare that she'd not only lived but often had to relive during her sleeping hours. It haunted her still and would until she took her last breath. At the rate danger kept finding her that would be sooner rather than later.

"Look at me, Chandra. Tell me that they didn't sense your power. You hadn't learned to hide your magik yet and I wasn't there to mask it from them. Tell me they didn't try to.... Oh God, I can't even say it." Ferran struck his chest again, driving the message home.

The wolves had done horrible things to her. She already knew that. Having him tell everyone around them would accomplish nothing.

"They tortured you before they took you within inches of dying. Had Gildas not sensed your pain, felt his granddaughter's life force being stripped from this earth, and alerted us to what was going on, you and everyone else would have died. Their intent was to wipe us out. To assure that our mates and future mates were destroyed. They got off to a fucking fine start, Chandra. How is my desire to see to it that we survive a bad thing?"

She tightened her grip on Fisk's hand. "Because you kill indiscriminately. You don't kill to protect yourself, Ferran. You kill for pleasure now."

Staring down at Fisk, Ferran rubbed his stubble covered chin. "Let go of him."

"He agreed to go in peace. Don't shed any more blood, Ferran. Please."

"Very well." Ferran's eyes flickered. A sign that his beast lurked just below the surface. "Let go of him."

Chandra did so reluctantly. Fisk lashed out with his good hand and caught her upper arm, slicing it wide open. Pain radiated through her. She cried out and jerked back. Ferran swept a clawed hand out and left Fisk's body falling one way and his head falling the other. Blood splattered up, hitting her in the face.

Turning quickly, Chandra covered her mouth as she fought not to be sick. The wound on her upper arm was deep and blood poured forth from it. She did her best to avoid looking at it or thinking about the body that lay in pieces behind her but it was next to impossible.

"Turn around and look at what your attempts at helping got you, Chan. Look at the thing you tried to protect. It tried, and would have succeeded, in killing you if I'd have given it a chance. Hell, it tried to take your arm off."

She shook her head. "Ferran."

"I told you to turn around, Chan."

"The lesson has been successful, Ferran," her grandfather said, sounding much closer to her than he should. "Holding the dove too tight will kill it. Is that what you desire? There is a reason Wesley forbids killings to take place around her, Ferran. It is not merely his need to spare Chandra from our very violent reality."

"Gildas, she needs to learn not to interfere in pard business. I gave her the opportunity to have a say, equal to mine, but she refused to take it. Right now she could be telling me not to harm anyone and I'd have to consider her suggestion. Believe or not, I would respect what my wife had to say." Ferran snarled. "She didn't take the opportunity, Gildas, and you didn't make her."

"One cannot force another to marry, Ferran. To do so would be the same as building your home on quicksand."

Ferran laughed. When he touched her back, she shivered. Leaning in close, he whispered, "We are far from finished, Chan."

She drew in a deep breath, fighting the nausea that rode her. "Gawd, Ferran, I can feel his spirit around us. It's desperate to hang on. It knows its going to hell." The nausea intensified and it took all Chandra had to keep it together. "You didn't have to kill him."

Ferran cupped the back of her neck. "You're wrong about this one, Chandra. I did have to. You just can't admit it's true. He would have killed you, even Gildas will agree with me. Hell, even another of his own kind would agree."

She cringed as she felt the dark spirits coming for Fisk's soul. Their cries, the haunting eerie echo they made sounded so loud in her ears that she shook her head. "Please, no more death."

Ferran dug his fingernails into the wound on her arm, sending pain radiating through her. "Concentrate on here, Chan. Stop drifting off into your mind. Places I can't reach."

"Chandra," her grandfather said. "Ignore the call of the dark spirits. They will take you with them if they can. The mountain has seen too much death. They are too powerful for one guardian alone. Ferran, you know better than to kill next to her. She has no one to hold her to us. If they decide to take her and she loses the internal battle, she will die."

Dark shadows spun around her, dancing a slow dance--the dance of souls. It was both captivating and deadly. She followed them, captivated by them even though their cries tore at her ears, sending pain through her skull. Still, she reached out as one moved to her. It whispered to her in a language only a select few living souls could understand. It was the language of the dead.

Come.

The spirits swayed, as did she. The haunting melodies filled her head, chasing away the pain. She had to touch it, touch them. They formed the shape of a large gray wolf and she knew then it was Fisk's soul trying to lure her but she couldn't stop herself.

"I have to get to him." Bucking back hard, she tossed the weight off her back, paying no mind to the fact that it was Ferran and reached out further, trying to make contact.

"What the fuck is she doing?" Ferran's voice sounded far away.

"The dead call to her, Ferran," Grandpa said, sounding even farther away than Ferran. "To kill one so evil in her presence has left the gate open for his soul to attempt to capture her own. The fact he was a shifter, a wolf, only intensifies that for Chan. To guide spirits on earth is part of her destiny. Part of who she has always been. Part of who she will always be. This much you knew yet you chose to ignore it. You also know that she has a severe handicap in comparison to other guardians--she is not a shifter nor is she immortal. This you knew as well."

"What is she looking at?"

"My guess would be that she sees whatever form the man you killed has chosen to show himself in. So far, it has not attacked." The need to follow her grandfather's voice was powerful but the lure of what lay before her was greater.

"How do you know it hasn't attacked?" Ferran asked.

"You will know when it does. It is not a thing a man who

claims to love Chan would wish upon her regardless of how displeased he is with her need for peace. You shall see why she seeks it firsthand. Her inborn need is to see all to safety so she will attempt to save him from the pits of hell. It matters not that he is evil, for Chan's destiny does not afford her the opportunity to pick and choose who she guides. She must guide all to their fate."

The shadow of the wolf continued to draw her attention. "Come on, it's okay. Follow me. You don't have to go with them," she whispered, putting her hand out slowly.

The dark spirits swooped down and struck her hard, sending Chandra hurtling backwards. She did her best to stop herself, but nothing worked. Ferran reached out to stop her, but the spirits thrust him aside. She struck a table hard, rolled off, hit the floor as the table toppled over on her.

"Gildas, I felt something!" Ferran cried out. "It wasn't Chan. It felt like...."

"Death," Grandpa answered. "Do you feel like more of a man now, Ferran? Does it please you to know that your need to teach Chandra a lesson has now left her in a battle for not only her soul, but that of all souls present?"

"What?"

"Yes, Ferran, you announce that she is a guardian, thinking that all along she had hidden it from you but she is not the type of guardian you think her to be. Chandra is not like others that guard a race of shifters and maintain peace, settle disputes and deliver death to those who deserve it."

Grandpa sighed before continuing on, "Chandra is a spirit guardian. Her greatest battles are fought with things that know no bounds, have no physical limitations. Should they win and destroy Chan prior to her own spirit guides coming to her aid then they will be unleashed upon mankind. It is why Chan will fight to the death--she has no other choice."

Fisk's breath caught. "I didn't mean to ... I didn't know. I thought she...."

Grandpa huffed. "You have always thought my granddaughter to be a bleeding heart. Weak because she does not carry the gene to shift into an animal like you, like me. Weak because she was terrified of what she saw you turn into, Ferran. And I do not mean your shifted panther form. I mean into a man who shows no mercy."

"How do I stop it?" Ferran asked.

"*You*, do not. It is a task that she must endure herself or that another of *her* kind must help with--another soul guardian. Even I am powerless to help her fight the dark spirits."

Another dark spirit fell from the air, scoring a direct hit. Chan screamed as pain ripped through her upper back. Scrambling to her feet she stood her ground, waiting for them to strike again. To her surprise, they seemed to fixate on the mystery man in the corner, near where her grandfather and Ferran still remained. That was odd. They never normally tried to steal another's soul when she was still able to fight freely.

"You will not harm him," she said, in the language only the dark spirits could understand, the language of the dead. The mystery man's brown gaze flickered to her and she could see the question in them. Had he understood what she had said? No. He didn't feel like someone with access to the dead. The spirits loomed over him still. "He is mine. You cannot have him."

To lay claim to another's soul was something Chandra had never done before. It was something a guardian would only do to protect their significant other, their spouse. But she didn't think twice about it. There was no way she would let them have the man.

"Mason will come with us," they whispered, in their native tongue. "We have waited a long time to take him."

Mason? Who is Mason and what the hell are they talking about?

"Chan, search your heart and you will find the answers to that which you seek," Grandpa said, somehow managing to break through the state of mind she was in when the spirits were near. It was testament to his power.

Search my heart?

"What your eyes and mind refuse to see and acknowledge, your heart already knows to be true."

Closing her eyes, Chandra concentrated on the name Mason. Instantly, the image of the mysterious man filled her mind. He was Mason, the one the dark spirits wanted to take with them. Another image quickly followed. This one showing Mason above her, dropping down and capturing her mouth with his. It was so vivid it felt real.

The dark spirits moved dangerously close to Mason. Her

heart pounded in her chest. She ran full force at them, diving into a handspring and tucking her legs to her chest as she went. Undoing herself, she kicked her foot out, sweeping her leg just over Mason's head and knocked the dark spirits away from him.

Chandra dropped to her feet on the table before him and stood protectively. "I told you. Mason is mine. You cannot take him," she said, still speaking the only way she could to the dark spirits.

"You shall die, too." The dark spirits flickered in and out as they did when she wore at their strength. They had a limited amount of time to either get back to the gates of hell with their soul or kill her.

"I will die to protect him, if need be. But know that I will take you with me when I go."

She searched the room for sign of Fisk's soul, but found none. He was hiding, toying with her. Something growled and struck her upper back with such force it sent her to her knees, teetering on the edge of the table. Blood ran down her shoulder.

Ferran rushed at her. He tried to bat at the nothingness around her but he wasn't like her, he couldn't fight them. They hit him hard sending him hurtling through the air. He landed on a table. It gave under his weight and he hit the floor with a thud.

The dark spirits spiraled back at her. She stood tall and put her hand out. Calling upon her power, her magik, she let it fill her. Something moved up next to her and she went to strike out but stopped the instant she locked eyes with the mysterious stranger named Mason.

"You're hurt," he said, reaching out for her. The sound of his voice rolled over her as though it were a power unto itself.

The dark spirits kept coming. Chandra went to push Mason out of the way but found him cradling her to his body. They hit and she released her power. Mason put his hand over hers and held it as the cold energy she held within filled the air.

"We will be back, *femgatia*," they whispered with a sickening scream. Chandra couldn't help but shiver. More and more they were referring to her as *femgatia*. Since there was no literal translation from the language of the dead to any other, the closest thing she could come up with was she-guardian.

Mason held tight to her. "Then it is you who will perish, for she is mine and you will not harm her," he answered back in the language of the dead.

She gasped a second before Mason brought his lips dangerously close to hers. "Make her sleep, old man. I know you can."

Chapter Two

Chandra walked out to find breakfast warming on the stovetop. The smell of bacon and eggs had been what had awakened her. She had no idea that she'd find fresh biscuits and a pot of coffee made, too. There was even a jar of homemade jam open on the table, meaning someone had gone down to the cellar and brought it up. Grandpa tended to avoid the place because Chandra's tools for laying souls to rest also resided down there and he thought it best not to tamper.

Glancing around the orange kitchen, Chandra smiled. It was perfect. After the night she'd had, she would have been happy with corn flakes in a bowl. Finding this treat was divine. It was heaven, pure and simple. The sounds of classic rock began to fill the house cutting into the euphoric feeling. Puzzled as to why, she followed it. Entering the dining room, Chandra glanced around for signs of someone home, but found none. That couldn't be right. Someone had taken the time to make breakfast and someone had turned the music on. Granted, the music could have been turned on by a spirit or ghost which did tend to visit her frequently but they'd never cooked for her before.

As she approached the bathroom she found the door open and the shower running. "Jeanie, I think I love you. With Wesley gone I eat corn flakes for breakfast." She laughed. "Milk is optional. I also don't normally sleep as well as I did last night." Chandra went to the medicine cabinet and grabbed her toothbrush. One of the extra ones she kept up there for unexpected visitors, like Jeanie, was opened and laying on the sink countertop.

"Aren't you the quiet one this morning." She put a dollop of toothpaste on her toothbrush and turned the cold water on low. "Hey, thanks for staying with me last night. I hate needing to have someone nearby after *it* happens. I hate the way it drains me. It's probably the only time I'm envious that I can't morph into some superhuman crossbreed and heal instantly. Okay, I was jealous that I couldn't do that when I twisted my ankle when we were seven too, so I guess I have cat-shifter envy."

As she brushed her teeth Chandra swayed her hips and danced around to the music, wearing only an oversized tee shirt and her undies. "Hey," she said, after spitting in the sink and carrying on with her dancing, still brushing her teeth. "How the hell did I get home last night? I remember something taking a bite out of my back and then the sexy guy who wasn't from around here grabbing hold of me."

Dancing around more, Chandra thought about the man in question. "Jeanie, I think he was like me. I think Mason can see and hear the dead. In fact," Chandra exhaled as the realization of it all struck her, "I'm almost positive I heard him speaking the language of the dead. The one I tried to teach you when we were in high school but you opted for German instead." Laughing, she ran her fingers through her hair, trying to get it to do something extraordinary. It wasn't cooperating.

"You know, I always love our one-sided conversations," Chandra said, sarcastically. "Don't get me wrong. Your quiet moments are wonderful and all but I could really use a springboard this morning. Plus, I'm rarely the one who has guy issues to discuss. Let me have my turn, will you?"

Chandra glanced at herself in the mirror. "Why don't I have any blood on me? If you let Ferran get me home and clean me up, I will hang you by your pink painted toenails, Jeanie. That son of a.... Never mind. I'm not going there today. I still don't understand how the two of you could come from the same womb." She put her hands up and danced with her back to the shower.

When Jeanie didn't respond, Chandra sighed. "Okay, I'm sorry. I know he's your brother and I know he wasn't always like he is now. You know, I hate when he throws what happened in my face like I didn't live it. I don't need to be reminded I was almost ripped into little pieces by a pack of werewolves. I was there. I'll never forget it. I'm not asking Ferran to stand and hold their hands singing campfire songs, Jeanie. I'm just asking him to understand that the ones who came didn't represent the whole. They weren't acting out the wishes of all werewolves."

Chandra finished brushing her teeth and pulled her tee shirt up and over her head, not fully taking it off, merely hooking it in her arms. "Hey, Jeanie, can you peek and see if my back is healed. Grandpa must have stayed late working his magik on me. I woke up feeling the best I've felt in years. I honestly thought I'd feel like a punching bag until Wesley got home and handled it for me."

Her brother had an amazing gift for healing and was the reason she was alive today. He'd been the one to tend to her wounds after the werewolf attack, leaving not so much as a scar on her body. "Speaking of Wesley, you do realize that he's going to try to kill Ferran if we tell him what went on. I'd rather not have anymore bloodshed and I'm sure you'd rather not have your brother's head severed."

Putting her back to the corner of the shower, Chandra waited for Jeanie to check her. "Jeanie, I, unlike you, am not immortal and I can feel myself aging waiting for you to look at my back." Thoughts of their time together flooded her and immediately a trip they'd shared to a fortune-teller popped into her mind. Chandra couldn't help but chuckle.

"Until that big strappin' man with dark hair, dark eyes, similar gifts as me and a tattoo of an eagle on his lush ass shows up and says 'let's spend forever together' I will surely die of old age in this spot."

Shifting her weight from side to side, Chandra tried her best to patient. "For the record, that fortune-teller you made me go to with you was a quack. She got so detailed for a minute there that she almost had me. But come on, tall, dark, and handsome is a bit vague. Granted, the tattoo thing was a bit different, but it's not like I'm going to walk up to every good-looking guy with dark hair and ask him to show me some ass. And you are not allowed to do it for me, Jeanie."

Chandra stopped and thought about what the fortune-teller had said. "Didn't she tell me that my future husband and my paths would cross many times before he'd come to me? That we'd know the same people but not know each other when we met? That he'd be in grave danger and our 'love' would have to overcome some big obstacles, but he wouldn't bat an eye at it all?"

Her stomach tightened at the thought of any man showing up in her life with everything she had going on. "What the hell made the lady think I'd want to hear that? What would I even say to Mr. Right? Oh, yeah, head on over. Everyone who lives around me, doing their best to control my every movement is a trained, supernatural, killer but hey, don't worry, if they do manage to kill you, I'll fight to make sure you don't end up in the wrong hands once you're dead."

She laughed at her own neurosis. "Remember when she told me something about my dream man, my Mr. Right, and a black wolf? Real funny, the cat and dog thing. You fell out of the chair laughing and I sat there looking like she'd just announced I was pregnant with sextuplets." Chandra shook her head. "Yeah, that was funny too until she told me I really would have six children. *Right.* I am not having any, let alone six. What the hell was she thinking? Even a supernatural male would have issues knocking his significant other up that many times. I really need to stop talking about sex. I've told you before about how horny I get after using my gifts."

It was true. After using large amounts of power, Chandra generally passed out and then woke with the urge to have sex. The mere thought of it made her entire body tense. "Damn, I shouldn't have brought it up. I was actually doing okay until I mentioned it. Now I'm going to be biting my lower lip and wishing I had a stiff one between my legs all day."

"Where's Mr. Right when I need him?" Shivering as the shower curtain opened and cool flecks of water sprinkled over her, Chandra bunched her shoulders up. "Can you just image my mystery mate's sperm? They probably have capes or something and the guy probably has like a zillion other kids out there because of it. Uhh, no thanks. I'll pass. That's why I don't want to put any stock in that dance to draw your mate to you. Everyone here, except you and Grandpa, is convinced that I'm free game for the men here to marry. I'm not. I don't care if I don't have the genes to shift. I'm not less of a person because of it, Jeanie. If Grandpa wouldn't have threatened to bring in human law, I'd already be married to Ferran. Not even Wesley could have stopped it from happening."

She shuddered. "At least you know Ferran would never allow you to be with someone like him--someone who has let the darkness take him over. He loves you too much to do that to you.

"Until last night, I never understood his protectiveness

with you but when I saw the dark spirits over the new guy at the bar, the guy who I'm sure could hear and see the dead, Mason, I couldn't breathe. The thought of the dark spirits hurting him terrified me more than anything ever has. Is that weird or what?"

Chandra shivered as a horrifying thought hit her. "Oh, gods, did Mason get out okay? Grandpa was hiding what Mason was from me and I'm guessing from Ferran and the others too, but I knew the second I laid eyes on Mason and felt him pushing back against the power on him that he wasn't human. Did they hurt him?" The idea sickened her. Swaying slightly, Chandra did her best to keep her composure. Passing out wouldn't do Mason any good.

"Tell me now, Jeanie. Tell me Mason made it out and went on his merry way." Fear like she'd never experienced before consumed her. Covering her mouth, Chandra shook her head.

"Jeanie." Tears filled her eyes. "Say something. Tell me that Mason made it out, that Ferran and his men didn't.... Oh, gods, I can't even say it. Jeanie?"

A large, warm, wet hand ran over her back causing her entire body to respond. Shocked, Chandra turned fast to find the mysterious man in question staring down at her. "Mason?"

He smiled.

Her gaze instantly began to run over his wet, olive-colored skin. His entire body looked as though it had been chiseled from the finest of marble. The water seemed to run down every path that her tongue wanted to take. She should have been outraged to find him standing there. She wasn't. No. She was horny and he was just the man to solve that problem.

When her gaze reached his groin, her mouth opened wide in disbelief. Sure, she'd assumed he'd be well-off in the 'what he was packin' area but she had no idea he'd be doing that good. His long, thick cock was a shade or two darker than his olive skin. It bobbed obscenely before her, almost touching her stomach as it did. The urge to drop down and take it in her mouth was great. That caught her off guard.

Tracing her way, slowly back up Mason's body, Chandra found him staring at her with a mix of amusement and fascination. Surging forward, she reached for him. The need to feel for herself that he was safe outweighed her better judgment. "They didn't hurt you."

* * * *

Mason stared at Chandra, still unable to believe that he'd not only helped her grandfather get her home but had volunteered to take care of her. He didn't even trust himself to be alone with her, how the old man had was a mystery to him. Now, as he soaked in the sight of her standing before him, one pink nipple showing from behind the slipping garment in her arms and her tiny panties hiding what he'd already seen, a mound with a thin strip of hair on it, he knew he should have run as fast as he could.

She was a temptress to the tenth degree and as much as he swore to himself that he wouldn't touch her, wouldn't risk becoming attached, he found himself reaching out for her. When he'd first heard her enter the bathroom he wasn't sure what to do. Any other woman, he'd have instantly tried to work his 'get laid' magik on them. This one was different. Something about Chandra made his pickup lines, smooth moves and whatever else Lily, his best friend's wife used to describe as his repertoire, seem pointless. Almost embarrassing.

The moment Chandra expressed concern for him, fearing he might have fallen victim to the prejudiced acting head of the pard, Ferran, his heart had melted. He was left no choice but to touch her. The need was even greater now that he'd seen the hungry way she'd looked at him.

"I thought they.... Oh, gods, you're okay." Chandra cupped her mouth, leaving the tee shirt that had been at least partially covering her breast, slipping more.

Mason took hold of her hand and put it against his chest. Heat flared between them instantly as their powers recognized one another. Never before had he dared to dream he'd meet a woman who would understand the call of the dead. It was something that had been passed down through the generations and even though his mother had not been Native American or a shifter, he'd managed to get the gene and the gifts from his father.

To have someone to share them with, to discuss things and who wouldn't think he was crazy when the spirits came to talk with him was a dream come true. To find out that person was also his mate was something Mason had never expected.

My mate?

He'd spent the entire night guarding Chandra, worried that the dark spirits or the pard would come calling again. Thoughts of her being his mate had plagued him. He wasn't looking for a wife. He wasn't looking for anything beyond a one-night stand, a quick 'pickle tickle' and a good time. Chandra wasn't someone he planned on but he now understood the pull to come to the bar. It had been her. She'd unknowingly summoned him, no doubt with the dance she had half-heartedly done. Running Elk, his great-grandfather and Shaman for his pack, was always teaching it to the females. It looked as though some other man had done the same thing for Chandra.

Running Elk would love knowing the dance had worked. He'd most likely never let Mason live it down.

The old ways are sacred and shrouded in mystery for a reason. His great-grandfather's voice echoed in his head.

Mason smiled. Yeah, the ways were a mystery for the sole purpose of confusing the hell out of his senses and leaving him wanting to not only bed the beauty before him but to pledge his life to her--for her.

Chandra ran her hand down his chest, causing his breathing to grow shallow. He needed her. His cock ached to be in her and his body burned to be allowed to simply sample her skin. But, she'd been through a horrible ordeal and his intent, for the first time in his long life, was to do the right thing. See to it she was safe. Mason had already done that. Chandra was safe now. He knew he should leave.

Just walk away and make it easy on all parties involved.

Put one foot in front of the other.

Do it.

Take a step.

The only move he made was to run his thumb over Chandra's lower lip. She closed her eyes and tipped her head back. She bit at his thumb, kissing it. They both made choked sounds, expressing the need between them. No woman had ever responded to his touch that quickly. Could she really be the one? There was one way to find out.

Mason took hold of her, lifted her quickly off the ground

and captured her mouth with his. The mint flavor of her toothpaste was still heavy but he could make out her natural taste just a bit and it drove his need to a whole new level. Growling, he thrust his tongue in hoping to devour her with the passion that burned through him. The second Chandra wrapped her long legs around his waist, he knew it was working.

He supported her weight with ease. Mason wanted to pull her through him, merge her body with his in ways that weren't even possible. Never before had he wanted to fully possess a woman and that's what he wanted to do to Chandra.

Snap out of it.

His cock dug at her, blocked from entering her by her now drenched panties. It was easy to judge from the smell in the air that her pussy was soaked with cream from her arousal but she was also wet from the lukewarm spray of water from the shower. His supernatural senses were on overdrive and if he wasn't careful, he'd lose control and shape shift. That wasn't something Mason wished to happen his first time with Chandra.

First time? You mean only time.

Mentally chastising himself for continuing to commit to her, he did his best to concentrate on Chandra. It wasn't too hard seeing as how her legs were around his waist and the scent of her arousal filled his head.

Continuing his tortuously slow exploration of her mouth, Mason pressed his cock head into her, knowing he couldn't really enter due to the barrier of material between them but needing to at the very least test her.

Chandra ran her hands through his hair, only serving to spur him on more. He bit at her lower lip gently, moaning from the feel of her body against his. The tee shirt she held fell to the tub floor with a wet smacking sound, leaving her nipples scraping against his chest. The need to touch them, feel them was great. Mason pressed Chandra's back to the tiled wall and slid his hand up her side. She shivered and he knew she was already on the verge of coming. He could smell it, sense it. Cupping her breast gently, Mason ran his thumb over her pebble-like nipple and she bucked against him as her kisses came fast and feverous.

Pushing the head of his cock towards her more, Mason

drew in a sharp breath at the same moment she did. Though he could only enter a bit due to the barrier between them, it was enough to feel just how tight and wet she truly was.

Damn, I'm going to take her. She deserves better than this, better than me.

"Don't say that," she whispered between kisses. "I want you."

Mason paused momentarily, knowing he hadn't spoken out loud. She'd read his thoughts, tapping into his mind without thought. Chandra picked then to nip playfully at his collarbone. The wolf within him roared to life, immediately acknowledging what Mason suspected--Chandra was his true mate.

Tell me to go, Chandra.

"No," she whispered, her lips pressed to his. If she realized she'd read his mind again, she didn't let on. "Stay."

Reaching down, Mason let a claw emerge from the tip of his finger and ripped the crotch of her panties open. They fell free of her body easily. She gasped but didn't pull away, didn't demand he stop. Instead, she slid her hand down and stroked his cock. He almost went to his knees from the sheer pleasure of her caress.

"Condom," she whispered.

Mason nodded, though he wasn't sure why. If he was right, if she was his mate, there was nothing in the world that would stop the beast within him from demanding to feel her, flesh to flesh. He wouldn't have a choice in the matter. He wasn't human, nor was he subject to their diseases. Chandra wasn't human either. Pulling out and not spilling his seed in her was the option he'd have to take because fucking her without the feel of her bare flesh to his would never satisfy the wolf in him--not if she truly was his mate.

"Mmm, I have some under the sink." Chandra kissed his jawline making it incredibly hard for him to concentrate on anything but the need to ram his cock into her wet core. "Condoms are...."

He turned and lost his footing on the slippery tub bottom. Mason pressed his hands to the tiled wall quickly to keep from falling and dropping Chandra. The action left him thrusting so deep into her tight vat that he went to the hilt.

She cried out in his arms, put her head back and seized hold of his upper arms, squeezing them tight, letting him know he was too big for her.

Mason tried to withdraw from Chandra only to find her hands and her pussy desperately pulling him back in. She felt too good to give up. So he didn't. Driving into her, he gritted his teeth to keep from coming but the fist-like hold her channel had on his cock made the task almost impossible.

"Mason," she panted. "More."

He did his best to slow his hips but the beast within needed this. It needed to know that its mate, his mate, was good and thoroughly fucked. A burning desire to feel her come all over him and to smell it hit him hard. Shifting his weight a bit, Mason stopped thrusting and pressed himself into her deep. He began to rub, swivel almost, move without actually pulling out at all. The position stimulated her clit while leaving their bodies pressed close to one another. It was as though he were stirring her to her peak. In a sense, he was.

"You like that, don't you?" he asked, knowing the answer but needing to hear her say it out loud.

She nodded, alternating kisses and tiny bites to his jawline and neck. "Yes. I like this."

"Then prove it."

Chandra took the lead, accepting his dare, riding him, increasing the sensations soaring through his body. She cried out, held tight to him as her channel contracted on his shaft, squeezing it to the point he knew he wouldn't be able to hold back.

Pull out. Pull out now.

"Mason."

The whisper of his name from her lips did it. His balls drew up and without thought, he let himself go. His seed shot forth from him, jetting into her, filling her womb. The beast within rose rapidly, threatening to claim the woman he continued to come into.

No, I don't need a mate. I've made it on my own this long.

Even as the argument against claiming her raced through his mind, he felt himself leaning down. His incisors lengthened and came in contact with Chandra's soft skin. He slid his tongue over her pulsing vein, more than able to hear her blood pumping. It excited him. She excited him.

"Chandra," he growled out in desperation, hoping she'd stop him.

* * * *

Chandra held tight to Mason as she felt him filling her to the brink with his hot cum. Her body seemed to wring every ounce of pleasure it could out of the experience. Suddenly, her power rushed up and out of her, colliding with Mason's, wrapping them both in a blanket of mystical proportions. It was glorious. Sharing this part of herself with another and having it not only returned but no doubt understood was almost too much.

Something pinched her shoulder lightly, but the magik around her quickly swallowed any sort of pain. Mason kept his head down as she ran her hands through his hair, moving her hips as she went, taking pleasure from his still erect cock.

"Mine," he said, so low she almost didn't hear him.

For a split second it felt as though she'd slipped from her own skin and rushed into Mason's. She could feel his heart beating as if it were her own. Smell the scent of their sex and feel what it felt like to have a beast within. It was odd, feeling the raw animalistic power that Mason held within him as if it were hers. He was struggling to control the beast, fighting to remain in charge.

The idea of Mason taking her savagely, bending her over and mounting her, excited Chandra in ways it shouldn't. Never before had she wanted someone to lose their inhibitions and let what nature intended flow free. Now, she did.

"Let it go, Mason. Set the wolf within free."

He pummeled into her, fucking her so hard that it should have been painful. It wasn't. It was exactly what she needed. She'd somehow become numb to herself and her desires years ago. Mason was breaking through that invisible wall she'd erected around herself and making her feel again.

The bizarre sensation was gone as fast it came on but the pull to be near Mason, to never let him go remained in its place. Chandra's mind was too satiated from pleasure to know or care what was happening. Her only hope was that it would never end. The feel of Mason licking her neck drew her attention to his face. His dark eyes looked as though they could see through to her soul. Maybe they could.

His jaw dropped as he began to thrust into her widely once more. The feel of the cool tile, the now cold water and Mason's hot body pumping into her was too much. Crying out, she hit her zenith and didn't bother calling her power into her. No. Chandra let it roam free, caressing, toying with her nipples, his balls, anything that could increase the pleasure.

The instant Mason's power joined hers Chandra cried out again, scratching her fingernail over his upper right arm so hard and deep she drew blood. Without thought, she leaned forward and ran her tongue over it, taking his coppery tasting blood into her mouth and swallowing it.

"Mmm, mine."

Mine? Why in the hell did I say that?

Mason rammed himself in all the way, held firm and began filling her again with his semen. It was as hot as he was and felt wonderful. Everything about him felt wonderful. Too good to be true.

"I don't want to pull out," he said, his voice low and his forehead pressed to hers.

"Then don't."

A manly chuckle came from him and it left Chandra smiling. "I should shut the water off. It's ice cold now."

"Funny," she ran her hands over his torso, "I was about to comment on how hot you are."

"Were you now?" The arch of his brow and the curve of his slight smile left Chandra staring at him in awe. He was gorgeous. Twenty-four hours ago she hadn't even known he existed and now she couldn't imagine her life without him in it.

Don't get attached.

"Why?" he asked.

Chandra shook her head. "What?"

"Why can't you get attached to me?"

Oh gods, I said that out loud.

She forced a smile to her face. A change of subject was in order. His cock was still hard and desire still hung in the air. He was as insatiable as Chandra was and that was hard to find. "Are you up for another round?"

Chapter Three

Chandra couldn't help but stare at Mason's arms as soap suds dripped off them. It was the slowest form of sensual torture she'd ever been exposed to. She wanted him between her legs again and seeing his buff body dripping with bubbles didn't help matters any.

Mason dunked a plate into the dishwater and began scrubbing it as Chandra dried the last one he'd handed her. "Did I thank you yet for that delicious breakfast?"

He chuckled. "Only about a half dozen times but I like hearing it so I won't complain."

"That's good because it was fantastic." Visually tracing his strong profile, Chandra found it hard to concentrate on making small talk while the need to have him between her legs still consumed her. He shifted a bit and rolled his shoulders. "You look tired. Did you sleep at all last night?"

"How are you feeling?" he asked, avoiding her question.

"That's a *no* on sleeping." Sliding her arm around his waist, Chandra gave him a tight squeeze. "Honey, you need to get some rest. Go lay down. I'm fine here."

Mason stiffened and she realized what she'd just done. She'd not only used a pet name but she was acting like they were lovers. Technically, they had had sex but that in no way entitled her to assume they were lovers in the sense that they were a couple. She didn't want that anyway. Did she? He was just a fling. A one-night stand. Right?

Pulling back, Chandra put her hands on her upper arm and rubbed. It was a nervous habit she developed shortly after the wolf attacks that left the pard numbers low.

"Chandra?"

"Hmm?" She lifted her eyebrows and did her best to play off having hung on him like a needy woman. That wasn't who she was. At least she hadn't been until he'd shown up in her life.

Mason reached out quickly and dabbed her nose with soapsuds. Laughing, she blew on them, sending bubbles up and into the air. Mason seized hold of her waist. His wet hands went up and under the white tank top she wore, seeking out her breasts. Her breathing grew ragged as he tweaked each of her nipples. Her nipples hardened.

"I love how you respond to my touch, Chan." Instantly, her inner thighs moistened. He chuckled. "See," he gave her a chaste kiss, "the minute I touch you, your body responds."

Chandra ran her hand over his smooth, bare chest, down his abs and stopped just before she hit the top of his jeans. Glancing down, she found his cock bulging against the thick material. "It appears to go both ways, Mason."

He took her hand in his and cupped it over his rock hard erection. "Oh, baby, you have no idea what you do to me."

Baby?

He called her a pet name, no doubt to make her feel less awkward. *He's too good to be true.*

"Funny," Mason toyed with her nipples, "I was just thinking the same thing about you, Chan. You're too good to be true."

Did I say that out loud?

She wanted to melt under his touch but she knew better. Nothing this good ever lasted. Chandra did her best to try to remain emotionally distant from Mason. It was hard. Something about the man called to her on levels she couldn't begin to understand. Easing her finger down the front of his jeans, Chandra eyed him carefully, doing her best to gauge his reaction. Was it purely physical between them? Would she ever know? Did it really matter?

"You think too much," he said, backing her up against the kitchen table. "Just feel, Chan."

Heat flared throughout her body as need pulsed through her veins. Giving into the primal urge to be one with him, she undid his jeans and wrapped her hand around his turgid shaft. "I want to taste you."

She didn't wait for an okay. No. Chandra kissed her way down his chest and licked a circle around his navel. The line of dark hair that started there acted as a guide as she ran her tongue down his lower abdomen.

"Chandra."

The very sound of her name on his lips made her wet. The minute her mouth came into contact with his cock, Mason hissed out in pleasure and laced his fingers through her hair. Sliding her lips over him, Chandra did her best to take all of him but had to add her hands to the mix.

She stroked the base of his shaft as she took him to the back of her throat. Mason's breathing was shallow and his body tight. She moaned and he did the same. "There, baby, right there. Yeah."

Spurred on by his encouragement, Chandra increased her pace, sucking on him as she went. Mason pulled her free of his cock and exhaled deeply. "Mason?"

His jaw went slack. "I need a minute."

"Mmm," she murmured as she captured his shaft with her mouth once more.

"Baby, no.... I can't hold it. Chan, baby."

She raked her teeth over his flesh gently but that was all that was needed. Mason's balls drew up as his cock twitched a second before he shot hot cum in her mouth. Chandra swallowed it down, careful not to miss a drop of his salty fluid.

Mason bent forward and used the table behind her for support. Shaking his head, he let out a soft laugh. "I can't believe I came that fast. Sorry."

Licking her lips, Chandra winked. "Don't apologize. Not for that. I love knowing I can make you do that."

He arched a brow in a challenging manner. "Oh, really?"

"Really," she said, rising to her feet.

In an instant, Mason had her lifted off the ground and deposited onto the kitchen table. Before she knew it, he had her skirt around her waist and was pulling her panties down her legs. "Mason!"

The mischievous grin he gave her told her she was in for it. "It's payback time, baby." He pushed her legs apart and stared up through hooded lashes. "I love the way you smell." He licked a long line up her slit. "Mmm, and the way you taste."

Tipping her head back, Chandra did her best to stay focused but the feel of Mason's tongue skating over her swollen clit was too much. She wiggled in an attempt to break free even though there was nowhere else she'd rather be. He pinned her to the table and continued his pleasure-filled torture.

He inserted two fingers into her and pressed upwards while licking her bud. Her inner thighs began to quiver.

Chandra clawed at the tabletop, needing something, anything to keep her grounded when all her body wanted to do was soar. It was too much. Too glorious.

"No more ... uhh ... no."

Mason chuckled into her pussy, not bothering to stop what he was doing. Chandra's orgasm struck with an intensity that left her bucking against him. He thrust his fingers in and began pumping them in and out of her. "Mmm, that's my girl," he whispered, lapping up her cream.

Exhaling, Chandra let her body go limp on the table. Mason rose over her and brought his face down to hers. She could smell her scent on him and for some reason that excited her.

He smiled. "Come home with me."

"What?" There was no way she heard him right. "I can't go home with you."

"Why?"

"I hardly know you."

Tipping his head slightly, Mason arched a brow. "Baby, you know me better than most."

"I don't even know your last name."

He kissed her quickly. "Blackwolf."

Her brow furrowed. "Blackwolf? That's an interesting last name. I wouldn't go telling anyone else around here. They're the type that kill anything that reminds them of a wolf. Your last name would get you shot for sure. A friend of my grandfather's has the same last name. I think he's Lakota but I'm not a hundred percent sure."

"You didn't happen to learn that mating dance from him, did you?" Mason asked, looking slightly pained.

Chandra couldn't help but smile. Mason had been watching her at the bar. He'd seen her doing the dance with Jeanie. She nodded. "Yes. Why do you ask?"

"Was his name Running Elk?"

She propped herself up on her elbows and stared at him with wide eyes. "You know Running Elk? How do you know...?" It hit her then as the air rushed from her lungs. "Blackwolf? You're related to him. You're a ... no ... Mason, no."

He sighed. "I would never hurt you, Chandra. You have to know that."

"Me? I'm not worried about me getting hurt. I'm worried about you. If Ferran finds out what you are, he and his men will kill you, Mason. I already can't let him know you spent the night as it is." She pushed up on him but he didn't budge.

"He'll figure it out sooner or later and I'm not about to run from some punk with a chip on his shoulder."

She snorted. "Ferran won't figure anything out because you'll be long gone by the time I see him again."

"No," he wagged his brows, "I won't."

"Yes," she pushed on his chest, "you will."

Bending his head down, he kissed her, careful to trace the edges of her lips with his tongue. She knew he'd done it on purpose to confuse her. It worked. Giving in, Chandra returned his kiss. As he pulled back, he smiled down at her and her chest tightened.

I could love him. It would be so easy to do and it would cost him his life.

"You worry and think too much, Chan." He kissed the tip of her nose. "If I don't stand up right now, I'm going to end up fucking you on this table and your grandfather said he'd be stopping by this morning. The last thing I want is for him to find me deep in you."

"No, that wouldn't be good," she said, chuckling as he stood.

He put his hand out to her and helped her up. Fastening his jeans, he winked. "Could love me or do?"

"What?" she asked, unsure what it was Mason was talking about.

"Nothing." He flashed his playboy smile. "I'll finish up the dishes and then I'm taking you away with me. We can take your grandfather, too, if you want. I have a cabin in the mountains. I think you'll like it. No. I know he'll like it."

Narrowing her gaze on him, Chandra licked her lip. "Are you a serial killer or something?"

He snorted. "No. Why?"

"Are you married?" She couldn't believe she'd never even thought to ask that. When he shifted and rubbed the back of his neck she drew back fast, covering her mouth as she went. "I didn't know. I wouldn't have. Oh gods. I can't...."

"Chandra."

She shook her head, wiping her palms over the red material of her floor length, slim fitting skirt. "What kind of man are you?"

He drew his lips in tight. "Chandra, listen to me."

Her temper flared. How dare he make her feel more than any man ever had and be married? How dare he do that to his wife? How dare he try to take her back with him? A sickening thought occurred to her. "Do you have children?"

Mason's hot gaze raked down the length of her and a slow smile moved over his face. "Maybe."

"Maybe? What the hell kind of answer is that?" Chandra pointed towards the back door. "Get out! Now."

"Chandra, there's no need for you to be upset."

"No need? Oh, you really are low. Out. Now."

If she didn't know better, she'd have sworn that Mason was trying not to laugh. When a tiny snort broke free of him, she knew that was exactly what he was doing. "Oh, this is funny? I'm sorry but I don't find the humor in it. I, for one, would never cheat on my husband--if I had one."

He snickered. "Good to know."

The urge to hit him upside the back of the head was great. She resisted. "How you could have someone sitting at home waiting for you while you stand here, being all *sexy* with me is disgusting. Get out before I call someone to remove you from the property."

Mason leaned against the counter and crossed his arms over his impressive chest. "No."

She couldn't believe her ears. "No? Are you mad? Get out! You saw what Ferran is capable of. If he finds out you're here and that you're a werewolf, his head might explode."

"Yeah, I did see what he was capable of and I have to say that if he wouldn't have killed the asshole, I would have." The serious look on his face told her that he was telling the absolute truth and that scared her. The last thing she needed in her life was a married, homicidal maniac. It wasn't as though things weren't eventful enough with a crazed acting head of the pard and the whole talking to dead people thing. She didn't need to add to it.

"Get out."

"I can't do that," Mason said, crossing one ankle over the

other looking entirely too smug.

The backdoor opened and her grandfather came shuffling through. He took off his fishing cap and held it against his matching fishing vest. When she spotted his waders, Chandra rolled her eyes. "Grandpa, you can't go fishing today. We're supposed to go into town."

"Going into town for what?" Mason asked, still leaning against the counter. "You don't need anything. You're coming with me, remember?"

"No, I'm not." Chandra pointed at Mason not wanting to hear him say another word. "You, get out now."

"Can't do that."

"Grandpa, tell him to get out!" She looked to her grandfather for support. That wasn't what she found. Instead, she found Grandpa staring at Mason with questioning eyes. When she peeked back at Mason she caught him nodding with a sly smile on his face.

"Is it done?" Grandpa asked.

"If you're asking what I think you're asking, Gildas," Mason said, "the answer is yes. It's done. I'd like to take you both home with me, if you want. I know that Running Elk would love to see you."

Chandra's jaw dropped. "Grandpa, tell Mason to leave before I throw him out."

"Afraid I can't do that, Chan. Seems to me the man has a right to stay considering what his new position with you is and all," Grandpa said.

Chandra's brow furrowed. "Position with me? What do you mean by that?"

Glancing at the floor, Grandpa's eyebrows raised. Chandra followed his gaze and spotted her panties lying near the leg of the table. Heat flared through her cheeks. "Umm, that's umm, yeah. Sorry."

Mason looked down and began to laugh. "That is what you think and I'll be damned if I apologize for making love to my wife."

"Your what?" Chandra asked, positive she'd heard him wrong.

"Wife." Mason raked his gaze down her slowly and settled on her abdomen. "I'm not one hundred percent sure if you're pregnant or not but if you are then the answer to your question about me having children is yes. If you're not, then it's a no."

Grandpa cleared his throat. "She is. I sensed it the moment I walked in."

Too shocked to move, Chandra just stood there staring at both men. "No. How?"

"Chan," Grandpa said. "I think you know how babies are made."

She growled and Mason laughed. "I don't mean how about that--and you are wrong about that. I am not pregnant. I mean how can I be his wife?"

"You might want him to explain the finer points, darling. I don't think you want me talking about it. It's sufficient to say that he claimed you and you accepted, like I knew you would."

"He did not...." She stopped when she thought back to their time in the shower. Slowly, the realization of it sunk in. Chandra reached out, needing something to steady herself. When she found Mason's arm, she took hold of it. "He did claim me."

"Yep. I sure did."

She glared at him. "Wipe that smirk off your face!"

"No." Mason licked his lower lip. "I'm your true mate. You know it. Running Elk knows it. Even your grandfather knows it."

"No. This can't be happening. There's no way that you're my...." Chandra stopped in mid-sentence and thought about Mason. He was like her--a soul guardian. He was a wolf--Mason Blackwolf. All that the fortune-teller had said was coming true. She shook her head, not wanting to believe that she could find her mate. "No. It can't be. You can't be my...."

Mason arched his dark brows, turned his back to her and did something Chandra never expected him to do--he mooned her. His tanned, apple-shaped ass was pure perfection, instantly making her wet. When she spotted the tattoo of a bald eagle on his ass cheek, she let out a choked gasp.

"I can't say I ever expected to have my grandson-in-law flashing his bare arse at me but I think I can rest assured that the two of you will produce fine babies," Grandpa said, doing his best to hide a laugh. "Now, pull your pants up, boy. We've got to get you two on the road before Ferran or his boys show up." Grandpa put his fishing hat back on, turned and hightailed it out the door.

Chandra headed out after him only to find a large red truck headed up her drive. Her heart went to her throat and she raced back into the kitchen just in time to find Mason walking out.

"Oh, no you don't," she said, pushing him backwards. "You can't leave now."

"But you just said that I had to get out." The smirk on his face said it all. He was screwing with her. She wasn't sure if she wanted to kiss him or smack him. So far, the urge to knock him out was winning. "I want to meet your guest."

"No. You really don't." She narrowed her gaze. "I'm still mad at you. You are a pig."

"I prefer to be called a wolf but you aren't the first woman to call me a pig so I guess I can live with it."

"That's not hard to believe." Rolling her eyes, Chandra gave Mason a good shove and shut the door. Mason winked at her through the window and it took everything in her not to call upon her own personal spirit guides to beg them to curse the man, not that they'd do it. If she had more time she would do it herself. As it stood, she had more pressing matters to attend to.

Grandpa glanced at her from across the stone driveway. "He'll not take this news well."

Chandra stared at Ferran's truck as it approached. "That's why I'm not telling him."

"Chan," Grandpa said, in a warning tone.

"I won't let Mason be harmed. This has all just been a big misunderstanding. I'm not his wife, his mate, his anything and I'm certainly not...." She stopped just short of saying pregnant because she didn't want to take a chance that Ferran's supernatural hearing would pick up on her.

The truck skidded to a stop. Ferran locked gazes with Chandra and got out quickly. "Hey, how are you feeling?"

"I'm fine. What brings you out here?"

He gave her a puzzled look. "I watched you get attacked by something I couldn't see or stop, Chandra. I came to with one hell of a headache and the need to make sure you were all right."

Not wanting to alert him to Mason's presence, Chandra smiled. "Thanks, Ferran. That means a lot to me. I'm fine.

Grandpa and I were just discussing how he's not getting out of going shopping with me."

Ferran laughed as he glanced at Grandpa. "How are the fish biting, Gildas?"

"Wouldn't know." He pointed at Chandra. "She's trying to get me to give up a prime fishing time."

"I could run you into town, Chan," Ferran said. "I need to pick up a few things too and it will give us time to talk."

Every ounce of Chandra told her to turn him down, that accepting his offer would only give him the wrong idea but the risk of him discovering Mason was too great. Forcing a smile to her face, Chandra nodded. "Grandpa, looks like you get to go fishing after all."

"Chandra?" Grandpa shook his head. "I don't mind. Really."

"Nonsense. Ferran is right. We need to talk, catch up, all that good stuff. Just give me a minute while I grab my sandals."

"Sure," Ferran said, eyeing her cautiously.

Chandra wasted no time. She ran into the house and slammed the door shut behind her. She didn't even need to look up to know how Mason would react. She could feel his rage radiating off him.

"You are not going anywhere with him."

"Yes, I am." She squared her shoulders and looked into his dark eyes. "I trust you can see yourself out while I'm gone. I had fun, Mason, and it was nice to meet someone who shares the same gift. Good-bye."

Chandra pushed past him and headed towards her room. Mason followed hot on her heels. "What the fuck is this? You don't really think that I'm just going to leave and never look back, do you?"

"Yes," she said, grabbing a clean pair of panties from her drawer. She slipped them on and turned to stare at Mason. Her stomach twisted into knots as she thought about what it would be like to come home and have him gone. But she didn't have a choice. The alternative, him dying, wasn't an option.

"Chandra, I claimed you. You are my wife--the future mother of my child." The pain in his voice almost broke her.

Somehow, she managed to maintain her composure. "I'm

none of those things, Mason Blackwolf. And you are to be gone by the time I get back."

"You're not going anywhere with that psychopath."

It was clear that Mason had no intention of going and Chandra had no intention of allowing harm come to him. Drawing in a deep breath, she prepared to do what needed to be done--lie to Mason to get him to leave. "He's not a psychopath. He's the man I was supposed to marry. He's the man I'm going to marry."

Mason growled out and slammed his fist into the wall. "You're going to have a fucking hell of a time doing that since you're already married to me!"

"I would rather," she swallowed hard, "die than be married to a werewolf. Just because I stand up for them doesn't mean I want to share my life with one."

He jerked back as if he'd been struck. Snatching her sandals, Chandra ran with them towards the kitchen door. It was cowardly but it was the only guarantee she had that he'd be safe.

Chapter Four

Ferran pulled up outside of her grandfather's bar and stopped the truck. Chandra glanced at him, waiting for him to explain his actions. Reaching out, he put his hand on her thigh and squeezed gently. "How's about we head in for a drink?"

She'd already spent the day shopping with him, doing her best to keep on a happy face when all she wanted to do was break down in tears at the thought of having chased Mason away. She almost asked Ferran to use his cell phone to call home and beg her grandfather to stop Mason but he'd been on it most of the day. Not only that, it would have been a dead giveaway that Mason existed.

"I'm kind of tired," she said, putting her head against his seat. "We had a long day."

"Just one drink." He put his hands up in an 'I'm harmless' manner. "A soda even. Just do me this favor."

Nodding, Chandra opened her truck door. "Ferran."

"Yes."

"Thanks for today. It was nice to see you again." She meant every word she said. It was good to see the Ferran she remembered again. He hadn't gone off on any hate tangents or made any sort of snide comments the entire day. Still, she could never love him the way she once had.

"Not a problem," he said, getting out of the truck.

As Chandra stepped out she stilled as an ominous feeling came over her. Nothing seemed out of the ordinary. Ferran came around and took her by the elbow. Instinctively, she jerked away from him. The sideways look he cast her set her nerves on edge.

"Ferran, what's going on?"

He shrugged nonchalantly. "We're stopping at your grandpa's bar for a drink. I thought that was obvious."

Ferran opened the door to the bar and music filled the air. It was loud, rhythmic with a definitive Native American vibe to it. Chandra headed in and spotted Grandpa sitting in his usual spot at the bar. He didn't turn to meet her gaze or acknowledge her at all. That was odd.

Walking in further, Chandra noticed that the place wasn't packed with its normal crowd. Instead, it was full of Ferran's buddies. The men who seemed to worship the very ground Ferran walked on. They thought him a savior after the werewolf attacks and agreed with him that the only good werewolf was a dead one.

She licked her lips. Something was off. She just wasn't sure what it was. "Hi, Grandpa. How was fishing?"

"I didn't feel much up to it so I didn't go. Did you have a nice day, Chandra?"

Didn't feel much up to it? The man had been in waders at the crack of dawn. Chandra eyed her grandfather carefully, unsure what was going on. As she glanced at Ferran's friends, it hit her that they were the ones listening to the music. The same music Ferran had been so quick to criticize the night before.

"Grandpa?"

Ferran moved up behind her and wrapped his arms around her waist. She tried to step out of his embrace only to find him pulling her back towards him. "Now, Chan, is that any way to react to my touch?"

"What's going on?"

"We've been over this already, Chandra." He hugged her tight and pressed his lips against her ear. "I forget, did you want a drink or soda? I know they say alcohol is bad for the baby and all but...."

Chandra froze. Baby? The music. Grandpa not wanting to fish. Her mind raced with it all and her stomach dropped out on her. "Did you hurt him?"

"Hurt who?" Ferran asked, kissing her neck and pressing his body to hers.

"Don't play games with me, Ferran." She shoved off him, just barely managing to break his hold on her. "Did you hurt him?"

Lifting his hands in the air, he looked around the bar. "I'm afraid I don't know what you're talking about."

"Did you hurt Mason?" she asked, not bothering to mask her fear.

"You'll have to be more specific," he tipped his head and stared out through narrow eyes, "after all, I'm a monster now. It's hard for me to keep track of who I've hurt."

Frantically, Chandra visually searched the bar and found no sign of Mason. "Grandpa, did they hurt Mason?"

"Gildas," Ferran said, his tone threatening. "I'll do it."

"You won't do a damn thing," Chandra spat. "Answer my question. Did you hurt Mason?"

He chuckled. "No. I didn't lay a hand on him. Why is he so important to you?"

She fought to keep her breathing under control but failed. "Mason! Where are you? Mason!"

Ferran's buddies took turns snickering. Chandra glared at them. "If he's been harmed in any way, I will personally kill each and every one of you."

"Chandra," Grandpa said, finally glancing in her direction. "You can't do that."

"Yes, I can. Where is he? You know. Tell me."

"Gildas." Ferran pointed at him. "If any soul could take hers, it would be mine."

"What are you talking about?" She shook her head. "You aren't dead. I only escort the dead, Ferran. Though, if you harmed Mason, you will beg me for death."

"Now, Chandra." He smiled and took a seat as if nothing was out of sorts. "Is that any way to talk to the man you spent the day with? The man you tried to keep from finding out you had another man in your house? The man you tried to hide the fact you're mated and with child from?"

"I'm not with...." Reaching down, she ran her hand over her lower abdomen and instantly felt sick to her stomach. "Oh gods, Mason wasn't kidding. I'm ... we're ... oh gods. What have you done to him?"

Ferran propped his feet up on the table. "The way I see it, you ran out on him the minute you saw an opening. I'm willing to let this go unpunished since it was really just a one-night stand gone horribly wrong. But, I'll need you to do a little something for me."

"I won't let you hurt my baby," she said, so fast it took even her by surprise.

"Gildas was quick to point out on the phone to me, when he was begging me not to slit your throat while we were out today that the likelihood of you carrying the baby through a battle with a dark spirit is slim."

"Mason isn't a dark spirit." She took another step back in an attempt to get all of the bar's occupants in her line of sight. "Where is he?"

Ferran folded his hands on his lap and offered up a smug smile. "Funny, you were so fast to run off and leave this Mason character all alone but now you act like you care. Do you care, Chandra?"

"Yes."

One of Ferran's friends snorted and Chandra made a mental note to kill him the first chance she got.

"How much do you care, Chan?"

She let her power up. "A lot."

"Do you love him?" Ferran asked.

She was about to say no but stopped. It was easy to visualize Mason's brown eyes staring down at her while he smiled. The way he made her feel by simply being in the same room as her was unlike anything she'd ever imagined. He was her Mr. Right--her true mate. "Yes. I love him."

"That's a real shame then." Ferran snapped his fingers and the back entrance to the bar opened. "Bring the piece of shit in."

Turning, Chandra found three men dragging a lifeless body in. When she realized it was indeed Mason and that he was covered in claw marks, she gasped. "No! Mason. Gods no. I'm sorry. I thought I could lead him away and keep you safe. I thought you'd go."

"He got a taste of that sweet pussy of yours, Chandra," Ferran said, appearing behind her suddenly. "No man walks away from that. Trust me on this one."

Rage consumed her. She spun around and thrust her fist out, catching Ferran's jaw as she went. His head snapped back and he let out a wicked laugh. "Whoohoo, that's it, Chan. Come on. Show me what you've got."

"Chandra," Grandpa said. "He's baiting you."

"If he wants me to kill him then he's going to get his wish." She kicked out and scored a direct hit to Ferran's gut. When he made no move to counter or protect himself, she paused.

"What's wrong, Chandra? Don't you have it in you to hurt me? Sure you do." He laughed. "Dig deep. You had no problem leaving me to travel the world. You had no problem shacking up with the very thing that drove us apart--a fucking werewolf!"

"Mason had nothing to do with those attacks and you

know it."

"He's one of them, Chandra. One of the filthy beasts that have no business living, let alone fucking our women." He swiped his hand over his mouth and came away with blood. "He even had the nerve to fuck my woman. Then he planted his seed in you, thinking you'd actually bring another one of their kind into this world." He snorted. "He's worse than the ones who came. He actually thinks he's good enough for you."

"He's more than I deserve, Ferran." Tears threatened to fall but she held them at bay. "Don't do this. Call your men off. Hurting him won't get you in my good graces."

"Don't you think I've figured that out?" he asked, looking every bit the part of the psychopath Mason had referred to him as.

The door to the bar opened and Bertin rushed in. "This has gone far enough, Ferran. Leave her husband alone."

"You knew?" Ferran asked, glaring at Bertin. "You did, didn't you? You probably knew the second the bastard walked in that he was Chandra's mate."

Bertin nodded. "I did and I also knew he was a good man. He'll take care of her and never harm her."

"He's an Indian piece of shit werewolf. They don't come any lower than that."

Chandra seized hold of a chair and whipped it at Ferran. It cracked over his head and knocked him to the ground. "He is my husband--my mate and the father of my child. You will treat him with respect because he is a better man than you ever were, Ferran!"

She went to finish the job and instantly found herself being wrapped in her grandfather's magik. It held her in place. "Grandpa, what are you doing? Let go of me. I can't protect Mason if I'm stuck like this. Let go!"

"Mason is dead, Chandra," Grandpa said, his voice low. "Do you not feel it?"

"No." She shook her head. "He's not dead. I'd know. He's not dead!"

"Check the bastard for a pulse." Ferran pushed to his feet and laughed.

"Nothing," one of his friend's said as they touched Mason's neck. "He's gone. Looks like she was too late to guard his soul."

"No!" Chandra tried to break free of her grandfather's hold but couldn't. Screaming out, she thrust her own power out, calling on the spirits for help. It was dangerous in her current state of mind but there was no way she was about to allow Ferran to get away with what he'd done. "Let go of me!"

"No. I will not allow you to put my great grandchild at risk."

Ferran charged Grandpa and Chandra was powerless to stop him. Bertin stepped to the side just as a flash of white blond moved in behind him. There was a snarl and then the thunderous sound of the spirits approaching. It took her mind a moment to process what it was seeing.

There, slamming Ferran to the ground was her brother Wesley. His long blond hair hung just past his shoulders and his normally blue eyes blazed with amber he swept a clawed hand out and over Ferran's throat.

"Wesley, no!" Grandpa shouted as Ferran dropped to the floor.

Panting, Wesley stared at Grandpa. "Are you hurt?"

Grandpa moved off the barstool with a speed Chandra had never seen him use before. He rushed towards her. "Wesley, get your sister out of here, now!"

"No, let the dark spirits come," she said, sinking to her knees. "Let them take me. I let him die. I shouldn't have left him. I should have stayed or left with him." She stared at Mason's lifeless body and let the tears she'd been holding in out.

Wesley took hold of her and lifted her off her feet. "Grandpa said go. You go, now." He took a deep breath in. "You're mated and you're," his eyes widened, "pregnant."

"Get her out of here!" Grandpa yelled. "Mason, she's not going to make it out before they get here!"

"Huh?" She choked back a sob. "He's dead."

"I know. I'm the one who killed him," Grandpa said, staring at her like she was the one spouting insanities.

"You what?" she and Wesley echoed.

"The minute Ferran called and threatened to kill him Mason knew what he was planning. He asked me to do it."

"Wait, let me get this straight," Wesley said, rubbing a hand over his goatee. "Chandra went and got herself mated and knocked up, then you got the okay from the guy to kill him?"

"Yep, that's about it. Now get her out of here."

She felt it then, the dark spirits coming for Ferran's soul. Something else entered the mix. Something warm, bright, full of power and goodness. Mason. Chandra pushed free of her brother's grasp and spun around to find Mason's soul poised and ready to attack.

"Take her and go!" Grandpa shouted. "She can't protect the baby and Ferran knew that. It's why he wanted someone to kill him. He knew he could take Chandra with him and open the gates to hell in the process."

"On that note--" Wesley snatched her up and rushed her towards the door, ignoring her protests on the way.

"Mason! No!"

Epilogue

Rolling over onto her side, Chandra did her best to ride the pain out. The cramping in her stomach worsened. She clawed at the sheets and exhaled slowly. It didn't help. Giving in, she nudged her husband. "Honey, I think it's time."

"Hmm?" he asked, peeking out from one eyelid. "Hey, baby, what's the matter? You didn't have another bad dream, did you? I'm fine. You're fine. We're all fine."

Her stomach tightened again and Chandra bit her lower lip as she took hold of his upper arm. "Mason ... it's ... time."

He jerked awake and touched her swollen belly. "Ohmygods, it's time. The baby's coming? Now?"

"Hopefully not right this very second but soon. We need to call your grandfather."

"Right." He went to stand and ended up falling off the side of the bed instead.

Chandra rolled her eyes and did her best not to laugh. "You aren't going to pass out are you?"

Mason got to his feet quickly and shook his head, sending a mop of dark hair flopping around. "I'm good. Are you good? No. You're having a baby. We're having a baby. Chan, sweetie, we're having a baby."

Another contraction hit as she tried to sit up. Mason was at her side in an instant, helping her to a seated position. "Breathe, sweetie. Breathe."

Arching a brow, Chandra gave him a hard look. "Get your grandfather or so help me, I will choke the life out of you and I will not allow my grandpa to use his magik to bring you back."

Mason looked pained. "You're not still mad about that, are you? I didn't have a choice, Chan. I knew Gildas was powerful enough to bring me back with ease. I had to fight Ferran and the dark spirits on their plane. It had to be done. You know that it did. I couldn't risk you or the baby."

She glared at him. "Running Elk now. Kiss my ass later."

"I love you," he said, planting a kiss on her cheek.

"I love you, too." She took hold of his ear and twisted. "Call your grandfather or the next thing I yank to the point of pain is your penis."

"Running Elk!" Mason shouted, his eyes wide. Chandra let go of him and he rushed to their bedroom door. The minute he opened it, she spotted her grandfather and Mason's standing there with identical shit assed grins on their faces. Mason drew back fast. "How did you...? I was just going to call you."

Running Elk patted Mason's shoulder. "Gildas sensed Chandra's pain and called me. We thought it best to come right over and not wait for you to phone."

"Remind me to yell at you both for having no faith in me later. Right now," Mason took a step back, allowing them to enter, "we've got a baby coming."

Grandpa nodded. "Yes, you do. She'll be here before you know it. Now, go wait at the door to let Wesley and Brayen in."

"Why are they coming?"

Running Elk winked at Chandra. "Because I called them. We will need them to pick you up when you pass out."

"Pfft, I'm not going to ... wait, Gildas, did you say 'she' just now?"

Grandpa nodded. "Yes. I thought Chan told you that you were having a girl."

"He wanted it to be a surprise," she said, preparing for her next contraction.

Mason paled considerably and staggered. "A girl? I'm going to be a daddy--of a little girl."

"Yes, honey. You need to calm down. You're the one who wants to have six kids."

His eyes rolled back in his head a second before he hit the floor. Grandpa and Running Elk laughed as they stepped over him. Chandra just shook her head. "That's not funny, you two."

They chuckled.

Chandra sighed. "Okay, it is funny but it's not nice. We can't just leave him there. That's my husband."

"We know. But that really is the best place for him at the moment. We'll wake him in a minute," Grandpa said, winking at her.

Chandra stared down at Mason and couldn't stop the swell of emotions that roared through her. "I love him so much." Another contraction hit. "I'm ... going to kill him. Six more my ass! Let me at him."

She reached out but was in no condition to move anywhere.

Grandpa nodded. "See, it's the best place for him because you can't reach him. He'll need all his body parts to make the rest of our great grandbabies," he said, patting Running Elk on the back.

The End

Printed in the United States
53000LVS00002BD/130-393